Aria thought she had escaped . . . from the ancient land of her birth . . . from the secret of her birth . . . from the one who shared her birth.

She was safe in New York, where no one knew who she was or what she was, and where brilliant scientist Michael Lansing gave her the love she desperately needed.

But Aria should have known that the world was too small a hiding place and love too fragile a shelter.

For now Thera was coming. Thera, her sister, her twin, her other half. Thera was coming, to claim all that the gods could give and Satan could want . . .

The Godchildren

The Godchildren

SHARON B. PAPE

CHARTER BOOKS, NEW YORK

THE GODCHILDREN

A Charter Book/published by arrangement with
the author

PRINTING HISTORY
Charter edition / April 1986

ISBN: 0-441-29450-2

Charter Books are published by The Berkley Publishing Group,
200 Madison Avenue, New York, New York 10016.
PRINTED IN THE UNITED STATES OF AMERICA

To my Mom and Dad
for believing in me

The greater the power, the more dangerous the abuse.

—*Edmund Burke*

. . . that what we believe is not necessarily true; that what we like is not necessarily good; and that all questions are open.

—*Clive Bell*

The Godchildren

Prologue

Crete: 1244 B.C.

The sun blazed, molten copper in the cloudless blue sky, matting the thin wool tunic against Anchises' back and thighs. Restless with the simple task of guarding his small flock, the shepherd dreamed of cool wine and clouds that would splash his burning skin with liquid cold shadows.

Above him soared the rocky peak of Mount Ida, taunting him with its permanent cap of mist. How cool it must be up there, he thought, feeling all the more miserable in comparison. A stand of cypress trees on the slope of the mountain caught his eye. The sun, not yet at its zenith, threw a ragged belt of shade before them. Anchises glanced at his sheep. There was plenty of grass to keep them busy. Surely he could take a few minutes to relax beneath the cypress trees. But he had barely stretched out, his back against one of the gnarled trunks, when sleep overtook him.

He awakened with a start, pushing himself to his knees to check on the flock. None had strayed. He hadn't slept long, judging by the angle of the sun; though it had whittled at his shade, it was still not directly overhead. He was trying to decide what had awakened him so abruptly when an image flashed at the edge of his vision. He turned toward it. It was far away, shimmering in a haze of heat. Anchises blinked several times to see if it would disappear, a creation of his sun-parched mind. But the image was still there, closing the distance between them. A woman. Even at this great distance he could marvel at her beauty, the regal grace of her posture, the

1

flowing lines of her garment. He watched transfixed, unable to believe she was real, unwilling to look away. She paused to pluck a few blossoms from the ruddy pink dittany that grew in wild profusion on the mountainside, and he noticed that animals were romping beside her. She tucked the flowers into her hair and moved on toward him again.

Anchises gasped and jumped to his feet. The creatures that surrounded her were no playful pets, but wolves and panthers. His heart tumbled in his chest; his mind raced frantically. What could he do? The woman was in mortal danger, as was his flock. There was nowhere to run, no shelter, and no time. They were close enough now for him to see the careful sweep of her flaxen hair pinned high on her head, the glitter of extravagant jewelry catching and reflecting the sunlight like miniature suns. Then he noticed the most extraordinary detail of all: The woman was smiling, laughing softly. And the wolves and panthers seemed tame, no more threatening to her than newborn lambs. Even as he came to this startling realization, the animals stopped abruptly and turned away from her, loping off the way they had come. She continued on toward him alone.

Her mouth was tilted up in the sweetest of smiles. Her eyes were locked on him as if he had been her destination from the beginning. Eyes that were the pearl gray of the first light of dawn, the pupils wide and hypnotic in spite of the sun. Her dress and veil were of a fine, almost luminous cloth, which Anchises had never before seen.

She came through the small flock of sheep without disturbing them. Anchises watched her progress, his feet rooted to the ground, his legs weak stalks swaying above them, the discomfort of the sun forgotten. As she came to stand before him, he was enveloped in her exotic scent.

Before he could think what to say, she had taken his hand in hers and settled lightly on the ground, drawing him down beside her. Her long, tapered fingers traced the lines of his face and sifted through his thick black hair.

"You are indeed handsome, Anchises," she murmured. "Perhaps the most handsome of your kind."

Anchises was about to ask her what she meant and how she knew of him, but she leaned closer and kissed him, her mouth so sweet against his that all his questions disappeared, his head spinning as if he'd drunk too much wine. When she drew back, he let her go reluctantly. She regarded him, gentle mischief in her smile, as she reached up to his shoulder where the *chiton* was fastened. She undid first one pin and then the other, allowing the garment to slip to his waist. Her hand roamed across the smooth, bronzed muscles of his chest for a moment before moving to her own shoulder where a dazzling jeweled brooch secured her robe.

Anchises watched her remove the brooch. He felt as if his heart would stop. Never before had he seen or imagined such beauty. He was shaken with desire for her. But who was she? Would she disappear if he dared reach out to touch her?

As if in answer to his thoughts she shook her head and moved into his arms.

Thirteen years passed and Anchises lived on in his rude shack at the base of Mount Ida. The woman of that magical summer day was no more now than the memory of a dream.

One evening while he ate his lonely supper there was a knock at the door. When he answered it, he found a boy standing there.

"I am Aeneas," said the youth. "Your son."

Bewildered, Anchises opened his mouth to deny it. But before he could, the boy went on.

"My mother has sent me to you, for she can no longer keep me with her. There are those whose jealousy overrules their judgment."

Anchises studied the boy as he spoke, and memories stirred in him: The golden hair and dove gray eyes had belonged to another. The dream had not been a dream after all. He held out his arms and drew his son to him.

1

Heraklion, Crete: September 23, 1986

It was night, and the perimeters of Knossos were well lit and well guarded, the excavated structures throwing arcane shadows across the silent countryside. One car traveled the narrow road that led from Heraklion to the site of the ancient palace. It moved slowly, as if the driver were trying not to shatter the peaceful night on which he had intruded. The car veered off the road onto a dirt patch across from the palace. Pebbles kicked up by the tires ricocheted off the undercarriage, sounding like a barrage of bullets in the stillness. The driver uttered a mild oath under his breath and brought the car to a stop beside a tiny house of smooth white stucco. He emerged from the car, a short, stocky man of sixty, and extended his hand to help a passenger out of the cramped back seat. But Thera drew herself out of the car, ignoring the hand, and walked around to where her grandfather Nicodemus was already waiting. The driver shrugged, eased the door shut with a soft thud, and joined them.

All three were dressed in pants and long-sleeved shirts in spite of the heat that had lingered past sundown. In the dark they might have been taken for three men, except for the cascade of blond hair that fell to Thera's shoulders. Together they approached the house. Dim light seeped around the edges of drawn curtains. Nicodemus rapped on the door. The curtains were parted; eyes peered out at the threesome. Then the door was opened just enough for them to pass inside, and quickly closed again.

Andreas towered over them, stoop-shouldered, as if ashamed of his six-foot-three-inch frame. He smiled broadly and clapped Nicodemus on the back like a benevolent giant.

"We were beginning to worry that you weren't coming," he whispered, his voice cracking, threatening to explode into its normal volume.

"I was late picking them up," Petros apologized. "I had a flat."

"Still, you are here and that is what matters. I'm glad we waited." Andreas escorted them into the center of a small room where nearly a dozen others waited, most of them older men and women. Muted greetings were exchanged.

Thera smiled and nodded at each of them until she came to Nikolas, who was leaning against a table in the far corner. She hadn't seen him there at first. The lamplight was dull and he had chosen the spot farthest from it, his black hair and eyes and the dark clothes he wore helping him merge with the shadows. Thera's smile faded beneath his stony glare.

"And had we not come, what would you have done?" she asked Andreas, her eyes never moving from the dark young man in the corner.

Andreas laughed abruptly, self-consciously. Thera always managed to make him nervous. The contrast between her blond hair and flawless olive skin was enough to take his breath away, but it was her manner more than her beauty that intimidated him.

"Well," he said finally, "I suppose we would have gone on. Nikolas could have led us. He is a Koraes, too."

"I see it is a good thing we are here, then." Thera allowed a sly smile to curve her lips. She could feel Nikolas's anger rise like a wave of heat from his body and rush toward her.

Nicodemus put a firm hand on her forearm, and she turned to him. His dark brows were drawn together ominously over his pale gray eyes, chastising her, at once demanding and begging that she stop. He loved her, but he also loved his great-nephew as he might have a son. He couldn't bear the animosity between them, but it had always been there. Nikolas forever jealous of Thera's power and position. Thera envious of Nikolas's place in her grandfather's heart.

For Nicodemus's sake Thera said no more. She would settle

matters with her cousin in her own way, in her own time.

The others, frozen during the confrontation, relaxed and shifted around where they stood or sat. Someone coughed. Nicodemus nodded to Andreas, who turned off the lamp. Flashlights were produced, and everyone withdrew to the sides of the room. Andreas knelt and began rolling back the rug that covered the wooden floor. Petros held a flashlight for him as he inserted a metal ring into a hole in the floor and lifted up the trapdoor. A musty, earthen odor poured into the room, but no one recoiled. It was an odor they all knew well.

Without a word Nicodemus went first, climbing backwards down the wooden ladder. Thera followed, Petros's flashlight illuminating the way from above, Nicodemus's from below. One by one they made their way down the ladder and into the tunnel, the damp, cool walls chilling them through their warm clothes. Andreas went last, slinging an old-fashioned goatskin flask over one shoulder.

The tunnel ran for fifty yards beneath the roadbed and on under the gates of Knossos, coming up in an unexcavated series of rooms, part of the more than fifteen hundred rooms that formed the original labyrinth of Knossos. As Andreas traversed the tunnel, he swept his flashlight over the walls and ceiling. The tunnel needed constant maintenance—shoring up walls, clearing away minor cave-ins, pumping out water. He had taken over the job from his father and considered it a privilege. Near the end of the tunnel he noticed a thin stream of water trickling down one of the walls. He made a mental note to repair it the next day as he caught up with the rest of the group.

Nicodemus and Thera were waiting in the first room, a small antechamber. Once everyone was together, they moved on, flashlights poking meager holes in the darkness, until they reached the largest of the rooms, the one they believed had been used as a sanctuary by King Minos himself. They proceeded slowly, taking each step with care, for the huge in-laid stones that made up the floor were uneven and half buried in earth. The assemblage stopped at the base of the stepped altar of solid limestone, Nicodemus and Thera alone ascending to the top.

Thera held the flashlight while her grandfather lit the propane lamp, carving a circle of light in the darkness. Now the faded red, blue, and yellow scalloped designs were distinguishable on the altar, and the wall behind it emerged in a dull red hue embellished with pictures of the bull and the labrys, the double-edged ax.

Thera lifted the priest's crown of woven myrtle leaves from the altar and placed it on Nicodemus's thick white hair.

"The water," he said, his features wavering strangely in the glow of the lamp.

Andreas came forward, ascended the altar, and slipped the goatskin from his shoulder. Nicodemus accepted it, pouring the contents into one of several stone bowls. He dipped his hands briefly into the water and stepped back. Next Thera and then Andreas passed their hands through the water. One by one, each member of the group approached the altar to take part in the ritual washing. When it was Nikolas's turn, his eyes strayed with silent fury to Thera standing beside her grandfather. She didn't return his gaze, knowing this would better serve to enrage him. Instead it was Nicodemus whose eyes locked on his, sending the same warning they had earlier issued to Thera. Nikolas turned away abruptly, jarring the bowl and causing the water to slosh over the sides. No one dared comment, yet Nikolas was certain he heard the cold peal of Thera's laughter echoing in his head.

With the water ritual completed, Thera dipped her hands into a second bowl and sprinkled barley grains around the altar as an offering. Finally Nicodemus resumed his place at the altar and raised his arms, palms upward.

"Minos, good and kind protector, son of divine Europa and omnipotent Zeus, we who have remained faithful throughout the ages entreat you and your great lord Zeus, the supreme god of the heavens, to listen to our humble prayers."

Thera raised her arms and, with the other congregants as echoes, repeated her grandfather's words. Before their voices had faded, Nicodemus went on.

"We who have never turned from you, we who have not followed the usurpers, the pretenders to your heavenly throne, we beseech you, mighty one, bless us and our loved ones with good health and good harvests in whatever work we do. You who control the wind, the storm, and the warmth of the sun, let peace be the climate of our lives.''

Thera again repeated the devotions, but though her voice registered the proper emotion, the performance was mechanical. The prayers no longer moved her. When she was a child, the ceremony and the eerie subterranean rooms had enchanted her, inspired her with awe. Now her eyes wandered to Nicodemus, continuing with the litany. Did he still believe in his gods? His gods. Were they not hers, too? No, not any longer. Then why was she here? She could have stayed home with her grandmother, who was no doubt praying to her Christian God, begging him to forgive her husband and granddaughter, the poor misguided fools whom she loved. Thera had accompanied Philina to her church once out of curiosity. But it had been like watching a show, and she had been completely unmoved. At least here, she realized, repeating the last of the prayers, at least here was what linked her to her past and her future. For if the gods themselves were long gone, their powers remained.

Nicodemus ended the ceremony with a few special prayers on behalf of his people. Petros's father was dying of cancer, and Petros hoped the old man could be spared further pain. Flora's son was to be married; she wanted a blessing of happiness and fertility for the couple.

Then the crown of myrtle was removed, the bowl of water emptied back into the goatskin.

Andreas led the way out with his flashlight. Nicodemus waited. He would extinguish the lamp and be the last to leave as he had been the first to enter. He watched as the last man disappeared into the antechamber. Thera should have followed, but she was staring into a dark corner of the room, lost in thought.

"Something troubles you," murmured Nicodemus.

"Yes," she said, turning to confront him. "Do you still believe in them—your gods, Minos, Zeus, and the rest of that Olympian circus?"

His sharp intake of air was answer enough. She could see the shock on her grandfather's face without the help of a lamp.

"I've startled you." She laughed softly but without warmth.

Nicodemus struggled to control himself. Thera had never been a passive, compliant child, but she was becoming more of a stranger to him as she grew older.

"How can you of all people say such a thing? How can you possibly doubt them?" His voice was hoarse with the effort of containing his anger. In this holy place how dare she be so irreverent? "You know what was given to you!"

"Yes, I know. I don't deny that the gods once were here. But they're not here anymore. Maybe they just got tired of our constant whining and our demands. For whatever reason, they no longer concern themselves with us."

"Then for you there's nothing left to believe in," said Nicodemus. And nothing left to guide or control you, he added to himself.

To Thera he looked old and weary in the dying lamplight, facial lines deepening into crevices, eyes sinking into hollows as if he were aging before her.

"I can believe in myself," she said firmly. She wanted to explain, but she knew he wouldn't understand and would never be able to accept her beliefs even if he did. She pitied him, calling to gods who no longer listened when all he had to do was look within himself. Their legacy ran in his blood, as it did in her father's, in her own, and in her sister's.

Her sister. Thera was reminded of the power that waited just beyond her reach, and her fingertips began to tingle with an almost electrical charge of anticipation. Over the years, as far back as she could recall, she had sought out every opportunity to exercise and develop her abilities, constantly extending her potential. When she was a young child, her experiments had been no more than a game, but the tenor of the game had changed with adolescence until now, at the age of twenty-four, it was a deep hunger, an appetite that only increased the more it was fed. But she could go just so far alone. She needed her sister.

Nicodemus caught the peculiar smile that transformed Thera's lips and then vanished as quickly as the flutter of an eyelid. What had become of the infant girl he had cradled in his arms and lulled to sleep with half-remembered songs from his own childhood? Several times when he had stretched his mind to try to understand her, tremors had taken hold and shaken him fiercely, and he had withdrawn, preferring after all not to know. But he had his suspicions. Suspicions the others must never guess at, or Thera would not live through the night.

"They'll be waiting for us," he said, turning down the lamp until it flickered out. He followed Thera out of the darkened sanctuary, through the antechamber, and on into the tunnel.

2

New York City: September 23

The darkness pressed in on her from every side, cold and dense, choking her with a bitter earthen smell. She was entombed. Panic, like an icy liquid, rushed through her. She opened her mouth to scream, but the sudden glow of a light startled her into silence. Voices were converging on her, foreign syllables linked together by echoes. Unaccountably she felt a wave of anger and bitter frustration wash over her, submerging her fear. Her teeth were clenching, her hands balling into fists. Yet even as these new emotions gripped her, she knew they were not her own. They'd been thrust upon her like ill-fitting clothes. She struggled to be free of them.

Aria bolted upright on the couch where she'd been napping and opened her eyes. But instead of being surrounded by the white walls of her studio apartment, she found herself still within the horrible dark place of her dream. Featureless shadows drifted past her; incomprehensible words vibrated in her head. Her heart was knocking furiously in her chest, but she was powerless to move, like a butterfly whose wings had been pinned while it was still alive. She fought for control. Control was the key. She willed herself to be calm. Remain calm and wait for it to be over.

She drew several deep breaths in spite of the acrid air and concentrated on where she ought to be. She imagined the convertible bed on which she'd fallen asleep, the red carpeting, the graphics on the walls, the red and white kitchen area, the armoire, and the table. Gradually the air began to freshen; the darkness receded. The voices were reduced to a vague hum like the sound of central air conditioning.

Aria closed her eyes, and this time when she opened them she was home. She emitted a long, choked sigh and shuddered violently. She had always made it back before, but what if there came a time when she couldn't return? Would she have to live out her life within the confines of those haunting dreams?

A staccato beeping from her watch set her in motion. Five-thirty. She was supposed to meet Karen for dinner at six. There wasn't time, but she desperately needed a shower and a change of clothes. Her jeans and shirt were clinging to her body with the clammy perspiration of fear.

Aria pushed herself off the couch and rushed toward the bathroom, tripping over the book of torts she'd been reading when she'd fallen asleep. She fell into a heap on the floor, muttering and rubbing an injured toe with one hand while pulling open the buttons on her shirt with the other. She hopped into the shower, hoping the cut would stop bleeding on its own; she didn't have time to fuss with Band-Aids.

At five forty-five she locked the door behind her, feeling refreshed and sane again in a flowered dress and sandals. It was still rush hour, but she managed to flag down a taxi, an expense she rarely allowed herself.

She settled back into the seat and made a conscious effort to unwind. The whole idea of having dinner with Karen was to take a break from the grind of studying and to relax. Studying—she'd have to get back to that book later tonight or Dr. Fischer would find her unprepared tomorrow. He always seemed to know when someone was behind. She wondered if he had some psychic ability. Then she wrinkled her nose and smiled wryly. Well, my dear Dr. Fischer, may you have as much pleasure from yours as I have from mine.

Karen was already holding down a table for two in the Greenhouse, a glassed-in section of the restaurant hung with enough greenery to almost fool you into thinking you were dining al fresco in the countryside. Karen said the area had originally been uncovered, but the owners had found it impractical. Customers who liked to linger over dinner had complained about the fine layer of soot that accumulated on their food by the end of the evening.

Karen looked up from a glass of rosé she'd been sipping.

"Don't say it. I know I'm late." Aria smiled, slipping into her seat.

"Only technically. I didn't expect you to make it before six-thirty, so six-fifteen is impressive."

"Maybe you should stop being punctual."

"And give up the only thing in the world I do better than anyone else?"

Aria laughed. "You do plenty of things better than I do."

"Name one," Karen demanded, suddenly sober.

For an awkward moment Aria was stuck for an answer. Karen was sweet and a dear, considerate friend, but she was plain to the point of being unattractive, and academically she'd had an uphill fight to enter law school and stay there.

"You're the best listener I know," Aria replied, relieved to have come up with such an honest response. "That's awfully rare these days, what with most people so tuned in to themselves."

"You're right," said Karen cracking a smile. "It's not a terribly exciting trait, but at least it's not common."

A waitress appeared to take their order, and they confessed they hadn't even opened the menus yet. She pursed her lips and told them she'd be back.

"I wonder what her problem is," Aria whispered, scanning the dinner selections.

"Probably boyfriend trouble. I think I'll try the seafood crepe."

"Good enough, I'll have the same. I'm not in the mood to make decisions tonight."

"Well, I'm still waiting for tonight's excuse," said Karen, once the waitress had taken their orders.

Aria's skin prickled with recollection. It had been over a month since she'd had one of those extended dreams. She'd begun to think gratefully that they were tapering off. Apparently she wasn't going to be that lucky. Forcing a smile, she said simply, "I dozed off reading for Dr. Fischer." She'd never mentioned the dreams to Karen, although she'd known her since they both started law school two years ago. She didn't know how to describe them without sounding totally irrational. Besides, putting those horrible dreams into words would only serve to enhance them, making them uncomfortably real again.

Instead Aria steered the conversation back to more mundane topics. They discussed their courses for the new semester and the possibility of taking a vacation together during intersession, preferably someplace warm and full of men. Karen had once confided to Aria that she enjoyed traveling with her partly because Aria always drew a throng of male admirers from which Karen had her pick of the overflow. Jealousy played no part in her feelings. She'd learned long ago how useless that was. Anyway, she would joke, where Aria was concerned, how would she know where to start? With the heart-shaped face, or the lustrous blond hair that hadn't darkened a shade since childhood, or the huge mauve-gray eyes?

By the time they'd reached coffee, Aria's side of the conversation was flagging. Answers of more than a word or two took a tremendous effort. She thought she might be coming down with the flu. She felt peculiar, in a familiar way. A combination of lassitude and a tingling as if her nerve endings had become supersensitive to the point of pain. Then it came to her. Not the flu, the aftermath of the dream. She'd forgotten how depleted they always left her. Depleted and yet charged with that curious sensitivity. She drank the coffee quickly, hoping it would help.

Karen had put down her own cup and was studying her.

"Late for another appointment?"

Aria shook her head, her mouth full of hot coffee.

"Okay, give."

Aria raised her eyebrows, puzzled, and managed to swallow the coffee.

"If I'm such a good listener, I think it's about time you told me what the problem is. You're really not yourself tonight."

"The problem is I should never take naps. I always wind up twice as groggy." She couldn't bear to say more than that. She needed to go home and immerse herself in her studies to the exclusion of everything else. Karen might be a good listener, and she might be able to understand the simpler manifestations of Aria's psychic abilities, but as for the rest—how do you explain that you spend half your life feeling that you're really somewhere else? How do you describe what it's like to be missing some important part of yourself that you can't even name? She'd tried to explain once before. "It's like having two arms and still feeling as if one's missing," she'd said.

"I know exactly what you mean," Karen had responded sympathetically. And Aria had thought that here at last was someone who did understand. But then Karen had gone on, "I feel that way whenever I try to hang wallpaper."

Aria had smiled and let it drop. Why should anyone else understand it? She barely comprehended it herself. Her own parents' reactions had been less than supportive the first time she'd tried to explain these sensations as a child of four. Her mother's face had crumpled, eyes wide with fear as if she'd been dealt a physical blow. Her father had taken Aria aside and firmly instructed her not to dwell on such things. At the time she'd been daunted and confused. Now, from an adult perspective, she wondered if they'd been afraid that their only child was going off the deep end? There were certainly enough times that Aria herself had wrestled with that same possibility.

Over the years she had learned to be circumspect about what she confided and to whom. Although precognition and telepathy were finally finding acceptance in certain scientific circles, deviations from these new norms could still raise eyebrows.

Karen was chewing on her lower lip. "I guess we ought to call it a night. I have tons of reading to do, too. But I had something to tell you, and it's completely slipped my mind."

Aria waited quietly.

"C'mon. Can't you be a little more helpful?" Karen prompted.

"I'm afraid it doesn't always work on command, at least not for me."

"That's it."

"It is?"

Karen was suddenly more animated than she'd been all evening. "Listen—I was checking out the bulletin board in the student union today. Always looking for a good deal on a car. Anyway, there was this notice asking for volunteers for an experiment in psychic research. It's being conducted by a graduate student as part of his doctoral work. It asked people who believe they may have demonstrable psychic ability to contact him.'' Karen rummaged through her purse as she spoke. "I wrote down his name and phone number. Here it is," she cried triumphantly and handed a small crumpled paper to Aria. "Doesn't it sound exciting?"

Aria took the paper.

"Well?"

"I don't know. I don't think I like the way it sounds. Experiment. Like lab rats."

"Don't be silly. Lab rats don't have ESP."

"How do you know?"

Karen looked crestfallen. "You're really not interested? I was sure you'd jump at it. I know if it were me . . ."

Aria shrugged. "I'm awfully busy just keeping up with all the work."

"Why don't you just give the guy a call? What harm could it do?"

"I guess," Aria replied without enthusiasm, and tucked the paper into her own pocketbook. It might be interesting to investigate her abilities with someone committed to psychic research. Someone who would deal with her scientifically, clinically, instead of with awe, fear, or cynicism. Then why didn't the prospect excite her? She felt like a mummy whose carefully wrapped layers were about to be peeled away. She wasn't altogether certain that she wanted to find out exactly what lay underneath.

She left Karen outside the restaurant, promising to give the experiment serious consideration, and walked to the corner to wait for a bus. Taking two taxis in one night was simply out of the question.

Aria stopped studying at eleven, unable to concentrate properly. The psychic research kept insinuating itself into her thoughts. She left the open law book on the couch and went to the table that doubled as her desk. She picked up the phone and dialed, hoping she wouldn't wake her mother, who often retired early.

Damos answered in a low voice, and Aria suspected he had

been reading in the study adjoining the bedroom. When he heard his daughter's voice, he became concerned. He and his wife had spoken with her just the night before. Short of an emergency, he couldn't imagine why she would call again, and at this late hour. She was a self-sufficient young woman who could cope with most problems on her own and who managed well with the money they had settled on when she began law school. In fact, as she frequently reminded them, she was keeping track of the amount and was determined to repay it after she became a practicing attorney. Damos hardly needed the money, but he was proud of his daughter's ethics and character.

He rose and closed the door to the bedroom while he listened to Aria present her dilemma.

"Surely you're not serious, Aria," he said when she'd paused.

"That's what I thought at first, but I must be or I wouldn't be debating it so furiously or calling you at this hour." She couldn't remember the last time she had sought parental advice on a decision. Even the determination to go into law instead of following her father in architecture had been completely her own.

"Don't do it."

"Why?"

"It would be a mistake." His tone was even, but Aria sensed the tension beneath it. She could picture his strong, chiseled features drawn taut across the bones as always when he was troubled, his hand running through the black hair that had only recently become seeded with gray. Here was a man who was open-minded in all of his attitudes toward life. Why then this one blind spot?

"That's it?" she pressed.

"Yes. Your studies keep you busy enough, I would think. Why open a Pandora's box?"

"Curiosity maybe. Don't you get curious about it sometimes?"

There was a long silence on her father's end.

"I don't want you to do it, Aria. Promise me you won't." The demand was implicit in his tone. Aria was nonplussed.

She'd expected a rational discussion, not an edict.

"I promise to give it a good deal of thought before I decide."

"That's not what I meant."

"I know, but I'm afraid that's the best I can do. I'm sorry," she added, feeling vaguely guilty, as if she'd let him down.

She hung up the phone more confused than ever. Had premonitions colored her father's reaction, or was he merely expressing the conservative fears of the middle-aged?

She sank onto the couch and retrieved the law book. She would just have to put the issue out of her mind for now, she told herself sternly. The last thing she needed was a hassle with Dr. Fischer tomorrow.

3

New York City: September 25

Aria walked full tilt into the man, sending his brierroot pipe flying from his mouth to clatter onto the tile floor. She'd been so lost in thought that it took her several moments to sort out her confusion before she could even apologize.

"Why the hell don't you watch where you're going?" the man bellowed at her, resetting the tweed cap that had flopped over his eyes in the collision.

"I—I'm sorry," Aria replied, retrieving the pipe. "I don't know why I didn't see you there." She brushed off the pipe and handed it to him with a sheepish smile. "I'm really sorry. I hope it's not broken." She looked up at him.

He no longer appeared angry. In fact the mouth above the white triangle of beard was smiling broadly back at her.

"That's okay. No damage done. You just gave me a start. And if I had to be jostled, I'm rather glad it was by you."

Aria felt a blush of color burn her cheeks.

"My only regret," he went on, "is that I didn't know it was coming. If I had, I could have enjoyed it more."

Two men who had seen the incident laughed good-naturedly, but Aria hurried away from them, the words trailing after her like a torn hem. How do I always manage to get myself into these situations, she wondered miserably. Maybe it was a sign that she shouldn't go through with the interview. No, she didn't believe in signs. At least not the kind you fell into by inattention. She giggled at her own nervousness, and at the last moment sidestepped a bucket that was catching a leak from the ceiling. It's just an interview, she told herself sternly. I don't have to agree to anything. And I won't sign any papers. I'm only here to satisfy my curiosity. I'll just take one thing at a time.

Room nineteen was near the end of a long hallway that was punctuated every few yards by a closed door, all of them beige metal with translucent windows and black numerals. Nothing distinguished number nineteen from the others. Aria checked the number on the slip of paper in her purse. This was the right room, the one he'd given her when she'd called that morning. She knocked. After a moment the door was opened, and she found herself looking into the warmest brown eyes she'd ever seen. The corners curved up, and bright flecks like gold dust danced in the irises. He held out his hand.

"Aria? I'm Michael Lansing."

She put her hand in his and was immediately drawn into the office. It was no more than a ten-by-ten-foot cubicle with a desk, several molded plastic chairs, a filing cabinet, and a two-shelf bookcase, all overflowing with folders, books, and papers.

"Aria Koraes," she murmured, her hand still trapped in his large palm.

"I'm glad you came, Aria. Have a seat." They both took in the cluttered office and laughed at the same moment. "Wait a sec—I'll make room." He dropped her hand and moved a pile of folders from one chair onto a teetering pile on another.

"I'm afraid I need to get organized," he said, nodding toward the empty chair.

"How long have you been working on this project?" Aria asked, settling into the chair.

Michael leaned against his desk. "A few months."

"I think you need a secretary."

"Graduate students the world over would applaud the suggestion, but I'm afraid it's not to be."

Aria laughed again, fully at ease with him. "How long does it usually take you to get organized?"

"I guess the truth is I'm a compulsive slob. Too interested in the ideas to be bothered with details like filing." His whole appearance, in fact, spoke of a casual disregard for the banal, a disregard that Aria found endearing. His hair was well cut, but the thick, sandy layers tumbled across his forehead, and he occasionally combed them back with his fingers. The deep cleft in his chin was nicked where he had cut himself shaving, and a shadow already marked where his beard would be. He wore an odd assortment of clothing that didn't really match but somehow managed to look well on his tall, lean frame: jeans, an oxford shirt, a blazer, and sneakers.

"So, Aria," Michael said, rummaging through the jumble on his desk. "On the phone you said you believe you have demonstrable psychic ability." He plucked out a yellow legal pad, causing a small avalanche of papers to cascade off the desk and onto the floor. "Could you be a little more specific?" He found a pen in one of his shirt pockets.

Aria was brought up sharply by the question. She'd almost forgotten why she was in the office. "I have precognitive visions," she replied, wishing she had met Michael Lansing somewhere else, anywhere else.

Michael was studying her. "Does it bother you to talk about them?"

Aria forced a smile. He seemed so concerned and intense. She didn't want to disappoint him. "I'm not sure. I haven't talked about them much with anyone before." She hesitated, searching for the right words, but there weren't any. "And there are other things—things that are harder to explain."

"Well, we don't have to go into anything you're not comfortable with." Michael put the pen and pad down. He was dealing with real potential here, he could sense it. But she was skittish, and he didn't want to scare her off. Better to keep the approach nonclinical for today. She was looking at him with a mixture of openness and anxiety that touched him, and he caught himself staring back at her, trying to decide if her eyes really were lavender. No. This was definitely not the way to deal with a prospective subject. Distance and objectivity were essential. Michael stood up abruptly.

"Can I get you some coffee?"

Aria looked around the room. "You have a coffeemaker hidden under something in here?"

He grinned. "If I did, I'd probably never find it. No. There's a machine around the corner in the hallway. It's not great, but if you're desperate . . ."

"Thanks anyway. I think I'll pass."

Michael paced a few steps up and back and then settled back against the desk again. "Would you like to know what my research is all about?"

"If I'm going to be a statistic in it, I guess I should."

"Okay. Basically I'm testing the hypothesis that hypnosis can elevate a person's psychic output and, secondarily, perhaps give the person some control over its manifestation."

Aria had tensed immediately. She could barely cope with the current extent of her abilities; the last thing she needed or wanted was to enhance them. If Michael hadn't mentioned control, she might have walked out the door right then. As it was, she stayed in the chair and listened as he rambled on, engrossed in his own explanations. But she stayed more out of a desire to remain with him than because she wanted to become a part of his project.

"Am I boring you?" Michael interrupted himself after several minutes."

"Not at all. Actually it's nice to hear someone talk about all this so scientifically."

"I take it you've had your share of ignorant remarks and stares of incredulity."

Aria sighed and nodded.

"I know. It goes with the territory. Have you ever been tested before?"

"You mean scientifically? No. When I was younger I used to fool around with friends a little, though. You know, they'd look at a card, and I'd try to guess what it was."

"Bad word—*guess*. You weren't guessing, were you?"

Aria shook her head. "No. I didn't have to."

Michael's adrenaline was pumping, but he tried to keep his voice neutral. "How accurate were you?"

"Well, I used to fudge it a little, so the kids wouldn't think I was too weird. Ninety percent right, I'd say."

"Would you object to some simple tests like those?"

"You mean with regular playing cards?"

"Except we don't generally use the picture cards. We use a deck of forty with the ace as one."

A card game. No more than she had done as a child. It didn't sound particularly threatening. Aria shrugged.

"I guess that would be all right, but I'm not sure I want to become involved in a full-scale experiment. I'll need a little time to decide, if that's okay."

"Of course it's okay," Michael smiled, and the gold flecks in his eyes lit up. "As long as you eventually say yes."

Aria couldn't help smiling back at him; he seemed to draw it from her, his warmth like a magnet.

"Mind if I take down some personal data for my, uh, files?" he asked.

Aria burst into laughter. "With your filing system I'm sure it'll be safe from prying eyes."

"Yeah," Michael agreed, retrieving his pad. "My own included."

They spent another fifteen minutes together as he took down Aria's history. She avoided mentioning the dreams that followed her beyond the threshold of sleep and the physical sensations that didn't relate to her surroundings. It wasn't that she didn't trust him; she was just—afraid. Afraid, after all, of the Pandora's box that frightened her father.

"One last thing," Michael was saying.

"What's that? I think you have everything short of my measurements."

"I can estimate those," he said with a crooked smile. "But I need your phone number."

Aria gave it to him. "For professional purposes only?"

"If you insist." But he knew the answer should have been an unequivocal yes. If she was to be a part of his research, their relationship had to remain purely professional. And she might just be his most important find yet.

Aria had risen and was extending her hand. "I'm glad we met, Michael. I'll be in touch soon with my decision. I hope I haven't wasted your time."

"No matter the outcome," he said, "it wasn't wasted." He opened the door for her and watched as she walked down the hall and out of sight. Her eyes were lavender. He would swear to it. Or at least lavender-gray.

4

Heraklion, Crete: October 3

Thera closed her office door behind her and stood for a moment in the hallway that linked the office area with the exhibition rooms. It was early evening, and the museum was silent. Gone were the guides and the tourists, competing to be heard in a cacophony of foreign languages. Aside from the guards, the only ones left in the building were Milo Stefanatos, the head curator, and his assistants, Demetrius and herself. She checked her watch. Milo was expecting her in his office in two minutes. He'd sent her a memo during the day. A memo generally meant a reprimand, the more formal the wording, the more serious the offense. She had a pretty good idea what tonight's censure was to cover, though she considered it unreasonable. She'd left the building earlier than usual yesterday. But the work load had been light, barely enough to keep the three of them occupied. The important pieces they were expecting from Knossos had been delayed to the end of the week. Milo simply enjoyed flexing his authority.

Passing the office next to hers, Thera could hear muffled sounds. Demetrius was still at work. Filing cabinets were opened and closed, a chair squeaked under his weight. Although she was sharper than he and worked more assiduously, she was fairly certain he had never received a memo. She was equally well aware that both Demetrius and Milo viewed her with barely concealed tolerance. Although sometimes astonished by her clever insights, they were still convinced she

24

belonged at home with a husband and a flock of children to care for.

A bubble of laughter tickled Thera's throat and tugged at her mouth. Foolish men. If she had her way, they would learn just how far superior she was. Her smile vanished, replaced by a tight line of frustration, her teeth clenched hard. If her grandfather had his way—he and the others—no one would ever know just what she was capable of. And worst of all, neither would she.

Thera found herself outside Milo's door, unaware of having covered the length of the hallway. She took a deep breath to muster her self-control. Milo didn't make her nervous, but he did irritate her, and it was sheer willpower on her part that had seen them through their first bloodless year together. She knocked.

"*Embros.*"

Thera entered the office, which was only slightly larger than her own, but with two windows. Milo was seated behind his desk, engrossed in papers laid out neatly on his blotter. The fluorescent ceiling fixture lent a sickly greenish pallor to his bald pate. Above his ears the patches of dark hair, usually plastered down, stood up in scruffy clumps, which he smoothed back absently as he looked up.

"Miss Koraes."

"Mr. Stefanatos," she said, mimicking his tone.

"Have a seat."

Thera chose the only available one in front of the desk. The other two were piled with cartons.

Milo interlaced his hands on the desk and waited for Thera to make herself comfortable. "I see no reason why we can't get right down to business," he said. "I asked you to come here this evening because I'm concerned about your commitment to this institution." He paused in case Thera intended to say something. He disliked conversations that interrupted or overlapped. When she didn't open her mouth, he went on.

"I'm sure you are aware how fortunate you were to have been appointed to a curatorship in this museum. How many other applicants, all quite well qualified, were rejected."

Thera watched the pasty surfaces of his face move as he

talked. The beginnings of a double chin made his head appear pear shaped. Didn't he realize how ridiculous he looked? How absurd he sounded? He had paused again.

"Is there a point to all this?" she asked as politely as possible.

"Of course there's a point," he nearly shouted at her. Then, controlling himself, he continued, "The point is, you seem rather eager to leave your office and your work."

Thera waited a few moments for her own anger to subside. "Because I left early one evening?"

Milo had risen from his chair and was standing behind it, stubby fingers pressed into the soft vinyl back.

"No. Because you often leave early."

"Once a month."

"More often than that."

"Prove it." The words came through clenched teeth.

"That's not exactly possible, since we don't punch a time clock around here. But I'm sure Demetrius would substantiate my claim."

"Demetrius!" Thera exploded, rocketing to her feet. "That obsequious little lump! You could accuse me of murder, and he would sign the affidavit just to get on your good side."

Milo was taken aback by the sudden palpable fury that seemed to leap at him.

"Now then, Thera, let's be reasonable," he murmured, holding up his hands as if he were warding off more than an exchange of angry words. "I think we've both gotten a little carried away here." He started to take his seat. "Please"—he nodded to her chair—"Let's go back, as they say, to square one."

Thera remained standing an extra minute, looking down at her boss. Under the intense scrutiny of those cold, flint eyes, his own skittered quickly away. Satisfied that she had the upper hand, Thera sat down again.

"So," Milo resumed, swallowing audibly and staring at his desk. "I suppose what I wanted to say to you was that I would like to see more evidence that you do not take your position here lightly."

"No, the truth is, what you really wanted to say is that you don't believe a woman belongs in my position, or in any position outside the home."

"No of course that isn't—I mean, there are certain—"

Thera thought she detected moisture beading on his upper lip. "Ah, Mr. Stefanatos," she said, aware she was committing the cardinal sin of interrupting. "As a student of archaeology and history, you are no doubt aware that there was once a time when goddesses as well as gods ruled the heavens and the earth."

"That's mythology," sputtered Milo whose face had flushed a spotty red at Thera's rebelliousness. "And even if the people back then did worship gods and goddesses, their beliefs are irrelevant to today's world. Next I suppose you'll be telling me you also belong to that crazy cult that still worships Zeus."

Thera's lips spread in a humorless smile. "No," she said softly, "I would never tell you anything like that."

"Then shall I assume we have come to an understanding about your performance here?" Milo's complexion was returning to normal. He was beginning to feel he was in command again.

Thera didn't respond immediately. She was thinking about the bird outside her bedroom window. The one that lay dead at the base of the cypress tree. It had been so much easier than she had anticipated, and all she'd experienced afterward was a mild headache. She remembered studying the bird, watching the way its heart had made the soft brown chest undulate. She had needed only to focus and concentrate.

"Thera?" Milo repeated.

Thera let her eyes drop to Milo's chest, centering on the left breast pocket of his shirt. Beneath it, within the cavity of his chest, nestled the heart muscle, the right auricle controlling the life-sustaining beat.

"Oh, yes, we've come to an understanding," she replied in a detached monotone. "But there is one thing you ought to know, Mr. Stefanatos."

"What's that?" he asked, eager for the meeting to be concluded.

"The past is never irrelevant."

Milo was about to ask her what she meant when the pain

gripped him. His heart seemed to leap out of control, beating in a wildly distorted rhythm. He clutched his chest, his face ashen, and slumped forward over the desk, scattering the neatly stacked papers.

Thera stood at the rear doorway and watched as Milo's stretcher was loaded onto the ambulance. Demetrius scrambled in beside him, and the ambulance sped away, sirens blaring.

Instead of leaving through the back door, she walked out into the museum proper. As she moved slowly through the rooms with their cases of ancient jewelry, tools, and fragments of a life long vanished, her tension and anger ebbed and she grew more relaxed. The museum always had a calming effect on her, its treasures not unlike her own—gifts from the past.

She stopped once in front of a tall display case where a golden ax was suspended at eye level, its double blades in perfect symmetry. This piece had not come from Knossos, but from the Diktean Cave. And although it was the only one the archaeologists had discovered there, it was not the only one that existed. Thera found herself smiling with secret pleasure. So much that Milo and Demetrius didn't know. And in better spirits she breezed on through the connecting rooms that led to the front entrance.

"*Kalinihta sas*, good night," she said airily to the uniformed guard leaning against the door.

"Have a good evening, Miss Koraes. *Tha idhothoume aviro.*" He held the door open for her. "I hope Mr. Stefanatos will recover."

"Yes," Thera nodded.

Outside it was not yet dark, but the light had a wan, diminished look to it, its colors having drained off into the sinking whirlpool of the sun. Thera struck out across the Platia Eleftherias, deserted now by the tourists, and headed home.

5

Heraklion, Crete: October 3

It was nearly dark when Thera arrived home from the museum. The apartment she shared with her grandparents was in one of a row of dreary three-story buildings that had lost their luster years before. The whitewashed facades had dulled to a yellowish gray, the turquoise shutters flecked with white where the warped paint had finally chipped off. There had been a time when Thera, fresh from the university in Athens, had considered moving to a newer, better-kept section of Heraklion. But she had quickly discarded the notion. For now the old house would do. She would be leaving soon enough, living her life far beyond the island of Crete.

She pushed against the heavy door with her shoulder, and it gave grudgingly, scraping and shuddering inward as if over the years it had grown a size too large for its frame. Inside, the spicy vapor of Philina's cooking had filled the air with the scent of garlic, onions, tomato, and lamb. Thera crossed the small, dimly lit lobby and hurried up the stairs. At the second-floor landing the aroma was so dense and rich that her stomach contracted hungrily and she could almost taste the *giouvetsi*. She had her hand poised to knock when the sounds of conversation first reached her. She couldn't distinguish individual words, but the texture of the voices was familiar. Nicodemus's gruff and hearty, the other deep but of a smoother timbre. Nikolas. Thera's hunger abated sharply. What was her cousin doing there? Nicodemus was usually careful to visit with him when she was at work, making sure their paths didn't cross unnecessarily. Keeping the spark from the kindling, as he would sometimes say. She groped in her purse for her keys. She didn't want Nikolas to open the door for her. This was her home. Not his. She could feel the old hostilities, like hot lava, rising in her. She turned the key in the lock and took a moment to settle her features into a serene expression, the anger carefully submerged behind the thick lashes and cool gray eyes. She opened the door and stepped inside.

Nicodemus and Nikolas were sitting directly in front of her at the dining room table. Nearly empty cups of Philina's strong coffee sat in front of them. They were so engrossed in conversation that neither of them looked up at her.

"And this source, this source is reliable?" Nicodemus was muttering gravely.

"Without question," Nikolas replied.

Thera flung the door shut behind her, causing both men to look up abruptly. Nicodemus appeared disoriented, like someone who'd fallen asleep on the job. Nikolas's dark eyes narrowed warily, but he produced a thin-lipped smile.

"Good evening, Cousin."

"Nikolas." Thera tossed her purse onto the battered desk that stood to one side of the doorway.

Philina poked her tiny head out of the kitchen. Her knot of gray hair had wilted, and dank wisps clung to her cheeks.

"I made *giouvetsi*, your most favorite, Thera *mou*. It's almost ready," she smiled broadly, her glittering black eyes all but lost in a net of fine lines.

"You work too hard," Thera said without conviction. But Philina had already disappeared back into the heat of the kitchen, and Thera could hear the slap of her feet as she scuttled about on the worn linoleum.

Nicodemus had straightened himself and was squinting at his watch.

"Aren't you home early?" he asked as Thera brushed her lips across his leathery cheek and took a seat beside him.

"A little late," she smiled condescendingly. "You were discussing a problem? Something I should know about?"

"A problem, yes. But there is nothing you can help with," Nikolas answered her.

Thera's smile dissolved. "Tell me and I'll decide that."

In the tense silence that followed, Nicodemus glanced from one to the other. He had to end the discussion and send Nikolas on his way or he and Thera would worry the subject forever like two dogs with a bone. He chose the most direct route.

"Nikolas has it on good authority that the archaeologists are about to begin excavating the section near the sacred altar."

Thera shrugged and tossed her head so that the blond hair fanned out around her face before settling to her shoulders. "Rumors. How many times before have we heard this same story?"

"It's no rumor," Nikolas snapped. "And even if it were, it's only a matter of time before they reach the altar."

"And when they do, there are still the caves."

"Is that your solution?" He laughed sharply. "I can see it was indeed well worth telling you."

Thera's face remained impassive, but her voice cut through the air like a blade. "I take it you have a better solution?"

"The caves are too far away, too inconvenient."

"I take it you have a better solution?" she repeated the challenge.

Nikolas wanted to reach across the table and strike her, feel his palm sting against the smoothness of her cheek, shake the smugness from those lips and eyes. But this was his fault. He had left himself open to her again. Impotent rage coursed through him. Blood rushed to his face and neck and burned behind his eyes. She was a spoiled child who had no right to the powers she claimed.

"When I do," he said tightly, his jaws clamped against the desire to shout at her, "I'll tell Nicodemus. And I assure you it won't simply be the first useless thought that pops into my mind." Brushing savagely at a thick lock of black hair that had fallen over his eyes, he started to rise.

"Children!" Nicodemus thundered, slamming his palms down on the table, making the cups jump and clatter in their saucers. "*Arketa*! Enough! We are not so many that we can afford to fight among ourselves." His voice softened, became conciliatory. "Are we not, after all, on the same side?"

Thera glanced at her grandfather and then at Nikolas, who was staring moodily at the table. Nicodemus was right, but not for the reasons he believed. In truth she had little to gain by fencing with Nikolas. She only degraded herself in the attempt. You are jealous and resentful, she thought, still looking at her cousin. You place yourself too high. But you are only a nephew. Not one of *us*. What a pity you don't accept yourself as you really are. You are useless, nothing more than . . . A new idea was tugging urgently at her mind. Nicodemus was speaking again, but she wasn't listening. A plan was forming. A new exercise. A new trial for her powers. It took Nicodemus's hand on her arm to draw her attention. She turned to him sharply, annoyed at having been disturbed.

"Thera, Nikolas has said good-bye."

She looked up to find her cousin standing near the door. She turned back to Nicodemus, a smile slowly curving the corners of her mouth.

"Grandfather, you're right," she said in a silky voice. "We shouldn't quarrel. But you're also quite rude. How can you let your nephew leave when dinner is barely a moment away?"

As if on cue, Philina appeared in the kitchen doorway, a tray in her hands.

"I'll see to an extra setting," Thera said, leaving the two men frowning with bewilderment at each other.

"Wonderful," Philina exclaimed, setting the tray down and crossing the room to Nikolas. "It's been so long since you've stayed to dinner. Come," she steered him back to the table like a small, determined tugboat guiding a powerful ship. "There's plenty, plenty."

There was little conversation during the meal other than Philina's continuous exhortations to eat more of the roast lamb with the orzo mounded around it. But no one seemed comfortable enough to eat much at all. Nicodemus chewed distractedly, breaking off a piece of the pita bread to sop up the fatty juices that ran from his meat. He was so absorbed in studying Thera that most of the juice ran down his chin and dripped onto his hand. He wiped it away roughly with his napkin. She was up to something. Of that he was sure. Never did she forgive so quickly. It was not her nature. And there was no one she loathed more than Nikolas.

Thera felt her grandfather's eyes on her, but she maintained her concentration. The plate in front of her, the table, the apartment itself were reduced to shadowy images that hung at the periphery of her mind.

"Thera *mou*, you eat nothing," said Philina. "I cook all day, and you eat nothing. Nikolas, you, too. Some more meat. Some orzo."

Nikolas put his hand up in protest as Philina tried to scoop another helping onto his plate. "No, no, thank you. This is more than enough."

Philina shrugged and shook her head. "Everyone wants to be skinny. It's not healthy. I don't know."

Nicodemus picked up the half-filled bottle of red wine. "*Krassi?*"

Nikolas extended his wineglass. Nicodemus refilled it and then his own. Philina's glass was virtually untouched, and Thera never drank alcohol. Having tried it once, she'd decided she didn't like what it did to her, the cloudy, off-center feeling. "I won't surrender any part of my mind," she'd declared when Nicodemus had asked her why she steadfastly declined even a glass of wine with dinner.

Nikolas sipped his wine and stole a glance over the rim at Thera. He was startled to find her staring directly at him. Her eyelids were partially lowered, sheathing her eyes, but he could still feel their full intensity. He wanted to look away, but that wouldn't do. He wouldn't give her that satisfaction. He continued sipping the wine, his fingers rigid around the glass stem, and stared back at her. She would have to look away first. They seemed to be locked on each other for hours, but he knew it couldn't have been more than a few minutes when Nicodemus ended the silent battle with a gruff attempt at conversation.

"Thera, tell me, has anything interesting arrived at the museum recently?"

Thera smiled, a small, knowing smile, and let her eyes drift, wide and innocent, toward her grandfather.

"Nothing remarkable."

Nikolas felt released, as if it had been against his will that she had held his eyes. But that wasn't possible. It had been his choice not to turn away. His neck was stiff. He swiveled it

gingerly and finished his wine in one long swallow. He ought
to excuse himself, thank Philina, and leave. But he sat where
he was.

"We had a little upheaval at the museum this evening,"
Thera was saying. "Milo had a heart attack."

"Such a thing. He's still a young man," Philina clucked,
rising. "If no one is eating, I'm going to start the coffee."

"I called an ambulance," Thera continued. "It's a good
thing I was with him or he might still be lying there." She
started to help Philina clear the dishes.

There was something about her tone that disturbed Nicodemus. Such a short while ago she had been involved in a life-
or-death emergency, yet she recounted it without emotion, as
if it were something she'd seen on a movie screen or a long
time ago. An icy foreboding stole through his body, and it
took a vast effort to shake himself free of it. He poured the
last of the wine into Nikolas's glass.

"Drink. Drink to health."

Philina served the coffee along with a tray of *bougatsa* that
she had baked earlier in the afternoon. Nikolas bit into one.
The cold, rich custard slid over his tongue, but he took no
pleasure in it. Whenever he looked up, Thera was staring at
him. He would never have admitted it to anyone, but he found
her particularly unnerving tonight. There was none of the
patent malice he usually saw in her expression, none of the
hatred or contempt he had learned to detect beneath the surface. But neither was her expression benign. She reminded him
of a velvety spider spinning lacy webs of death. The urge to
leave welled up in him again. He swallowed the pastry with a
mouthful of coffee. All that wine was making a weak fool of
him. She wouldn't win so easily. He would stay awhile, and if
he made her uncomfortable, so much the better.

Nicodemus gave up trying to understand Thera's behavior
and decided instead to enjoy what appeared to be a temporary
truce between the two beloved children. Buoyed by the warm
glow of the wine, he launched into a story about a friend's
fishing boat.

Nikolas tried to pay attention, but his eyes kept moving
back to Thera. At one point she smiled, and he found himself
smiling, too. Where was the hostility? A new sensation flared

in him, and he realized he was now looking at her not as an adversary but as a woman. Her steely eyes were muted in the lamplight, the defiant thrust of her jaw softened, her whole posture more pliant. He knew that such a transformation was unbelievable and yet he believed it. He knew more powerfully than ever that he should leave, and yet he was more than ever determined to stay. He was at war within himself, and that part which was realistic and instinctive was losing. He could feel his tensions ebb and with them his defenses. Worst of all, he didn't care. What harm could come of sitting here and listening to his uncle's fishing tales?

Nicodemus drifted from story to story with little regard for chronology. A tale from his early days as a fisherman was followed by an anecdote he'd heard only yesterday at the wharves he still frequented. Philina, who had heard all the stories before, nibbled at a pastry with tiny, critical bites, nodding as if to compliment herself. She slipped an extra one onto Thera's plate.

Thera ignored the cake. She had sampled something far more satisfying than a simple confection. Nikolas's resistance was giving way. She had made it past the first barriers. But it was not over yet. She would have to be careful and diligent now, for she could still fail. The intensity of her concentration was causing a small pulsing of pain between her brows, but success would be worth the discomfort.

"Excuse me, Grandfather," she said. "I've developed a headache. Maybe a little fresh air . . ." She started to rise.

"So I've given you a headache," Nicodemus grumbled good-naturedly. "I can take a hint."

"It's time I left, too," Nikolas found himself saying. It was late, and he had proven himself by not running off sooner. He kissed Philina, thanking her and complimenting her on the meal, said good night to Nicodemus, and followed Thera out the door.

They walked down the stairs in silence, but once outside Thera turned to him.

"Perhaps you wouldn't mind taking me for a ride before you go home? It's so still tonight, and a breeze would help my head."

She made the request without any apparent guile, but still

Nikolas hesitated. This is Thera, Thera, an inner voice reminded him. Beware. No one changes in a matter of hours. Least of all Thera. But the voice was thin and remote like an isolated violin playing a different tune from the rest of the orchestra. He wanted to take her in his car. He wanted to be with her. He wanted . . . He couldn't understand why, but it scarcely mattered.

"Nikolas?" Thera had moved closer to him.

"Why not?" he said with a nervous laugh. "Come on."

The car was parked at the curb, unlocked. Thera slid into the passenger seat, rubbing at the spot between her eyes and smiling.

Nicodemus was standing at the window when Thera climbed into the car. His brow was pinched in a frown, and he ground his teeth. This sudden reversal of Thera's was more than merely peculiar. It troubled, even frightened him. Was this, then, the beginning? He stood at the window long after the car's taillights had disappeared, searching for answers in the empty darkness.

For some time an alarm had been sounding deep in his core. And there had been the dreams as well. To another man they might have been no more than a recurrent and uncomfortable nightmare, but not to him. A spasm rocked his body at the memory of them. Raging black-green thunderheads boiling up over the horizon, hurtling together over a clear blue sky with such intensity and speed that the world shook beneath them. Within seconds they obliterated the sky, the earth, everything. They roared around him, and their fury vibrated inside him. They filled his nose and throat until there was no air to breathe. He was wrenched awake, gasping and trembling in a pool of sweat.

What would happen, or when, he didn't know, but he had no doubt that something momentous, perhaps even monstrous, loomed ahead. Philina's hand on his back startled him. He jerked around to face her.

"What is it?" he growled. "Why must you sneak up on me?"

Philina blanched and drew her hand back as if she'd been burned. It was hard to recognize her Nicodemus in the angry old man he had become during these past weeks. He had never been particularly tender or romantic, but neither had he ever treated her unkindly. Lately he'd been lapsing more and more often into moody silences, snapping answers to ordinary questions. At dinner tonight she had thought, hoped, that his old good humor was returning. But now a stranger stood before her, glaring at her with eyes that seemed not to see her at all.

"Well, what is it?" he demanded.

"Nothing. I . . . I was wondering what was so interesting outside, that's all."

"Thera just rode off with Nikolas," he grumbled.

"And this disturbs you?" she inquired in a small voice, trying to understand why it should. Wasn't Nicodemus always complaining because the two didn't treat each other with the respect due family?

Nicodemus threw his hands up in frustration. "Yes, this disturbs me. And if you bothered to think about it, if you used your head, old woman, it might even disturb you!"

Philina's mouth moved in silence for a moment, struggling with a rage and pain that would not work themselves into words. Tears blurred her vision, and she turned and walked away.

Nicodemus slumped against the arm of the couch and rubbed his open hand across his face. What indeed did he find so disturbing? If he couldn't cope with Thera's whimsical behavior, how could he hope to deal with the stuff of his dreams? He owed his dear Philina an apology.

He found her in the bedroom, a small black shape hunched over on the edge of the bed. There was no light on, only a diffused glow from the hall. He sat down beside her.

"I'm sorry. Sorry." He reached for her hand. She didn't resist, but let it rest inanimate in his callused palm. "I know I've been difficult lately." The words did not come easily.

Philina tilted her head to look up at him.

"I'm a foolish old man, my dear, and I've been troubled. I'm afraid it's gotten the better of my nerves and my good sense." He hadn't wanted to tell her this, to worry her, but it was the truth and the only excuse she would accept.

Philina's distress evaporated with concern. No amount of pain could permanently cloud the fact that she loved this man.

Her fingers curved around his. "What is it?" she whispered, her throat still thick with tears.

Nicodemus sighed deeply. "I don't know. Something will happen. It waits just ahead of us."

A chill flashed along Philina's skin. "The dreams again?"

He nodded.

"Perhaps it's nothing," she said, but the words held little conviction. Nicodemus had always had the gift of dreams, in his case a dubious gift. More often than not, they presaged tragedy and death. Although she'd been a skeptic when she'd first met him, she'd quickly come to accept this ability of his as fact. They had only dated twice and had been well chaperoned. They'd barely known each other when Nicodemus had shown up at her house unexpected and uninvited. He'd claimed she would be needing him. She'd protested, appalled by his aggressiveness and arrogance, and told him to leave. He in turn had refused to go and had settled himself on the ground in front of her house. Not two hours later a policeman and a priest arrived to inform her of the accident that had claimed her parents' lives. Philina had collapsed. Nicodemus had been there to catch her and see her through the ordeal.

Now there was even a modern name for it—psychic ability, the sixth sense. Giving it a scientific label did little to lessen the impact though. And looking into Nicodemus's troubled gray eyes, she trembled at the prospect of what must lie ahead.

Nikolas had taken the road south out of Heraklion. They had passed the ruins of Knossos over a quarter of an hour earlier. As they drew near the village of Archanes, the countryside leveled out into a plain, and vineyards fanned out on either side of the car looking like an exotic stunted forest in the glow of the headlights. During the ride they had exchanged only a few words, and Nikolas still felt vaguely uncomfortable. Whenever he turned from the road he would find Thera watching him with a smile that teased at his defenses. He was attracted to her and suspicious of his own feelings.

"How's your headache?" he asked.

"A little better," she lied. Actually the pain was increasing, drumming behind her eyes and tightening in a band around her head. She'd been at it for too long. But she was learning and that made the pain bearable. Apparently a long period of concentration was more difficult than the shorter, more intense focus she had used earlier on Milo. It couldn't be helped, the situations were different. Nikolas was not the easy prey Milo had been, and because her goal was loftier, her method this time was far more intricate—the difference between wielding a meat cleaver and using a surgical laser.

"Could we stop and walk for a while?" she asked.

Nikolas shrugged. "We could drive into Archanes if you want to walk."

"No, right here, I mean. It would be so nice and quiet. I'd just like not to hear anything. Not even the car engine."

"All right." Nikolas slowed the car to a stop on the narrow dirt shoulder of the road, the right-side tires digging into the cultivated field. He watched Thera open the door and step out. He decided to sit in the car and wait for her. No sense in both of them stumbling through the furrows in the dark. Her golden hair was shot through with silver in the moonlight, and a sudden breeze molded her thin dress to her long, tapered legs. He felt his body responding in spite of himself. A well of heat erupted in him and flashed through his groin and down along his thighs. What in hell was happening to him? That was Thera out there, he told himself. Thera, who had always been anathema to him. Nothing had changed. She was motioning for him to join her. He shook his head angrily and looked the other way. Let her take her damn walk and get back to the car. It was late, and he had to be up early tomorrow. Why had he driven all the way out here anyway? Why had he agreed to take her for a ride at all? He wanted nothing to do with her. He turned to his right to call to her, to tell her that they were leaving. But she wasn't there. He scanned the field slowly. She couldn't have walked out of his range that quickly. She must have stumbled and fallen among the low trees. He started to open the door and stifled a scream. She was standing at his window, smiling at him. She'd crossed behind the car and come up on him unnoticed. She opened the door.

"Come walk with me." Her voice was sweet, cajoling, but there was an authority in it that he sensed more than heard.

"No, it's time to go, Thera. Get back in the car. We're leaving."

She reached for his hand. "Just for a minute."

He flinched at her touch, yet couldn't bring himself to draw away. She led him from the car and through the rows of vines drooping under their burden of grapes. His mind was numbed. Thoughts withered before they could become whole. They walked to the far side of the field where a few acres had been left fallow. Thera stopped and turned to him, close to him; he could feel the fabric of her dress flutter against his pant leg. Her fingers entwined in his were a live current that sparked desires deep inside him. His instincts screamed danger. He wanted her desperately and as desperately wanted to run from her. Emotions collided in him with such ferocity that his body swayed like the grape leaves in the wind.

Thera's smile was gone. Her eyes were opaque, hypnotic, the brows peaked with intensity. The pain was savage. It bit into her brain and exploded in her skull. Nikolas's face swam before her, the struggle an agony mirrored in his black eyes. She was almost there. If she put her mouth on his or moved her body against him, he would capitulate. But that wasn't enough. She focused more sharply, tensing as the pain roared through her.

Nikolas felt it happen, felt his will crack and shatter beneath hers. It was as if the fingers that held his hand now held his mind as well. Strangely, he didn't care. Surrender was a relief after the battle. He didn't know why he had fought so hard. He was consumed with an exquisite passion, stronger than any he had ever known, and nothing mattered but to touch her, to feel his mouth on hers, to be part of her, to love her.

His mind seemed to awaken some time after his body, for he found himself sitting up on the hard earth. The moon had set, and the breeze had stiffened. He shivered and realized he was naked. Half-formed thoughts slid through his grasp like minnows through a child's hand. Another chill shook him, and instinct made him look around for his clothes. They were strewn about haphazardly, his shirt near one hand. He grabbed it up, but his arms were limp and rubbery, and it took him several minutes to pull them through the sleeves. He spotted his pants several yards away, and that was when he noticed her. She was leaning back on her elbows watching him. Suddenly the confu-

sion was gone, and in its wake came a stunning clarity. Nikolas remembered. Anger and repulsion ripped through him.
How could it have happened? It was incredible that this delicate young woman could have controlled him so completely.
Yet there was no other explanation. Whom could he tell? Who
would believe what had happened here tonight? Nicodemus
had made a grave error when she was born. She should have
been put to death before her eyes ever opened.

Thera rose. She picked up his pants and tossed them at him.
In spite of the dense black of the moonless sky, he could see
her face clearly as if it were outlined by a peculiar light. She
was drawn with fatigue, and hollows like charcoal smudges
framed her eyes, but she was smiling, a sly, self-satisfied smile.

"I have to go now," she said offhandedly and turned to
walk back toward the road. Nikolas could hear his keys jin-
gling in her hand. "I'll drop the car off at your apartment."

Shame and an impotent rage seethed in him. He would
jump up and seize her and rip her apart. But his body, still entombed in a heavy lethargy, would not respond. It took all his
strength to spit a few indistinct words at her retreating form.

"You pay, Thera. Some—someday you pay."

Thera didn't stop. His words were of no consequence. She
had succeeded, but it had been vastly more difficult than she
had anticipated. And more costly. She needed to sleep. It was
convenient that Milo would not be at the museum the next day
to question her absence.

6

New York City: October 3–4

"I didn't think he'd ever stop," Aria groaned as she and Karen filed out the door of the lecture hall.

"Stratford likes the sound of his own voice," Karen said, stopping abruptly with her hand on Aria's arm. "You know, you don't look right." They were standing in the middle of the hallway, breaking the tide of other students like a jetty.

"Oh, I'm fine," Aria assured her. "I just need a couple of aspirin for this headache." She touched the bridge of her nose and winced. "It came over me right after we got into Stratford's class." She started walking again, obliging Karen to fall in beside her.

"Come on downstairs so I can get water to take my aspirin. You've got time for a cup of coffee."

The cafeteria was nearly deserted. A few students were scattered around the room with mugs of coffee and open law books in front of them. Aria chose a small corner table and watched Karen pick her way through the maze of tables, balancing the tray. She sat down opposite Aria.

"Here you go. One water, not a drop spilled."

"Thanks." Aria took two aspirin out of her purse and swallowed them with a mouthful of the water.

Karen sipped her coffee. "You've been getting a lot of headaches lately."

"I know," Aria said dismally. She had never been susceptible to headaches before, and she was becoming increasingly concerned over this sudden incidence of them.

"Look, maybe it's just eyestrain from all the reading we have to do. Why don't you get your eyes checked? It might be as simple as that."

"I suppose I should," Aria agreed, but privately she doubted that an ophthalmologist would have the answer. Her eyes weren't bothering her at all, and there'd been no change in her vision.

Karen opened her mouth as another possibility occurred to her, then shut it abruptly. The movement hadn't gone unnoticed.

"Were you going to say something?" Aria prodded.

"I didn't want to sound like your mother." Karen hesitated. "On the other hand, I'd feel responsible in case . . ."

"In case what?"

"Do you think the headaches could have anything to do with the experiments you've been doing?"

Aria shook her head. "I don't think so. All Michael's had me do is some card guessing. It's so easy it's almost boring."

"Michael, is it?" Karen smiled slyly, and Aria found herself smiling back. Just the thought of him was enough to make her momentarily forget the throbbing in her head.

"Well, it's silly to be formal when we're going to be working together. Besides, he's an awfully nice guy. I should thank you for pushing me in his direction."

"I was wondering what changed your mind about volunteering."

"I haven't actually committed myself. I've just agreed to a couple of simple tests."

"How are they going?"

"Okay, I guess. Michael makes a lot more out of them than I do. He can't believe the accuracy of my scores. He says I perform better than anyone he's ever found."

"Oh, really?"

"Wipe that smirk off your face. I haven't even seen him outside the office."

"How big is the office?"

"Very funny."

"Are you disappointed?"

"You know, I think I am. But he seems determined to keep our relationship purely professional. Either that or he's just not interested."

"Now, there's one I don't believe."

Aria put her hand up to her head. She was suddenly disoriented and queasy. The aspirin wasn't helping. In fact the pain was more intense than ever.

Karen took a last swallow of her coffee. "You're looking a little green. Think you can make it through Fischer? We've got exactly three minutes to his class."

Aria took a deep breath. "I'm sure going to try." She gathered up her purse and books and followed Karen toward the door. "But I don't think I'll be able to keep my appointment with Michael this afternoon."

Karen slid her tray onto the return stack and shook her head. "You're too conscientious. In your place, I'd say the hell with Fischer and go home and take a nap until it was time to see Michael."

Aria never made it to Michael's office. After Dr. Fischer's class Karen took her home in a taxi and left only when Aria, lying on the couch with a cold cloth on her forehead, protested that she was fine and there was nothing more that could be done for her. With Karen gone and the apartment quiet, Aria slid into a deep sleep. She didn't awaken until the next morning, nearly fifteen hours later. The headache, although not entirely gone, was reduced to a dull ache more like the memory of pain than the pain itself.

Michael phoned in the afternoon, concerned because it was unlike Aria to miss an appointment.

"I'm sorry, Michael. I should have called. I had this really monstrous headache, and I fell asleep. The next thing I knew it was morning."

"When you sleep, you really sleep," Michael laughed. "I must have called half a dozen times last evening."

Aria found that peculiar, but said nothing. Usually a footstep on the staircase or a door closed down the hall was enough to awaken her. The telephone was no more than six feet from where she'd been lying.

"Are you feeling better?" he was asking.

"Yeah, just sort of bruised."

"Well, if you're up to it, I could see you today."

"You work on Saturdays, too?"

"Whenever I can get hold of a volunteer. Listen, we'll take it easy. If you feel even a twinge of the headache returning we'll pack it in."

Had it been anyone else, Aria would have declined. She felt strangely depleted, hung over from the pain and the long hours of sleep. But the opportunity to see Michael, even professionally, was too tempting to resist. And the alternative was to spend the day doing laundry and studying.

"Just give me a couple of hours to pull myself together," she agreed. "I seem to be stuck in first gear."

Michael arrived at his office an hour early, too restless to wait at home. He tried to work, but couldn't concentrate on the tables of statistics in front of him. As much as he hated to admit it, he was as eager to be with Aria as he was to test her. He had become emotionally involved in spite of his pledge to remain detached.

When she finally walked into his office, he regretted having suggested that she come. Her face was waxen, pinched with fatigue, making her eyes appear larger and giving her an air of great vulnerability. His initial reaction was to gather her in his arms. Instead he ushered her gently into the one padded chair behind his desk.

"Are we trading places today?" she asked with a wan smile. "Or do I look as if I might break?"

Michael was frowning at her. "You didn't have to come, you know."

"I'm fine, really," she insisted, realizing as she said it that she did feel better just being there with him.

Michael brought her some coffee from the machine and was relieved when a touch of color returned to her cheeks.

Aria put the cup down with a grimace. "That stuff is awful. It could revive a corpse."

"It works better than smelling salts." He grinned.

"I'm ready for anything now. Bring on the cards."

"I thought we'd try something different today." He was already shuffling through a heap of manila folders and envelopes on top of the filing cabinet. Aria wondered if there was anything actually inside the cabinet. He withdrew a small stack of the envelopes and set to work clearing off his desk, explaining as he worked.

"This is called picture drawing. It's a free-response method that tests the extent of a person's psychic abilities. Only trouble is, it's hard to evaluate. With cards either you guess the three of diamonds or you don't. With picture drawing, it's sometimes hard to determine whether a response is close enough to be considered correct." He slid the last of the papers onto a growing pile in the corner of the room.

"Ah, my car keys," he said, scooping them off the now clear blotter. "I've been looking for them for three weeks."

"You've been locked out of your car for three weeks?" Aria laughed.

"No, of course not. I may be disorganized, but I've learned to live with myself. I have a spare set. In fact, a friend keeps a third set for me. A very organized, efficient friend." He pocketed the keys and set unlined paper and a pencil in front of her. Then he pulled one of the plastic chairs up to the other side of the desk and sat down with the envelopes in his lap.

"I'm going to give you one sealed envelope at a time. Inside each one is a carefully wrapped picture. You may have it near you, but you may not touch it. You are to draw what you perceive to be in the envelope." He slid the first one across the desk close to her paper.

"Have you ever done this sort of thing before?"

"No, never," Aria replied, intrigued by the new test. But as she stared at the yellow envelope a memory flashed through her mind. It had been back in junior high school. She'd received her report card and was afraid to show it to her father because she had done poorly in history. Damos had read the anxiety in her eyes when she handed the report to him still in its manila envelope. He never opened it, but tossed it onto the table and pulled her into his lap, hugging her close to him.

"You mustn't let it upset you so, Ariadne," he'd said. "One C is nothing. Nothing. And confidentially I was never very fond of history myself."

At the time Aria had been too overwhelmed with relief to question how he had known what was on the report card without having seen it.

"You can start anytime you like," Michael said.

For a moment Aria thought of mentioning her father's psychic abilities, but she decided against it. Michael would only want to test him as well, and Damos would hardly be a willing subject. When Aria had admitted to him that she had, after all, started doing some minor experiments with Michael, he had been clearly agitated and unhappy. It would be best to keep Michael off the scent. She looked again at the sealed envelope beside her and tried to concentrate. It wasn't difficult. After a few seconds an image took shape in her mind. She reached for the pencil and with a minimum of strokes sketched a fairly good representation of the Eiffel Tower. She handed the paper to Michael, who marked the back with a number, which he also printed on the envelope. Aria tried to read his expression, but couldn't tell if she'd been correct or not.

"Do you know which pictures are in the envelopes?" she inquired.

"Yes and no," Michael replied. "I selected them and inserted them, but I have no idea just which ones I'm handing you or in what order. Ideally, someone else should have made the selection, but I'm all I've got. Besides," he added with a twinkling smile, "I'm extremely honest and trustworthy." He handed her the second envelope.

Aria worked her way through nearly a dozen pictures, some of them drawings of single objects, others of complicated scenes or designs.

"I think that'll do us for today," said Michael, collecting and numbering the last paper and envelope.

Aria pushed back from the desk and stretched her arms over her head. "No argument." She rose and went around the desk to Michael. "Is it against the rules for me to see how I did?"

"I don't know how it can hurt. Just don't try to explain the drawings, okay? They have to stand on their own merit."

"Not a word." Aria perched on the edge of the desk and watched Michael match up the envelopes and the pictures with the corresponding numbers. The first one, the Eiffel Tower, was correct, and Michael was clearly impressed. With each succeeding picture she could see the extent of his wonder grow until he put down the last one and looked up at her, mouth slack, eyes so intense that the gold flecks appeared to be on fire.

"Any impartial judge would call every one of these correct," he murmured as much to himself as to her.

"But I reversed the buildings on this one," Aria pointed out quickly. "And I have an extra elephant over here." She felt compelled to point out that she hadn't been absolutely right. Although she wanted to please Michael, she didn't want him to regard her as an anomaly, some rare scientific find. She wanted him to see her as an ordinary woman. One he might someday wish to date.

Michael shook his head, a slow smile of amusement curving his lips. "You're a tougher critic than my adviser."

"I just don't want any unfair advantages."

"Don't worry, I haven't given you any." He'd only meant to pat her knee reassuringly, but his hand rested there and he found himself staring up into her face. Neither of them wanted to be the first to move or break the silence. Then at the same moment they both stood up.

"Thank you for coming in today," he said.

Aria reached for her purse. "It was interesting. Better than the cards."

"I have other good ones, I promise. When can I see you again? I mean, when can we continue?" Flustered, he straightened his corduroy jacket, and Aria noticed that two of the buttons were hanging by a thread.

"Next Thursday? And remind me to bring along a needle and thread—you're falling apart." She touched the buttons.

Michael thought he could feel her fingertips all the way through to his skin. Next Thursday was too far away. The tests could wait, and he had other volunteers to see and material to collate. But *he* couldn't wait. Not till Thursday. He glanced at his watch.

"If you're not in a hurry, we could go somewhere and have dinner."

"No, I'm in no hurry. My laundry will wait for me. It's very devoted."

"Great," said Michael, already chastising himself for breaking the rules. "If I work you this hard on a Saturday, the least I can do is make sure you have dinner and get home safely." He'd deal with his conscience later.

They decided on a restaurant near Michael's school that specialized in oversized hamburgers and crisply broiled potato skins with cheese and bacon. They drank red wine and talked easily, opening up their lives to each other, the food growing cold on their plates as if they'd been hungrier for the bond than for the nourishment.

"I think people are waiting for this table," Aria observed finally. The check had been placed on the table over half an hour earlier, and now a busboy was clearing their coffee cups while the waiter lingered impatiently over them.

They were swept outside on a gust of cold wind that whispered of winter not far ahead. Aria shivered in spite of the sweater she was wearing.

"Wrong time of the year to leave your coat at home," Michael said, shrugging off his corduroy jacket and putting it over her shoulders.

"Now you'll freeze," Aria protested.

"Not me, I'm hot-blooded. Besides, now you can keep me warm," and he held her tightly against his side as they walked.

Michael insisted on seeing her home. He told himself it was only because of the dangers that lurked in the city. But he wasn't that gullible. The truth was he didn't want to let go of her. He didn't want the night to become a memory.

Aria was silent during the cab ride back to her apartment, wondering what she would do if Michael wanted to make love to her. She rarely allowed men to spend the night with her. Not that she was old-fashioned, but she did need to feel some emotional bond with a man before she could allow any physical intimacy. It had nothing to do with morality. She had just learned early on that sex on the purely mechanical level held no appeal for her, and she no longer gave in to desires that would fade well before the night was over. Tonight, though, she seemed to be a mass of nerve endings, her senses all sharper in spite of the wine. They short-circuited her logic and overwhelmed her. By the time the taxi stopped in front of her building, she knew that if Michael wanted to stay she would let him.

The studio apartment that had always been spacious enough for her alone suddenly seemed smaller with Michael there. He wandered around, trying to stay out of her way while she fixed Irish coffee. Then they sat on the couch that opened into a bed and drank their coffee and talked some more, the words like invisible threads they were weaving between themselves. Aria was more than ready when Michael finally bent to kiss her, cupping her face in his hands as if she were a fragile crystal he was afraid of shattering.

They explored each other's bodies with the same patient intensity with which they had at first explored each other's minds. Aria could feel herself opening up to him, the deep, private core, which she had always kept inviolate, unfurling under the glow of his touch. Even as she surrendered her being entirely to Michael, she knew without question that he was giving as much.

7

Heraklion, Crete: October 13

Thera dried herself briskly and slipped on her underwear. She plucked her watch off the shelf above the sink. The crystal had fogged from the steam, and she had to wipe it against her slip to read it. Eight-thirty. She'd lost track of the time. She didn't want to be late today. Milo was back at the museum, his doctors frankly baffled by his case. Although he'd apparently suffered a massive heart seizure, their tests and machines recorded no abnormalities. Finally, unable to present any credible excuse to keep him longer, they had discharged him. Thera used her towel to wipe the mirror. She wasn't suddenly interested in pleasing Milo with her punctuality, but several new acquisitions were due in from Knossos and the grateful curator had offered to let her work on them. Was it his way of thanking her for acting so quickly and possibly saving his life? Thera smiled at herself in the mirror and stroked mascara onto her lashes. Or did he perhaps realize that his life actually did rest in her hands in a much more tangible way? Was he trying to appease her as one would an angry goddess? The idea appealed to her, but she knew it wasn't likely. Milo's beliefs were cast in cement and immutable. He was merely acknowledging the human act, not the superhuman one. She ran a brush through her hair, pulled on her robe, and left the bathroom.

She dressed in her bedroom, the same small room she had occupied since her earliest memories. From the kitchen she could hear Philina singing tunelessly, which meant Nicodemus had already left for the day. She never sang when he was

home, since he protested, though gently, that her voice grated
on his nerves. Even at this early hour he was probably down at
the waterfront talking with cronies or helping out on a friend's
fishing boat. In spite of his official retirement, forced on him
by an ailing back, his life had changed little. Thera couldn't
comprehend such a static existence in one who harbored so
much potential. She had always looked upon her special gifts
as a resource to be exploited, whereas Nicodemus considered
them one more burden to be borne.

Thera slid her feet into sandals and went to see if there was
coffee. A harsh buzzing had erupted outside, causing Philina
to suspend her singing. She watched Thera pour herself coffee.

"That's all you want?" she said, straining to make herself
heard above the noise.

"I'm late." Thera mouthed the words. She took the steaming mug over to the living room window to try to locate the
source of the disturbance.

In the small park across the street, two workmen were saw-
ing down a dead tree. Although the park was deserted at this
hour of the morning, they had cordoned off the area as an
extra precaution. Thera sipped her coffee and watched them
work. One of the men was in his forties, the other barely out
of his teens. They were both wearing short-sleeved shirts that
capped muscular arms already glistening with sweat. The tree
was thick and gnarled, and their saw was having trouble biting
into it. They stopped for a minute, and the older man wiped
his forehead with a cloth he kept hanging out of his pants
pocket. Then he nodded, and they set to work again.

It occurred to Thera that she could easily do the job that
they found such a struggle. She'd been moving inanimate objects since she was seven or eight. She had never tried anything
heavier than a stuffed animal or a vase, but she was fairly certain the tree would pose no problem. It had been more than a
week since her confrontation with Nikolas, and though it had
taken her longer than she'd hoped to recuperate from that
night, she was now wholly recovered.

The men had finally made some progress, and the tree was
notched to ensure that it would fall away from them into the
roped off area. Hardly a real challenge for her anymore, she

thought ruefully. Of course, she could throw it the other way
. . . an interesting prospect. She took a last swallow of the coffee and set the cup down on the windowsill. She focused her
mind on the tree, willing it to defy the machine that gnawed at
it and the gravity that pulled at its weakening side. She thrust
all her energy toward it, but the resistance she met caused her
to jerk back sharply. She rested a moment, frustrated and
puzzled. No dead tree could be more difficult than snapping
Nikolas's will had been. Perhaps she was too far away. The
men had sawed almost through the trunk to the point where
the tree would topple from its own weight.

Thera ran from the apartment, down the stairs, and out
onto the street. She locked her concentration onto the tree and
summoned all her strength. She could feel the tree give under
her efforts. It seemed to groan with indecision as the machine
thrust it one way and she pulled it the other. The branches
swayed violently, clawing at the sky for balance. The men
worked on, oblivious to the battle they were engaged in, expecting the tree to fall into the roped-off area, as they had
planned.

Out of the corner of her eye, Thera saw a group of young
boys coming along the sidewalk toward the park. They were
on their way to school, juggling books and lunch boxes and
running around one another so that they appeared to be playing rather than walking. The smallest boy had a ball that the
others were trying to keep away from him. They tossed it teas-
ingly back and forth over his head. They had almost reached
the park when the ball rolled free and the little boy made a
dash to retrieve it. Thera saw him running even as she felt the
tree wrench under her power. Another instant and it would
fall for her, but the child would be in its path. If she released
her hold, it would go the other way and fall harmlessly into the
safe area. The power surging through her was sweet and seductive, demanding fulfillment. As she pushed the tree over, a
nearly sexual gratification flooded her body.

The tree cracked, lurching sharply toward the workmen.
They shouted and ran. But the boy, engrossed in catching his
ball didn't hear them in time. The dead timber crashed onto
the sidewalk. He was pinned under its branches like the prey
of some black skeletal being.

Thera rushed across the street to him. She helped the workmen lift him out and away from the tree. He was limp in their arms, his hair already darkly matted with the blood that flowed from a gash on his temple. She instructed them to call an ambulance, and then she sat down to wait, cradling the child's head in her lap. The distance had thwarted her at first, but it had been easy as soon as she was close enough. With practice she might be able to increase her range. There was a new challenge to consider as well—focusing on two targets simultaneously. Had she been able to do that, she might have deflected the ball at the same time she brought down the tree. An intriguing possibility. But there were limits that even practice wouldn't overcome, and she knew that she was closing in on them. She would need her sister.

8

New York City: October 13

"Blood! There's too much blood!" Aria's cries roused Michael, who bolted up and switched on the lamp beside the bed. He saw her sitting in a tangle of sheets, eyes wide open, staring at some invisible horror.

He shook his head, trying to clear away the haze of sleep. "Aria, what is it?" He was sure he had misunderstood her. "What did you say?"

Aria kept staring at the sheets. "Blood. He's losing too much blood." The distress in her voice was so genuine that Michael looked at the bed again as if expecting to see something he had missed the first time. Then she looked up and through him as if he weren't there. Her mouth hitched up in a smile that immediately mutated into a grimace. She started crying. Michael was shaken. He didn't understand what was happening, but it was obvious that Aria needed to be comforted. He folded her in his arms, stroked her hair, and whispered her name. Her body was rigid and unresponsive for a long while. Then he felt her shudder and relax as if whatever had gripped her had suddenly let go. Finally the crying diminished to a subdued hiccup-like sob.

"I'm okay now, Michael," she murmured haltingly.

He held her away from him and studied her as if to assure himself that she really was all right. "That must have been one hell of a nightmare," he said.

"More than a nightmare." The words had tumbled out before she could stop them. She wanted to tell him about the dream, but how could she explain it without sounding insane?

"What does that mean?"

Aria thought of detouring around the subject, but telling him a lie would be like driving a wedge into their relationship. Sooner or later he would have to know it all.

"I wasn't sleeping," she said. Suddenly cold in her sheer nightgown, she pulled the covers up around herself. "At first I was asleep, but then I woke up. I was wide awake during the worst part." She hesitated. "I just wasn't really here."

Michael's brows drew together, and he looked at her bewildered. "Of course you were here. You were right here with me the whole time."

"Was I?" Her voice made it a challenge rather than a question, and Michael was forced to remember her blank eyes and the barrier he had felt between them when he held her.

"Some part of me was lost in that dream, Michael. Or maybe it would be truer to say that the dream wouldn't let go of me. It hung on, superimposed itself over my real life."

"That doesn't make any sense. I've never—"

"I've never heard of anything like it either," Aria said for him, her voice threatening to crack. "Unfortunately that doesn't seem to stop it from happening."

Michael leaned back against the headboard and drew her against him, needing to comfort himself as well as her.

"It's happened before?"

Aria let her head drop onto his shoulder with relief. She had finally told someone, and he hadn't called Bellevue yet.

"Only twice in my life until recently," she said. "But this episode was the second one in less than a month."

Michael was silent, trying to put the fragments of her story into some kind of logical framework.

"Does it mean I'm going crazy?" Aria asked after a few minutes. She tried to keep her tone light and playful, but Michael could hear the anxiety threaded through it. He kissed the top of her head.

"I hardly think you qualify," he said. For the past two weeks he had spent all his free time with her, and he was as sure as a layman could be that the only extraordinary things about her were her physical beauty and her psychic talents. Could there be a psychic connection to the dreams, he wondered. He proposed the possibility to her.

"After all," he said more firmly, as the idea took hold in his own mind, "dreams are one kind of brain wave activity. And so is extrasensory perception. The brain is the seat of it all. You may just have overactive brain waves, my love, and unusually elaborate dreams."

"I guess that could be it," Aria agreed halfheartedly. His explanation sounded plausible enough. Then why wasn't she able to accept it? The more she thought about it, the clearer the answer became. Michael's facile explanation couldn't account for the emotions that enveloped her in those dreams, emotions that were so completely alien to her that she felt mortally threatened by them.

Michael turned off the light and slid down under the sheets again. He pressed himself along the length of her hoping his warmth could draw off the cold and fear he still sensed in her. His hands and mouth caressed her body, tracing the silky swells and hollows as if he were touching her for the first time. Aria moaned softly, arching her hips against him, grateful for the intense rush of desire that swept away the last vestiges of the dream and its hold on her.

She awakened to find Michael propped on his side looking down at her. Rectangular shafts of sunlight fell through the vertical blinds, spotlighting the dance of a thousand swirling dust motes.

"How are you feeling?" Michael asked, his eyes narrowed with concern.

Aria yawned. "As if I could use a good night's sleep."

"Now, you can't lay all the blame for that on me." Michael kissed her and got out of bed. "I am going to make you the most incredible brunch you've ever tasted," he said. "Guaranteed to exorcise even the grimmest denizens of the night. You just stay right there and rest."

Aria watched him pad across to the bedroom door in his pajama bottoms and realized how much she enjoyed just looking at him. His body had the lean, healthy musculature that came from playing tennis and swimming rather than the oversized bulges that resulted from bodybuilding. Michael disappeared through the doorway, and a moment later she could hear him moving about in the kitchen. She snuggled down under the quilt, which smelled faintly of his cologne, and surrendered to the languor that always succeeded the dreams. She felt warm and secure here in his loft; she'd liked it from the moment she'd walked in. Once a huge open expanse, it had been partitioned into two bedrooms, a living room, kitchen, and bath. The high ceilings and spare furnishings imparted a feeling of spaciousness in spite of the dividing walls. Because of the building's location in Chelsea the loft was convenient; Michael shared the rent with another graduate student who had temporarily moved in with his girl friend. Michael didn't think that relationship would last, but while it did, he and Aria had the loft all to themselves.

Having seen Michael's office, Aria hadn't been at all surprised by the chaos of objects she found everywhere. But, as she remarked to him, she didn't understand how one person with so few furnishings could create such a whirlwind effect. In her own apartment such confusion would have irritated her. In Michael's she accepted it as normal and right. And it was here they stayed whenever they were together. After the first night in her cramped studio, it was clear that they needed more room. Aria liked the arrangement, staying in her apartment alone during the week when she needed to concentrate on her law studies, going to Michael's on the weekends, like taking a vacation. In his loft she could immerse herself totally in the feel of him. Everywhere she looked and touched and smelled there was something more to add to her sense of him. She was dozing off again when he came to the doorway.

"Brunch is served," he announced.

Aria stretched luxuriously, reluctant to leave the comfort of the bed. Michael helped her into her robe and pulled her out to the kitchen.

"All I have is a package of English muffins," he apologized with a sheepish smile as he poured the coffee. "I forgot to go shopping."

"Good," Aria said with a laugh that became a yawn. "I think that's about all I can handle."

While they ate, Michael tried to make conversation, commenting on the movie they'd seen the night before, suggesting ways they could spend the Columbus Day holiday. But Aria was inattentive and listless. She drank her coffee, her cheek propped up on one hand. Michael reached across the table and covered her free hand with his.

"Whatever those dreams are, they take a lot out of you, don't they?"

She nodded.

"I've been thinking—there may be a way to get to the root of them."

Aria looked up, a hopeful glimmer brightening her eyes.

"Now, I can't guarantee anything, but hypnosis just might help." Michael saw her flinch and felt her hand contract under his. "Does that frighten you?" he asked, perplexed.

Aria rose abruptly and walked away from him to the window. The sun was a small fiery patch in the cloudless October sky. She could feel the heat of it through the glass, but it did nothing to warm her. Had she taken on her father's fears? Perhaps Damos was right. Some things were better left unexplored.

"I *am* afraid," she said finally, staring down into the street below. "Right now I'm still able to keep the lid on it, most of the time anyway. If I take that lid off—I don't know . . ." Her voice trailed off. She heard Michael's chair scrape back on the floor. Then his arms were turning her around to hold her. The fine hair on his chest was smooth beneath her cheek, and the beat of his heart comforted her.

"Without light, a dark room can seem pretty terrifying, even to an adult."

Aria knew what he was trying to say. The sensible part of her believed it. But another part of her eschewed sense and logic, and she believed that also.

"Is hypnosis really safe?" she murmured, her head nestled just below his chin.

"Yes, absolutely. It's a clinical technique that's been used successfully for decades. I wouldn't have even suggested it if I had the slightest doubt."

What if hypnosis could really put an end to the dreams? Aria wondered. It was tempting. She did trust Michael implicitly. She had to let go of her father's fears and superstitions sometime.

"Okay," she said, moving back far enough so that she could look up at him. She managed a smile. "Go get your pendulum."

Michael smiled back at her, and she could see the gold flecks in his eyes reflect the sunlight from the window. "I don't use a pendulum."

He had her lie down on the bed, and he closed the blinds, turning the room into a gray twilight. Then he pulled one panel aside so that a single bar of sunlight slid across the ceiling, and he went off to hunt for his cassette recorder. Aria waited, stiff and anxious, wondering if he would be able to put her under, and half hoping he would fail. Michael returned with the recorder and a kitchen chair. He placed the chair beside the bed and sat down.

"Okay," he said. "I want you to look up at the light on the ceiling and listen to me." His voice was low and measured, vaguely seductive. "You're going to relax your muscles. You're going to start with your feet. You can feel it beginning in your feet. Your toes are loosening. Like a peaceful wave, the relaxation is flowing up into the muscles of your legs. Your calves are becoming soft and heavy. The wave is moving up into your thighs, carrying tensions away. Your muscles are becoming limp, loose, totally at rest. You feel as if you are sinking, melting into the bed. The bed alone is supporting your body. It's so restful. You're giving yourself up to the peace and comfort of it." Michael continued in his soft monotone, instructing her to relax each part of her body until he reached her eyes.

"You're so relaxed now, so completely at peace, it's impossible to keep your eyes open any longer. Your eyelids are so weary, so heavy. Your eyes are tired. You cannot see distinctly anymore. You want only to close your eyes. Close your eyes."

Aria's eyelids quivered and closed. Michael leaned over her. He lifted her hands and started them turning about each other. When he moved away, she continued the motion until he told her to stop. Satisfied that she was well into an intermediary trance, he started the recorder and set it on the night table.

"You are resting very peacefully, Aria," he said. "We're going to take a look into some of your dreams. What you see or smell or taste will not be real and cannot harm you or anyone else in any way. You will not be frightened or upset. I want you to go back now to the dream you had last night and tell me what you are seeing.''

Aria lay immobile on the bed. Michael repeated the command, but it was several moments before she responded. When she spoke, her voice was so thick and indistinct that Michael repositioned the recorder.beside her on the pillow.

"It's dark. We follow the small light. It smells funny."

"What does it smell like?"

"Wet and old.''

"Have you been here before?''

"I know this place.''

"Are you with anyone?''

"Yes. Almost everyone is here.''

"Who are these people?''

"My people.''

"Who are your people?''

"Mine.''

Michael would have liked to pursue that line of questioning further, but he sensed he had reached a dead end. He decided to try stimulating her memory with the little he already knew of the dream. "Can you see the blood?''

"No blood here.''

Michael hesitated, puzzled. "Is this the dream you had last night?''

"Not a dream.''

"If you are not in your dream, then where are you, Aria . . . ? Aria?''

Aria didn't reply. Her face remained expressionless. Michael leaned over, studying her, wondering if she had slipped into a deeper trance than he had intended. Not that the possibility alarmed him; he could still wake her at will. She was just more likely to perceive things other than those he requested.

Without warning, Aria's eyes flew open, startling Michael so that he rocked back hard on his chair, nearly toppling it backwards. Before he could right himself, Aria shattered the stillness, her voice hollow and vibrating like an echo of itself. She spoke louder than she had before, but Michael had no idea what she was saying. She was speaking in a foreign tongue. Baffled and intrigued, he tried to figure out which language it was. His own study of foreign languages had been limited to three frustrating years of high school French and a semester of college German meant to enable him to read scholarly papers in his field. He remembered little of either language, but at least he could say with certainty that she was not speaking either one.

He started questioning her, hoping to nudge her back into English, but his words had no impact on her flowing, incomprehensible monologue. Then her voice took on a peculiar urgency, and within seconds she was screaming abrupt, terrified phrases. Although Michael didn't understand the words, he knew she was panicked and on the verge of hysteria. He ordered her to speak English. She paid no attention.

A cold, slippery fear was insinuating its way into Michael's mind. What if she could no longer understand English at all? What if she didn't respond to his command to awaken? What if . . . ? Michael jerked his head in a hard, angry motion. Everything would be all right, he told himself, as long as he didn't lose control. But control and objectivity were harder to maintain when emotions interposed themselves. Aria was not just another volunteer for his study. He had fallen in love with her the day he met her, and he was desperately afraid of hurting her. His self-confidence began to shatter as he looked at her lying there, but not really there at all. He inhaled deeply, as if he were sucking his courage back in. He leaned close to her ear.

"Aria," he said sternly. And when she didn't pause in her own one-sided conversation, he called her name again, louder. And again. Her eyelids closed, and she fell silent. Michael lowered his voice, afraid to exhale the sigh of relief that had welled up inside him. She wasn't out of it yet.

"Can you hear me now, Aria?" he asked, trying to keep the trembling out of his voice.

"Yesh," she replied, slurring the word.

"Good. Very good. It's almost time to wake up. Nothing that you saw or heard will linger to upset you. You will feel well rested. I am going to count to three, and when I reach three you will be awake. One, two, three."

Aria's eyelids fluttered open. She turned lilac gray eyes to Michael and smiled.

"Did it work? Was I hypnotized?"

Michael forced his mouth into a lopsided smile. "Yeah," he said, his voice whispery with relief. "Do you remember anything?"

Aria shook her head. "Did you get it on tape? I'd love to hear it." Michael's expression was peculiar as if someone had done a poor job of pasting a smile on his face. There was no reflection of it in his eyes. She couldn't see the gold flecks at all.

"You don't seem very pleased." She sat up and faced him. "What deep, dark secret did you uncover about me?" she asked playfully, though she was afraid he had indeed uncovered some awful truth that would prevent him from ever loving her again.

Michael took her hands in his. "Nothing awful, I assure you. Perhaps *strange* would be a better description."

"Well, I'm waiting."

"What foreign languages do you know, Aria?"

She shrugged. "A few scraps of French and Spanish. I never stuck with either one long enough to become fluent."

Michael picked up the recorder. He rewound it and played it back for her. Aria listened raptly. At the point where she heard herself switch languages her eyes shot up to Michael's.

"That can't be me, Michael," she protested. "I don't even know what language that is. Do you?"

Michael stopped the recorder. Listening to the tape with her, one possible explanation had occurred to him.

"You told me your parents immigrated here from Greece, right?"

Aria nodded.

"Could that have been Greek you were speaking?"

"Even if it was, how did I learn it?"

"Maybe you heard your parents speak it at home and your subconscious picked it up without you even realizing it."

"No. They never spoke Greek. Not even when English was still new and difficult for them. I remember once or twice my mother lapsed into Greek, but my father insisted she stop. It was almost as if he wanted to sever every bond they'd ever had with their homeland. I don't know why. It's something they won't discuss."

Michael was frowning at the floor. "Still, there has to be some logical, scientific explanation."

Logic, thought Aria, as a sense of foreboding crept through her. Now that the lid had been lifted, would logic or science ever again be enough?

Michael was talking to her. She tugged her mind back from her fears to listen to him.

"Do you think your parents would be willing to translate this tape for us, if it is Greek?"

"As I told you, they don't like being reminded of their heritage. But maybe since it's just a matter of translating a few words . . . We can try. The worst they can do is refuse. Besides," she added, a genuine smile brightening her face, "it would be a good excuse to have you meet them." In spite of her father's staunch opposition to her participation in the psychic testing, she believed that once he met Michael he would like him.

"Why do I feel as if I'm about to be thrown to the lions?" Michael asked wryly.

9

Heraklion: October 19

Philina was already asleep when Nicodemus and Thera returned home from Knossos. There was a low light on in the kitchen, and a fresh pot of coffee was brewing on the stove.

Thera poured a cup of the coffee.

"Do you want some?" she asked her grandfather, who stood watching her from the kitchen doorway.

Nicodemus shook his head. What he wanted was to talk to her. There never seemed to be a time when they were alone together. At home Philina was always around, and he and Thera only went out by themselves if there was a meeting at Knossos. He thought of the days when she was a child and he would take her to the park to play or down to the waterfront where she loved to watch the ships and the fishermen. He remembered beaming with pride when his friends would remark on how bright she was and what a beauty she would someday be. Looking at her now in the dim kitchen light, he was as overwhelmed as ever by that beauty. But he could no longer see the child she had been. She was like some strange treasure he had found—no, rescued—not a part of him at all.

And there was the troubling business of her relationship with Nikolas, which he'd been unable to fathom since that night he'd seen the two of them drive off together. From what had appeared to be a budding friendship had developed an animosity more virulent than ever. Nikolas had refused to discuss the matter with him, other than to grumble about Thera abusing her powers. But the bitter hatred Nicodemus had sensed in his nephew had made him recoil physically and recalled to his mind the angry thunderclouds that still ripped apart his dreams.

Although he was reluctant to alienate Thera further, he had to seize this opportunity to speak to her, to try to find some answers. He would need to be calm; he must not badger her or be too demanding. He hoped he had absorbed some of Philina's gentle ways over the past forty-five years.

Thera had moved to the tiny table with two chairs that stood in one corner of the kitchen. Nicodemus took a cup down from the cupboard and filled it from the pot on the stove.

"I guess maybe I will have a little after all," he murmured, not really wanting the coffee but needing an excuse to join her.

Thera made no comment. They sat and drank their coffee together, the silence so dense Nicodemus thought his words might sink into it like stones and never reach her ears. How should he begin? He was paralyzed with indecision and misgivings as if he confronted an adversary and not this girl he'd raised from infancy. Irritated with himself, he forced out the first words.

"So," he said, "it seems I was prematurely optimistic."

Thera turned to him, her slender eyebrows arched.

"A couple of weeks ago when Nikolas was here for dinner, I would have sworn the two of you were actually tolerant of each other and perhaps even becoming friends." He studied her face as he spoke, hoping to read something there that she might not offer verbally. But her expression was inscrutable, as smooth and constant as if etched in marble.

"You have nothing to say to this?" he prodded gently.

"I didn't hear a question," Thera replied.

Nicodemus felt his hackles rise at the subtle mockery of her tone. He had to struggle to keep his own voice neutral.

"Was I not correct about what I saw and heard that night?"

Thera's smile was condescending. "You probably exaggerated."

"But you did drive off with him."

The smile faded. "Not much escapes you."

"You're wrong," he said ruefully. "As of late a great deal seems to escape me. Perhaps you wouldn't mind explaining it to me."

"I had a headache, and I thought the fresh air might help, so Nikolas took me for a ride."

"A friendly gesture on his part, to be sure. Is it my imagination, then, that the last two times we all met at Knossos the two of you didn't exchange a word, not even a civil greeting?"

Thera hesitated a moment before responding, and in that brief instant Nicodemus read dissimulation.

"We wound up arguing that night. Over something trivial. I don't even recall what it was anymore. Look, we aren't meant to be friends, Nikolas and I. It's as simple as that. If it distresses you, I'm sorry." Thera rose and went to put her cup in the sink.

Nicodemus chewed on his lower lip. She wasn't sorry. He had never known her to be sorry about anything, he realized with sudden clarity. In fact he wondered if she understood the meaning of regret. How had he and Philina failed to instill in her concepts as important as compassion and sympathy? How many more of their values had merely splashed over her, unabsorbed, like water over a mouthless vase.

Thera was already at the doorway, but Nicodemus had more to say. He turned in his chair to face her. "There's something else."

Thera stopped where she was and waited. She was weary of the inquisition, yet she knew it would not be wise to raise too many questions in the old man's mind.

"There are those who say you make unjust use of your powers," said Nicodemus.

Thera was immediately alert. She'd counted on Nikolas's pride and fear of disbelief to keep him from exposing what she had done to him. Had she underestimated him? She stepped back into the kitchen.

"*Who* says this?" she demanded.

"That is unimportant," Nicodemus said with a wave of his hand.

"Maybe to you it is, but not to me," Thera said sharply. "I wish to know who my enemies are."

"Enemies? That's a strong word. You believe you have enemies?"

"I believe jealousy brings with it enmity. And I know there are those who are jealous of me."

"You mean, of course, Nikolas."

"Can you deny that he covets my position and my powers?"

Nicodemus shook his head. He was no more blind to his nephew's faults than he was to Thera's.

"I doubt he would ever try to do you harm unless he was badly provoked."

"Provoked!" she thundered. "I provoke him with my very existence." In the dim light her pupils were wide, black wells, the irises no more than flinty bands of gray around them. "Just what in hell has he accused me of anyway?"

The discussion had deteriorated into a confrontation. Nicodemus needed to regain control of it.

"Thera!" he said sternly, raising his voice over hers, "you are overreacting. Calm yourself. No one has made any specific accusations."

"I see," she said, her voice reduced to a murmur.

Nicodemus was baffled. Not only didn't she demand more details, but the tight line of her mouth had softened into the curve of a smile. Her whole posture seemed to relax before his eyes. Whatever threat she had felt had clearly passed. He could let it end here, but he had one last thing to say.

"Enemies and accusations aside, Thera, there is something that troubles me."

Now that she was certain Nikolas had revealed nothing condemning, Thera regretted her outburst. Irrational behavior would not serve her well. She'd have to be more careful, especially around Nicodemus, who could see beyond the spoken word.

"What is it that troubles you?" she asked amiably, leaning back against the refrigerator. Let him ask his question. She would be careful to set his mind to rest.

"I know how little you revere the gods of late, and I wonder if perhaps you begin to place yourself above them?"

"Above them?" Thera laughed. How can I place myself above what no longer exists? she thought. But she said only what her grandfather wanted to hear. "They are the gods. I am only a woman."

Nicodemus nodded. "You are a clever woman. Sometimes, I think, too clever. But in the end you will fool no one but yourself. Do not mock the gods, Thera. They may not be as near as they once were, but neither are they so far away that they don't know what passes here."

"I'll try to remember that," she said lightly, walking over to him. "And don't you be so quick to believe what others say about me." She bent to kiss him, and her lips were as cool and dry as stone on his cheek. "Don't worry, you haven't raised a fool." She turned and left the kitchen.

Nicodemus stared with dissatisfaction at the coffee gone cold in his cup. He had said all he had intended to say, yet he sensed he had accomplished nothing.

Thera lay awake in bed and waited. She was tired, but the strong coffee was keeping her from sleeping. That was why she had taken it. She listened to the sounds of her grandfather preparing for bed in the next room. The soft thump of his shoes as he dropped them to the floor, the clink of his belt buckle hitting the chair where he left his clothes overnight, then the shuffling of his bare feet to the bathroom and back again a few minutes later.

She waited. It wouldn't be too much longer. Nicodemus always slept easily. She stared at the ceiling. Cracks and peeling plaster had given it the appearance of a relief map with rivers and mountains. The reflection of a car's headlights swept across it like a sudden sunrise, then plunged it back into darkness again. Thera strained to hear her grandfather's heavy breathing, but the wall that separated them was too thick, and her heart was making too much noise of its own. She waited a while longer, and when she felt quite sure that he should be asleep, she got up.

She moved down the hallway slowly, taking care to avoid the spots where she knew the wooden floor would creak. She stopped just outside her grandparents' door, held her breath and listened. Now she could hear the even rhythm of their breathing. Satisfied, she slipped into the room. Her eyes were accustomed to the dark, and she made her way easily around the bed, sidestepping Nicodemus's shoes to reach the chair near the window. She felt for his pants in the pile of clothing there. Taking hold of them by the heavy belt, she lifted them up. She slid her hand into one pocket and then another until she found the keys. She grasped them tightly and drew them out, careful not to jingle them. Then she put the pants back on the chair and left the room.

With the help of the flashlight that Philina kept in a kitchen drawer, Thera quickly found the key she needed. It was smaller than the rest, and she had often seen her grandfather use it. It unlocked one drawer of the desk that stood to one side of the apartment door. Thera located the drawer and slid the key easily into its lock. When she turned the key, the mechanism clicked, sounding like a gunshot in the stillness. Her heart tumbled wildly in her chest. She took a deep breath to steady herself. She didn't fear discovery, just the inconvenience it would cause, the need to alter her plans and schedule. No sound came from her grandparents' bedroom.

Her heart slowed. She pulled the drawer open, shining the flashlight over its contents. There were various documents, including a brittle yellow one that appeared to be her father's birth certificate. She paused with it in her hand, wondering if there was a birth certificate for her somewhere. She had come into the world under such a veil of secrecy that she doubted it had been documented anywhere. The thought didn't bother her. In fact, she rather liked the idea. It made her somehow less mortal. Gods and goddesses had no government papers attesting to their births. Although the lack of such a paper had made it difficult for her to obtain a passport, that feat had not been impossible. One simply had to find the right people and pay the going rate.

She replaced her father's certificate and rummaged farther back in the drawer. This time she withdrew a packet of airmail letters held together with a rubber band. She pulled one free and, holding it under the flashlight, tried to find the return address. There was none. She looked through all of them, but they were all the same. The writer of those letters had been very discreet. And Nicodemus had gone a step further by obliterating the postmarks. He'd left nothing to chance. The address existed only in his head.

Thera stood there in the dark, frustrated but unwilling to admit defeat. Finally she took the letters and the flashlight over to the dining room table. Perhaps within their contents she could find some clue Nicodemus had failed to censor. The

last, most recent, letter proved to be of some help. It was
dated nearly a year ago, and things could have changed since
then, but Thera doubted it. It seemed as if the letters were
meant to keep Nicodemus abreast of the basic currents of their
lives. Any important changes would have brought another letter. With a growing smile of satisfaction she reread the sen-
tence that would put her on her sister's trail.

Thera returned the letters to the drawer and locked it. She
replaced the flashlight; then she made her way back to her
grandparents' room. She skirted the bed and quickly crossed
to the chair. Her foot struck Nicodemus's shoe. She stumbled
and fought to regain her balance, but she was pitched too far
forward. She fell to the floor with a crash. The whole room
seemed to shake with the impact. The keys flew out of her
hand, jangling like a series of discordant chimes. She lay there
trying to ignore the pain that was shooting up through the
knee she had landed on, and wondering frantically if they
would believe she'd been sleepwalking.

After a moment she realized Nicodemus was still snoring
peacefully. Only Philina was stirring. Thera could see her covered form moving around on the far side of the bed. If she
were to turn on the lamp to see what had made the noise, she
would easily spot Thera sprawled there. Thera waited, expecting that at any moment the room would be drenched in light.
But Philina settled down, and after several more minutes she
seemed to have fallen back to sleep.

Thera drew herself up, wincing as she put her full weight on
the injured knee. Then, bent over, she groped along the floor
until her hand closed over the keys. She took care to replace
them in the same pants pocket from which she had taken
them. That done, she limped quietly back to her room and
eased herself into bed.

Sleep didn't come easily to Thera. And when it finally did
overtake her, it brought with it the same disturbing dream she
had experienced every night for more than a week. Like a pho-
nograph needle stuck in one groove, the dream played over
and over again in her mind. She was trapped underground,
stalked by a figure brandishing a bloody double-edged ax. The
ax was striking in its clarity. Everything else was dark and
amorphous. The more Thera strained to see, the more re-

stricted her vision became, until there were only the sparkling curves of the blades dripping with the viscous red blood.

Ordinarily Thera didn't worry about her dreams, although they could be as prophetic as Nicodemus's. But the power and persistence of this particular dream was awesome. It left her unrested and edgy. It stole her concentration at work. It eroded her confidence. Still she would not consider changing her plans.

10

New York: October 19

Aria was quiet as the car sped along the expressway toward her parents' home on Long Island. She was feeling anxious and vaguely guilty. When she'd called to ask if she could bring Michael out to meet them, she'd avoided mentioning the hypnosis or the tape. Over the phone it would have been too easy for Damos to refuse to translate it. In person she stood a better chance of talking him into it. She kept telling herself that she hadn't actually lied about the purpose of their visit. She did want her parents to meet Michael. She'd been dishonest only by omission. But somehow that didn't alleviate her discomfort.

As they drew nearer the exclusive North Shore community where she'd been raised, her apprehensions multiplied. She wanted Michael to like her parents, and she wanted their approval of him. But the encounter might be doomed if it started under a cloud of deception. It was too late to do much more than worry about it. She'd thought of asking Michael not to bring up the tape during this visit, but she knew how eager he was to hear the translation. And although he had listened patiently when she'd tried to explain how much Damos objected to her participation in the experiments, he clearly did not understand the depth or complexity of the problem. Against her better judgment she'd even mentioned Damos's psychic abilities, hoping in this way to make his reservations seem more credible. Still Michael failed to appreciate the resistance they would face. Defeated, Aria had given up. Aside from his rampant disorganization, Michael's only flaw appeared to be his blind devotion to his work. He would sacrifice almost anything to its advancement. Dispirited, she wondered if that might someday include her.

She turned to look at him. He didn't seem to mind her silence. And if he was nervous, he was masking it well. He had his window open to the fresh October air and seemed to be thoroughly enjoying the freedom of the highway after the tangled traffic they'd left behind in the city. He was singing along with the radio, beating an accompaniment with his open hand on the steering wheel as if it were a drum. He glanced at her and smiled.

"You're staring at me. I have great peripheral vision."

"I'm trying to figure out why you're not nervous."

Michael shrugged. "I don't believe in advance worrying. Besides, I'm sure you're doing enough of it for both of us." He took one hand off the wheel and held it out to her.

Aria sighed and slipped hers into it. His touch comforted her, and some of his confidence seemed to pass into her as if by transfusion. She was, after all, an adult now; what she did with her life and with whom she shared it were her decisions, hers alone. Her parents would accept Michael. They had no choice.

Michael had maneuvered the car into the right lane. Their exit was just ahead. Despite the renewed spark of courage, Aria was glad she had refused her mother's invitation to stay for dinner. If friction developed between Damos and Michael, they would all be spared an uncomfortable meal. Oh, hell, she thought, Michael was right. She did worry in advance.

Michael stopped singing when they left the highway so he could concentrate on Aria's directions. They swung along curving two-lane roads heading toward the Sound. Between the trees with their fiery autumn leaves, he caught glimpses of sprawling ranch houses and white-columned colonials set far back on manicured lawns that were still summer green.

"I've never been around here before." He whistled through his teeth. "Not bad."

The road sloped down suddenly, and as they came out of a hairpin bend, the silvery blue of Long Island Sound sparkled off to their left.

"We're almost there," said Aria. "Be ready. It's going to sneak up on your left. There it is now."

The blacktop driveway was nearly hidden in the overgrowth of trees and bushes that had usurped the shoulder of the roadway. If Aria hadn't pointed it out, Michael would have driven right by it. As it was, he had to swing the wheel sharply, spewing pebbles in all directions.

The driveway ran at a steep angle up to a parking area large enough to accommodate several cars. Michael pulled in between a late model Lincoln and a retaining wall. Above the wall rose the house, its stone base looking as if it had been hewn from the rocky cliff itself. The upper portions were all redwood and glass, cantilevered out over the water.

Michael's mouth dropped open for a moment. Then he turned to Aria. "I'm impressed."

"If an architect's house can't be impressive, whose can?"

"This isn't just impressive," Michael replied. "This is expensive."

"You can see my father is good at what he does. He's won a lot of awards, and he's always in demand." Aria got out of the car, then turned back to Michael, who was still staring through the windshield at the house. "Don't tell me you've finally developed stage fright." She laughed.

Michael grinned at her. "Maybe just a slight case of awe."

Aria's mother met them at the door.

"Mom, I'd like you to meet Michael Lansing. Michael, my mother, Helena Koraes."

Helena was a petite woman with Aria's full, engaging smile. Otherwise, with her black hair and eyes, she looked nothing like her daughter. She had a quiet warmth and reserve that tendered friendship but didn't overwhelm, and Michael liked her immediately.

"I'm so glad Aria brought you out here to meet us, Michael," she said in a soft, accented voice as she drew them into a vaulted entry illuminated by skylights. She took their jackets and led them along a wide marble hallway to a wood-paneled room that was lined on three sides with bookshelves. The fourth wall was entirely glass with a magnificent view of the Sound, the Connecticut shore a dark smudge on the horizon.

Damos Koraes was sitting at a sleek rosewood and chrome

desk in front of the windows, writing. He put down his pen and stood when he heard them enter. He embraced Aria; then he shook Michael's hand. His gray eyes, nearly the color of Aria's, were startling beneath the black eyebrows. Michael felt strangely naked under their scrutiny, and he had to remind himself that he had nothing to hide from this man.

"Your home is a masterpiece," he heard himself saying. Although it was true, he disliked resorting to flattery to win approval or friendship.

"Thank you," Damos replied with a careful smile.

Michael wondered if his psi abilities included telepathy. Discomfited, he moved away to look out the window.

Aria caught her father's eye and mouthed the word "please." Damos nodded ruefully. Although Michael's work represented a threat, he appeared to be an agreeable enough young man. For Aria's sake Damos would do his best to be pleasant. Besides, if he was unfairly rude, he would only succeed in pushing her more completely into Michael's arms. He joined Michael at the window.

"Mesmerizing, isn't it?" His tone had changed, become less formal, more conversational, as if some invisible barrier had been withdrawn.

Michael detected it and understood. There would be a truce between them for Aria's sake. Perhaps with time they would learn to be friends. "Yes," he replied. "I can stare at it by the hour. For some people it's fires. For me it's the water."

"For me, too," murmured Damos. "I've always been drawn to it. That's why I built my house here."

Michael was casting about for something neutral to say when Helena asked if he'd like a drink. He turned back to her. She and Aria were still standing in the center of the room like referees at a sparring match, alert and watchful.

Michael came up beside them. "White wine would be fine."

Aria smiled at him hopefully, and he smiled back with more enthusiasm than he felt.

Helena returned with the wine and a snifter of brandy for Damos, and they sat in the overstuffed leather chairs around a hammered brass table in one corner of the room. Michael drew Damos into a discussion of architecture, posing questions about future trends and regional differences. Initially

Damos's responses were courteous yet simple and to the point. But once he saw that Michael was genuinely interested, he spoke more freely and intensely, sitting forward in his chair, forearms resting on his knees.

Aria and Helena stayed at the periphery of their conversation for a while and then, as if satisfied that the two men were doing well enough, began to chat between themselves. But even as she appeared to be absorbed in Helena's words, Aria was still monitoring the other conversation. And when Damos deftly steered the subject to Michael's work, she felt her heart trip and accelerate. It was inevitable that he should inquire about Michael's work, and indeed it would have been patently impolite for him not to show some interest, but Aria knew what precarious ground they had entered upon.

Damos leaned back in the chair, the brandy snifter in his hand nearly empty.

"Tell me, Michael, does the scientific community still regard your specialty as a poor and unwelcome relation or has it finally accepted you?"

Michael grinned and brushed back the hair that had fallen near his eyes. "I can tell you appreciate the problem. We've definitely made some progress in gaining acceptance by the more orthodox branches, but we're still very much second-class citizens."

The exchange seemed harmless. Aria wished it would stay that way. Perhaps Michael would reconsider broaching the subject of the tapes. Surely he wouldn't want to disrupt this tenuous harmony they'd established.

"Do you yourself have psychic abilities?" her father was asking Michael.

"No, I don't. At least none that are clearly developed. I guess that's why the field has always fascinated me. It's something outside my own experience."

"I would think that could be dangerous."

"In what way?"

"Dabbling in matters you cannot truly understand."

Aria drew in her breath and held it. Nothing had changed in Damos's outward bearing, but his voice, while still measured and amiable, had acquired a subtle cutting edge. She glanced at Michael to see if he had noticed it. But Michael was totally absorbed in his favorite topic, and if he had sensed any change in Damos's tone he wasn't reacting to it.

"I don't think a doctor necessarily has to experience cardiac arrest in order to recognize and treat it," he replied. "Or for that matter, a psychiatrist doesn't have to be schizophrenic to help a patient with that disorder."

"You are overlooking one fundamental difference, Michael. In medicine and psychiatry there is a body of established knowledge on which to base decisions, a starting point of some substance. In your field there is nothing but guesswork and experiments. Psychic research is still in its infancy. You're not even sure what you are dealing with, where the ability originates, what forces control it, what forms of energy fuel it. You are like a blind man performing brain surgery by trial and error. I can't help being concerned for the safety of the patient."

Michael saw Damos glance meaningfully at his daughter. Apparently she had not overestimated his fears, after all. And as much as he hated to admit it to himself, Michael knew how valid Damos's concern was. He remembered with terrifying clarity the loss of control he had felt when Aria had slipped away from him during hypnosis. And he still could not understand or explain the phenomenon of her extended dreams.

"You're probably right about one thing," he said. "At this early stage it would be a great help to have people with personal experience and insight actively work in the field and help to develop it. People like yourself and Aria."

Damos drew himself upright. He finished the last of the brandy and put the glass down so hard on the brass-topped table that Aria thought it would shatter. Helena jumped, startled by the sudden shift in mood.

"You know I object to my daughter's involvement in your research," Damos said stiffly.

"Yes. But the decision to participate was entirely hers. She was not coerced in any way."

Except perhaps by a blinding attraction to you, Damos thought as he looked from Michael to Aria. But he simply said, "I didn't imply that she had been."

There was a long moment of silence, and Aria seized the opportunity to try to save the deteriorating situation by relating an anecdote about one of her law professors. Helena laughed, but Michael and Damos only nodded and returned to their topic as if there had been no interruption.

"Perhaps you'd like to know specifically what we've been doing," Michael said.

Aria closed her eyes and groaned inwardly. Michael was going to bring up the tapes.

"Yes, I would," Damos responded.

Michael spent the next few minutes describing the card tests and picture drawing he had done with Aria. Damos listened, his expression alert but unrevealing.

"The last thing we tried was hypnosis." Michael waited to see is there would be a reaction. He saw the lines around Damos's eyes and mouth deepen with the strain of maintaining his composure. Aria had been right. He was risking his future relationship with her father, but he doubted the older man would let him withdraw now. He looked at Aria. She had poured herself another glass of wine, and her hand trembled slightly as she reached for it. He was sorry for driving this wedge between himself and Damos, sorry for causing her so much anxiety. He wouldn't say any more unless Damos asked. Whatever else was revealed would depend on him alone.

"And?" Damos prodded.

"And?"

"What were the results of the hypnosis?"

"Inconclusive, I'd have to say."

"Why? What was the problem?"

"Something minor, really."

Damos was frowning at him. He'd have to be more explicit.

"Under hypnosis Aria lapsed into another language. I suspect it was Greek." He paused. "Would you be willing to translate?"

Damos rose abruptly. He pushed between the chairs and strode to the window. The sun was already low on the horizon, giving the water a glazed, ceramic appearance. Anger and distress churned inside him. Michael was a fool who didn't realize what he was tampering with. For that matter, neither did Aria. Maybe they had been wrong not to tell her, but they'd thought it too dangerous for her to know.

When Damos turned away from the window, his face was

taut and controlled. Deep shadows hardened the angles, and only his pale eyes seemed animated.

"You are dealing in things that can be disastrous," he said in a low, harsh voice. "Were you to walk through a mine field you would be in no greater danger. I cannot say more than this, though I know it is not enough. I know that neither of you believe me. To you I am an old man tied to old-fashioned ideas. I cannot forbid you to continue in these experiments, Ariadne, I can only hope you come to your senses in time."

Michael's face had clouded over as Damos spoke. Although he didn't believe Damos's concerns were legitimate, he knew they were real enough to him. He wished he could somehow allay those fears.

"I would never do anything to hurt Aria," he said.

"I believe you mean well," Damos replied, his tone suddenly weary and defeated. "But if you continue on your present course you will reach a point beyond which you will no longer have control."

The statement puzzled Michael. For that matter, a great deal of what Damos had said was couched in cryptic, vague terms. Michael would have probed more deeply, but he knew any such questions would only alienate Damos further.

Helena brought from the kitchen a tray of cheeses and French bread. She set it down near Michael and Aria.

"Please try some," she invited cheerfully. "I buy them at an excellent little cheese shop in town."

Michael was not at all hungry, but she was making such a valiant effort to save the afternoon that he felt it would be rude to decline. He sliced off a piece of the Brie and spread it on a chunk of bread.

Aria broke off a piece of the hard crust and nibbled on it absently. Listening to them argue she had come to a simple conclusion. The only way to prevent herself from being used as a pawn between her father and Michael was for her to choose a side and stick to it. Since the hypnosis was a fait accompli, there was no sense in trying to wish it away. And she wanted to know what was on that tape as much as Michael did.

She brushed the crumbs from her hands and stood before Michael could speak again. She went to Damos who was leaning against his desk like a contender waiting for the next round to begin.

"Dad, I understand your concern," she said softly. "But the tape is a reality. All we want is a translation of it. Michael could have it translated by someone at school, but we'd rather have you do it."

Damos studied his daughter. Her eyes and hair glittered in the fading light as if they had drawn off and stored the last of the sun's radiance. It had always been so difficult to deny her anything. And what she said now made more sense than she knew. It would be far better to translate the tape himself than to let a stranger do it. At least he would have some measure of control. He put his hand up to her chin and held it for a moment, enjoying the gentle symmetry of her features.

"Is there such a thing as love without worry?" he whispered so that only she could hear.

Aria rose up on her toes and kissed his cheek. "Thank you."

Damos withdrew a small cassette recorder from a desk drawer and followed Aria back to the circle of chairs. Helena had turned on two lamps that threw a mellow, rosy glow across the room.

Damos slid the recorder onto the table and took his seat. "Let's see what you have there," he said to Michael.

Too stunned to say anything, Michael watched Aria rummage through her purse for the tape. What could she possibly have told her father, or promised him, that would account for this sudden reversal in his attitude?

Aria found the tape, and Damos slipped it into the recorder. They sat staring at the spaces between the chairs as Michael's voice and then Aria's filled the room. At the point where Aria switched languages, Michael glanced at Damos. He saw no indication of surprise.

"Is it Greek?" he couldn't refrain from asking.

Damos nodded brusquely and held up his hand for silence. Michael looked across at Helena. Her eyes were flitting back and forth from Damos to the recorder to Aria and down to her own hands, which were moving nervously in her lap. She kept trying to engage Damos's attention, but he would only stare ahead of him, his face a mask of concentration.

Michael wondered why she was so agitated. Was it just because Aria was using a language she supposedly didn't know? Or did Helena's reaction have more to do with the content of those words? The tape was nearing the end. He could hear himself counting Aria out of the hypnotic state. Then there was silence. Everyone looked up expectantly at Damos.

"Dad?" said Aria.

His face relaxed into a smile, and he shrugged.

"You didn't say anything spectacular, Ariadne. You describe a darkened room. There are others with you, though you don't say who they are. And then it seems as if you become frightened. It was at this point that Michael awakened you."

Aria appeared disappointed. "Is that all of it?"

"Not word for word, of course, but a synopsis."

Michael thanked him, then looked again at Helena who was busy rearranging the cheeses on the tray. Feeling his gaze, she lifted her head. She tried to smile, but her lips merely twitched up at the corners, then drew straight once more. He wanted to ask her if she had anything to add to Damos's translation, but he knew that would come dangerously close to calling Damos a liar.

Aria sighed. "It doesn't sound much different from a lot of dreams I've had."

Damos studied her for a moment. "I'm glad I was able to ease your mind."

Aria stood. "And maybe we've eased your mind as well," she said, "now that you see how innocuous these experiments really are."

"There's one thing I don't understand," Helena remarked.

Damos looked at her sharply.

"How could Aria have been speaking Greek if she never learned it?"

"It's conceivable she picked it up subconsciously from hearing the two of you speak it," Michael suggested, curious to hear what they would say.

Helena started to protest. "But we never—"

"Oh, yes," Damos interjected quickly, "that's quite possible. Aria was no more than a toddler when we switched completely to English, so she probably would not remember it."

The explanation made sense to Michael. Although Aria had told him she'd never heard them speak Greek, she might have been too young to have accurate memories of that time. She may simply have stored the knowledge on another level of consciousness, which they'd tapped into during the hypnosis. But Michael had developed another, more intriguing explanation.

"I've been toying with another theory," he said. "Telepathy. Maybe in a hypnotic state Aria is able to draw information, thought patterns, directly from a receptive source such as you, Mr. Koraes."

"I've never heard of anything like that," Damos retorted.

Aria sensed another confrontation building. "I'm afraid that discussion will have to wait for another time," she said brightly. "Michael, we have to get going or I won't be prepared for class tomorrow."

Helena brought them their jackets. "Perhaps the next time you'll be able to stay for dinner."

"Thank you. It was nice meeting you, Mrs. Koraes," Michael said warmly. "Mr. Koraes." He turned to shake hands with Damos.

"I'm glad we had this opportunity to meet you, Michael." Damos's voice was cordial but cool.

"If I could have the tape back. . . .?"

"I'm sorry, I didn't realize you still needed it." Damos plucked the tape out of the recorder and handed it to Michael.

"For my research records," Michael said as he pocketed it. "The scientific process demands proof."

Damos nodded. He had hoped Michael would forget about the tape and leave it behind. There was always the possibility that he was suspicious enough to seek another translation.

Aria kissed her mother and came up to Damos. He drew her into his arms and held her close for a moment.

"Be careful," he whispered, wishing she were still a little girl he could protect.

"Was that the disaster I think it was?" Michael asked, once he'd maneuvered his car down the driveway and back onto the road.

"I've had nightmares that are worse, if that makes you feel any better."

Michael turned to her and smiled, the warm, easy smile that tipped his eyes up at the corners. Aria felt lighter, as if she had shed a coat that weighed heavily on her shoulders. As much as she adored her parents, it was only when she was away from them that she could sometimes escape the mysteries that crowded her—mysteries Damos seemed to understand but refused to explain.

"Does your father always talk in riddles?" Michael asked.

"Only when it comes to these psi powers of ours. I know it makes him sound a little paranoid. Believe me, I've tried to figure it out myself. And my mother's no help at all. She acts as if I'm Torquemada of the Spanish Inquisition if I even bring up the subject. I don't know, maybe he suffered some deep, dark trauma having to do with E.S.P."

"I know a good shrink."

"Come on, Michael, you're fairly perceptive. Do you think he would go?"

Michael shook his head. "One thing's clear—he loves you very much." He guided the car onto the expressway.

"I know."

"And your mother is a lady in the finest sense."

Aria opened her window a crack. Her head felt stuffy. Probably a mixture of too much wine and too much tension. Michael's voice was muffled. It was hard to concentrate on what he was saying. Ahead of them the sun was an overturned orange cup spilling its light below the horizon. Behind them the sky was already swathed in night. Her skin prickled uneasily. The darkness seemed about to overtake them as they tried futilely to outrace it. She heard Michael calling her name. She turned to him. His face was fragmented, as if she were seeing it through a kaleidoscope.

"Aria. Did you hear me?"

"No, sorry." The words were leaden on her tongue.

"I said I'm going to have someone at school translate the tape again. I'd like an exact word-by-word transcript of it."

The remark, buffeted by the heaviness in the air, took several moments to reach her and register fully. When it did, a sudden tidal wave of anger swelled inside her.

"You bastard! How dare you?" she exploded, shaken by her own vehemence. Although she didn't care for the implication inherent in Michael's statement, she didn't understand why she was reacting so violently. She heard herself lashing out at him, as if she were an impotent observer.

"You're saying my father's translation was a fabrication, a lie! That he's our enemy! Well, look to yourself, Michael. I know who my enemies are!"

Michael snapped his head around to look at her. Her face was luminous, and even in the darkened car her features were distinct. She was staring at him, her eyes glowing with a steely brilliance, her lips twisted into a malevolent curl.

Aria could see her own confusion mirrored in Michael's face. She struggled to explain that she hadn't meant it, but the words were lost somewhere inside her and darkness was consuming her.

A horn blast shattered the silence. Michael swung the car back hard into its lane.

"For God's sake, Aria," he said, trying to keep his eyes on the road. "If you're that adamant about it, we'll forget it. I wasn't calling your father a liar. I'd just like to see a literal translation. It would be easier to work with than the paraphrase he gave us."

He waited for a response from her, and when none came he pulled his eyes from the road to glance at her. She was slumped against the passenger door, her eyes closed, her face lost in shadows. He called to her, but she didn't move. Indifferent to the irritated blasts from the cars behind him, Michael slowed and pulled off onto the shoulder of the highway. He switched on the emergency blinkers and leaned across to her. As he came nearer he could discern the peaceful rise and fall of her chest. His initial fears abated. He stroked her cheek and called her name. When there was still no reaction, he took hold of her shoulders and shook her, gently at first, then roughly.

Aria's eyes blinked open. The car had stopped. Michael was only inches away, staring at her, the skin between his eyes deeply furrowed.

"Michael, what is it? What's wrong?"

Michael sighed. "I don't know. Do you remember what just happened?"

"I remember watching the sun setting and then . . . we had a fight, didn't we? I'm not sure why, but I remember feeling an uncontrollable rage."

Michael recounted what he had said about the tape and how she had reacted.

"It was so unlike you that it really took me by surprise."

Aria thought for a moment. "The strange thing is, I'm not even sure the tape was really the cause of the anger. It just suddenly erupted and needed a focus, so it settled on you."

Michael knew how desperately she wanted to understand what had happened to her, but he couldn't supply a comfortable answer. His own thoughts were in chaos. Her behavior had been radically inappropriate and out of character. He found himself considering mental aberrations and just as quickly discarding them. Insanity was an unthinkable explanation. He reached for her hands. They were dry and very cold. As he rubbed them, he could feel the cold spread into his skin.

"Have you ever experienced anything like that before?" he asked.

Aria shook her head. Tears welled up in her eyes and trembled on her lower lids. "I'm frightened, Michael," she whispered. "Do you think my father was right? Did that happen because of all the tests and the hypnosis?" She blinked, causing the tears to roll off her lashes and down her cheeks. "Maybe there are powers in me that I can't control."

Michael brushed at the tears with his fingertip. "I honestly don't see a connection, but we're not going to take any chances. No more tests or hypnosis for you. At least not until we figure out what's been happening."

Aria leaned her head against Michael's shoulder. Although her mind was in turmoil, there was a comfort in knowing that he placed her above his work.

Michael took her back to his loft. She had classes the next day, but she didn't want to be alone that night. She didn't care if she had to wake up at dawn in order to go home and change and collect her books, as long as she could spend the night in the security of Michael's arms.

She fell asleep almost as soon as she closed her eyes. But Michael lay awake well into the early morning hours trying to make sense of what had occurred. Parapsychology might be a new science, but it had its set of fundamental laws, and Aria seemed to be operating outside of them. As important as she was to his project, he couldn't risk experimenting with her anymore. Not until he had a clearer understanding of the dynamics involved.

He looked down at Aria and smiled. She was nestled in the crook of his shoulder, her arm across his chest, one leg flung over his as if to prevent him from disappearing during the night. He strained to pick out the delicate curve of her profile in the darkened room, and he was jolted by the memory of how she had looked in the car screaming at him. Her face had been fully illuminated then as if someone were holding a light to it. They might have been traveling under a street lamp at the time. But even as he considered that possibility, he knew it wasn't the answer. The reflection had been too bright, and besides, that section of the expressway had no lights.

Another hypothesis was working its way into his mind. He'd read an article a year or more ago about the work Soviet scientists were doing in parapsychology. They connected psychic ability to a life energy they called bioplasm. They even claimed to have developed a technique that enabled them to photograph this energy as it flowed from the body. It was said to show a pulsating glow that radiated from the hands or eyes or from the entire body of certain individuals. Could it have been such a bioplasmic glow he had seen around Aria? Perhaps her psychic abilities were so advanced that the energy was at times visible even to the naked eye.

Michael was well aware that the Soviet theory was rejected as thoroughly unscientific and invalid in the United States. But lying there in the dark where everything seemed possible, he could no longer dismiss it so casually.

11

Heraklion: October 20

Thera swept into the Olympic Airways office like a blast of cold air. She'd already spent her entire lunch hour at the bank where the crowds, the petty regulations, and the general ineptitude of the personnel had pushed her to the brink of outrage. She'd come perilously close to striking out, but she knew there were times when it was best not to draw too much attention. And this was surely one of them. Instead she had to satisfy herself with a verbal lashing of the arrogant young bank officer who made it so difficult for her to close out her small savings account. Not only did he give her endless forms to fill out and demand every scrap of identification she could produce, but he had the audacity to address her by her first name and study her with a lascivious expression that said he approved of what he saw.

By the time Thera was through lambasting him, his swarthy face had gone colorless, except for two spots of high color on his cheeks, and he had sunk several inches in his chair.

When she stormed into the airlines office she was still burning with indignation. A solitary man was being helped at the counter while two unoccupied clerks chatted together. She surveyed the scene with bitter relief. It was fortunate she would not have to wait. She had no intention of wasting any more of her time and her patience, both of which had been dangerously depleted.

One of the women behind the counter smiled as Thera

marched up to her. "May I help you?"

Thera made no attempt to be cordial. Few people were worth that effort.

"I want a one-way ticket to Paris on Friday the twenty-fourth," she said tersely.

The woman dropped her smile, and her tone became all business.

"I'll see what we have." She punched the information into a computer. "There's a ten A.M. flight on the twenty-fourth."

The rest of the transaction took only five minutes. Thera paid for the ticket in cash and left with it in her purse. Before returning to the museum, she stopped to place a long-distance call to Arlette Marceau who had roomed with her at the university. Arlette was thrilled to hear that Thera was coming to Paris and insisted she stay in her apartment. When Thera hung up, she was calmer and in better spirits. Everything was falling into place. She headed back toward the museum. Milo was next on her list.

The door to his office was ajar. She could see him behind his desk, his head cocked to one side, listening to Demetrius, who was standing a few feet away speaking rapidly and gesticulating.

Thera knocked on the doorjamb and stepped in. Milo turned to her, his lips pursed in irritation. Demetrius jerked his head around to see who dared intrude so rudely.

"Good afternoon, Mr. Stefanatos," Thera said. "Demetrius." She nodded stiffly at him and, without waiting for a reply, turned back to Milo.

"I'd like to speak to you, if I may." Although the words were deferential, her tone was commanding.

Anger erupted in Milo. Anger at having been interrupted, at her rudeness, at her imperious tone. It boiled and rumbled along the corridors of his brain. He would have enjoyed disciplining her right there in front of Demetrius. But he fought down the rage, reminding himself how much he owed this woman. Had it not been for her quick action, he might not be sitting here at all. He swallowed hard, his Adam's apple twitching as if a great lump of frustration blocked his throat. Why did he feel neither warmth nor gratitude toward her, but rather a subtle uneasiness that crept like an icy liquid through his bowels?

"All right, Thera," he said tightly. "I'm sure Demetrius won't mind if we finish our discussion a little later."

"Whenever it's convenient for you, Mr. Stefanatos," he said, glowering at Thera. His hostility had become more open since Milo's attack, as if he resented her having been Milo's savior. Ordinarily Thera would have exacted revenge for this treatment, but now she was too preoccupied to bother. Demetrius was no more than an irritating fly that buzzed at the edge of her awareness.

He brushed past her, shutting the door behind him. Thera waited until she heard his footsteps retreating down the hallway. Demetrius was not above lingering outside to listen.

She approached Milo's desk and without invitation sat down in the chair across from him.

"I need an indefinite leave of absence," she said without preface. "The reason is personal. I don't expect to be paid except for the two weeks' vacation due me."

Milo was nonplussed both by the content of the request and by the arrogance with which it was delivered. He drew himself up in his seat, his loose jowls bobbing above his starched collar.

"I'm afraid that is out of the question. There is work here that must be attended to."

"Hire someone to work in my absence with the understanding that when I return the substitute is to leave." She'd almost said "if I return," but she'd caught herself in time.

"You don't know when that will be."

"Correct."

"The position requires a highly trained person. Such an individual will demand a certain degree of job security."

"Jobs are harder to come by than pride. You'll find someone," said Thera, her gaze unwavering.

Milo felt the hairs on his arms prickle and his stomach and throat contract as if he were suddenly frightened. It made no sense, yet he couldn't shake off the anxiety that gripped him. He ran a trembling hand over his bald crown, which was clammy with perspiration.

"Such a thing is without precedent," he said, his voice high and thin as he struggled to maintain his poise.

"Then you will be a trendsetter," Thera replied.

Taking the remark as a joke, Milo forced a brittle laugh. But when he looked at Thera's face, the sound was choked off abruptly. Her eyes were steel knives plunging into him.

"Everything will work out," she said. "You shouldn't worry so. You don't want to bring another attack upon yourself, now, do you?"

Milo felt his heart quiver as if it had access to knowledge still denied him.

Thera had risen. "I'll write up the paperwork for my leave. I'll have it here for your signature before the end of the day."

He watched her walk to the door. He had to call her back, be firm, make it clear that what she was asking was impossible. That if she left she would in effect be quitting. But he was engulfed in a miasma of fear and weakness. A weight pressed against his chest, and his lunch rose in his gorge. He said nothing. And once Thera had disappeared down the hall he was relieved that he hadn't spoken. Later he would pass it off to Demetrius as his own brilliant plan for ridding themselves of Thera. As for himself, on some instinctive level he knew that as long as Thera was gone he would be left in peace.

On Friday it rained. The wind drove the water in sheets that chattered against the windows. Thera was up before dawn listening to its dismal rhythm. Nicodemus would not be going to the waterfront today, and that meant her departure would be made more difficult. She hadn't yet told her grandparents she was leaving. It was imperative that no move be made to stop her. She had planned on telling Philina that morning and leaving it for her to explain to Nicodemus. Thera was no coward, but she was practical, and her grandfather could be an awesome adversary if he chose to be.

She heard the clanging of pots in the kitchen. Philina was awake, preparing breakfast. That meant it was six-thirty. The old woman never slept later. Thera got out of bed. Moving quietly and relying only on the muted light from outside, she went through her closet until she found the suitcase from her university days. It would be colder where she was going, the winters harsh in contrast with the springlike winters of Crete. She would take only the essentials and outfit herself properly once she arrived there.

After she had packed and dressed, she went to the window. The sky was a bleak gray with filmy black coulds hanging just above the treetops as if they'd been caught there. No signs of clearing. Thera straightened her shoulders, picked up the suitcase, and walked out of her bedroom. Her heart lifted hopefully when she came to the dining area and saw that Nicodemus was not in his usual seat. She set her suitcase down just outside the kitchen doorway.

Philina was squeezing oranges, the sharp citrus smell mingling with the aroma of the coffee brewing on the stove. Thera yearned for a cup of the coffee, but she had no time to waste if she wanted to avoid Nicodemus.

Philina put down the orange rind she was holding and wiped her hand on a dish towel she had tucked into the waistband of her apron.

"*Kalimera sas*, Thera. Good morning."

Thera bent her cheek to her grandmother's kiss. "Where is *Papous* today? Not out in this weather?"

"No, asleep still. The poor man lay awake half the night because of the dreams." She clucked. "Terrible dreams. But you—you are up early today," she added cheerfully. "A special meeting?"

"Actually a little trip. I didn't say anything before because you know how Grandfather is. If it were up to him, I would never go anywhere," Thera said with a disarming smile.

But Philina was frowning, her eyebrows flexed with consternation. "'You know he has good reason."

"I know I can't live like some exotic bird in a cage. My roommate from the university invited me to visit her in Paris. I won't be gone very long." Thera paused, then added entreatingly, "I need to get away, have a little breathing space, see something other than the museum, the sanctuary, and this apartment."

Philina was touched by the intensity and innocence of the appeal. Surely a week or two visiting a friend would bring no harm. "I think you should at least explain this to him yourself, and say good-bye."

"You know that will only lead to a fight," Thera replied sadly. "I thought perhaps—"

"You thought perhaps you could sneak off like some runaway, some criminal," Nicodemus's voice boomed from the doorway.

Philina and Thera swung around to face him. He stood with his hands on his hips, his hair sticking up from his head like porcupine quills, his eyes red from lack of sleep.

"I only hoped to avoid such a confrontation as this, because there can be no resolution that is agreeable to both of us." Thera's voice was calm, but there was a defiant cast to her eyes and mouth that screamed her determination. "I am going to see Arlette. My ticket is paid for. My suitcase is packed. The only problem as I see it is that you don't trust me."

Nicodemus was momentarily left speechless by the candor of her last remark. She was right. The only problem was one of trust. Unfortunately, trust was a luxury he could no longer afford. He had forfeited his right to it when he bargained for her life. He crossed the kitchen and stood toe to toe with her before he spoke again.

"You have admitted to me that you no longer hold to our old beliefs, and yet you would have me trust you not to do what is proscribed by them."

The impasse had been reached. It was obvious that neither cajolery nor tears would sway him. Her only weapon was strength. She tossed her head.

"In any case I am going." She started to walk around him, but he seized her arm in his steel trap of a hand.

"Tell me, Thera, by the almighty gods to whom you owe so much, where are you going?"

"To France. To visit Arlette."

The stakes were too high. Nicodemus needed to be sure. Only one option was left to him. He mustered his energy and drove his mind into hers, probing for the truth.

Thera felt the intrusion, but she had anticipated it and her defenses were strong. She didn't need to block him completely; in fact she didn't want to. It was over in less than a minute. Nicodemus withdrew. He relaxed his grip on her arm.

"Now do you believe me?" she snapped indignantly.

The old man sighed heavily. "Yes. I'm sorry. I knew no other way."

Thera pulled free and strode out of the kitchen. She picked up her suitcase. Philina and Nicodemus were watching her forlornly like two worn-out relics of her childhood left behind on a shelf. She put the suitcase down again and came back into the kitchen to embrace them both. It was conceivable that she would never see them again.

12

New York: October 24

What had started as an autumn drizzle changed into a wintry ice storm as the bus carried Michael to Fordham Law School at West Sixty-second Street. With the sudden onslaught of sleet and hail, traffic slowed to a crawl and there was the high-pitched whine of tires struggling for traction on the slick pavement.

Michael checked his watch and looked out the window. The bus hadn't moved more than a dozen yards in the last fifteen minutes. Scraps of information were relayed back row by row from those in the front, like an impromptu news service. There had been an accident. The police were on the scene.

This last update Michael could confirm from the wail of sirens. He peered out the window again. The unseasonal storm was wreaking havoc with traffic. They were still at least five blocks from the school, and he didn't relish the idea of walking it in this weather. As he debated his limited options, there was a loud crack of metal against metal. He strained to pick up the latest scoop as it filtered back through the bus. Another accident. A fender-bender. Just ahead of them.

That did it. Michael rose and hit the stop tape. The driver, in a benevolent mood, and probably wishing he could just walk away from the mess, too, opened the rear door, and Michael exited.

The wind whipped ice pellets against the back of his neck where they melted and trickled down into his shirt. He yanked up the collar of his trench coat and hunched his shoulders, burrowing his face as far inside the coat as he could. He shouldn't have been so impulsive. He should have gone straight home and telephoned Aria with the news. But he had been too agitated, too restless, had needed to be on the move. After waiting nearly a week for an appointment with Dr. Yannatos, he now had the tape fully translated verbatim, and Michael couldn't sit still any longer.

He hurried along the crowded sidewalk, slipping and swerving around other pedestrians as if he were on a slalom run. His hands stung from the abrasive wind and ice, but he didn't dare shove them into his pockets; he needed them for balance. Bad weather for October.

He tried to anticipate Aria's reaction when she read Yannatos's translation. The day after her peculiar outburst in the car she had agreed easily enough to have an outsider translate the tape. But had she agreed because she felt it would confirm what her father had already told them or because she, too, had doubts and wanted the unexpurgated truth? Michael hadn't probed. She might not have known the answer herself at that point. Today they both would. He only hoped she wouldn't be too distressed.

When he reached the steps of the school he pulled back his sleeve to check the time. He was late. Aria's last class had been over for five minutes. It was entirely possible that after his long trek he had missed her. Then he caught sight of her golden hair billowing out in the wind as she ran across the street at the next corner with another young woman.

Michael dashed down the block after her, his feet skidding out from under him, his arms flapping for balance. He called her name, but he was moving into the wind now, and it threw his voice behind him like a strange echo. By the time he reached the corner, the light had changed, and Aria and her friend had reached the other side of the street. He shouted to her, cupping his hands around his mouth. Aria's companion swiveled her head toward him. Michael called again. The friend touched Aria's arm and pointed in his direction. He could see the puzzled expression on Aria's face dissolve into a smile of recognition.

When the light changed, Michael ran across to her. He hugged Aria to him. Her cheeks were red and wet, her hair speckled with ice crystals. She seemed to sparkle all over. He smiled and nodded at the other young woman.

"Michael, this is Karen Bailey, my dearest friend. Karen—Michael Lansing."

Michael shook her hand, and they all ducked into the protected doorway of a store.

"What are you doing up here on a day like this?" Aria asked.

Michael's smile became tentative. "I have something to show you."

"That's right—today's Friday. You saw Yannatos."

"Yes." Michael thought he detected a note of apprehension in her tone.

"Well . . . did he translate it?"

"Yes."

"I've never known you to be so short on words, Michael." She saw him glance obliquely at Karen. "Oh, its okay. Karen knows about it."

"Maybe we should go somewhere out of this weather." He was stalling, and he wasn't sure why. Hadn't he rushed here specifically to let her read the translation? Then why was he suddenly so reluctant even to talk about it? He was about to suggest stopping for hot chocolate when Karen spoke up.

"Aria, why don't you get Michael home. He's soaked. I'll catch my bus, and you can tell me about the tape tomorrow."

Before either of them had a chance to reply, Karen was moving out of the doorway.

"Nice meeting you, Michael. Speak to you tomorrow, Aria."

Michael looked at Aria and shrugged. "Your place or mine?"

They chose Aria's, which was closer. Even so, by the time they reached her building their hair was dripping wet. Aria started the coffee, and she and Michael took turns using the hair dryer while it brewed. She didn't press him for any details of what Yannatos had said until they were curled comfortably on the couch holding mugs of hot coffee.

"I'm ready now," she murmured.

Michael pulled a folded paper from the pocket of his plaid

flannel shirt and held it out to her. He watched her as she read it.

"You're not very surprised," he said when she handed it back to him.

"It's more explicit, more detailed than my father's translation. But I expected it to be. Still, my father didn't actually lie."

Michael's usually direct gaze faltered and dropped to the coffee mug in his hands. That, he thought, was a matter of degree. In his opinion Damos had omitted and diluted so much that his version was patently false.

Aria set her cup down on the table. "You feel my father lied to us, don't you?"

Michael chose his words cautiously. He wanted Aria to understand his position, yet he didn't wish to hurt her. "I would say he consciously misled us."

She nodded, and Michael felt encouraged to go on. "I mean, an underground chamber is hardly a darkened room. And 'becoming frightened'—I think that's how your father put it—is more than simple understatement when someone is stalking you with an ax that's already dripping with blood."

Aria shrugged and smiled weakly. "He probably didn't want to upset me. Let's face it—his version is a whole lot more palatable."

That might be so, Michael considered, trying to be open-minded. But he couldn't bring himself to dismiss the lie that easily. "Do you think that was your father's only reason for watering down the translation?"

Aria looked at him solemnly. "I think there are things to be afraid of, Michael. I think he wants to protect me."

Michael didn't doubt that she was right on that count. If he only knew what Damos meant to protect her from, he might become his willing ally. He decided to let the subject drop. Aria seemed satisfied enough with her conclusions. And even if Michael wasn't, he would gain nothing by trying to poke holes in her logic.

Aria carried their empty cups to the sink, and he wandered to the window to see if the storm had abated. It was dusk, but the streetlights hadn't come on yet. The world had melted into a monochrome of gray.

"I can't tell if it's still sleeting or hailing out there," he remarked when Aria came up beside him.

"Does it matter? Were you planning on going somewhere?"

"Well, I only have these soggy clothes I arrived in."

"We could always hang them near the radiator overnight to dry," she said with a mischievous smile.

Michael circled his arms around her narrow waist and drew her up against him. "Is that a proposition?"

"Invitation. I like the word invitation so much better."

"In either case, I accept." He bent his head to kiss her. His evening beard prickled her skin.

"You need a better razor," she murmured, her mouth still touching his.

"I've tried them all. It's just the Neanderthal in me."

Aria laughed and the sound vibrated between their lips. She was glad Michael was staying, and not just because her body longed for his. She needed his strength and his humor. She couldn't face another night alone this week. Although Yannatos's translation had been on her mind, it had not been the principal cause of her distress. She drew back from Michael. She suddenly needed to unburden herself, and if anyone would understand, Michael would.

"How prophetic do you think dreams really are?" she blurted out.

He was about to tell her jokingly this was not the time to discuss dream research, but he could see from her expression that the question hadn't been playful.

"That depends on who the dreamer is."

"Me."

"Have you had precognitive dreams in the past?" Michael asked with growing interest. This was one detail they'd never discussed.

"A few. None that were remarkable. At least not yet." The last was said with a rueful twist of her lips.

Michael took her hand and led her back to the couch.

"You're not talking about those extended dreams now," he said, still holding her hand.

Aria shook her head. "These are just run-of-the-mill nightmares, unless of course they come true."

"What were they about?"

"The most violent natural phenomena you can imagine: earthquakes, blizzards, tornadoes, tidal waves. You name it, I dreamed of it this week."

"What makes you think these dreams are prophetic?"

"I'm not really sure. Maybe the clarity of them. There weren't any of those vague details or the non sequiturs you usually get in dreams."

"Just that?"

"No. Did you ever read Nostradamus?"

"The French prophet? I've never read his work, but I've certainly heard of him."

"He predicted horribly destructive weather patterns for the last part of this century."

"Did he give a reason for them?"

"No. He just said they would happen. And so much of what he predicted for the past few hundred years *has* come true." Her voice was small and strained, her eyes imploring Michael to give her an answer he didn't have.

"You think your dreams are prophecies of the same kind?"

"Maybe."

Michael combed his hair back with his fingers, but it fell stubbornly down toward his eyes again. What would happen would happen, he reasoned, whether Aria believed her dreams were precognitive or not. Peace of mind was all he could offer. Time would determine the rest.

"Or maybe they're just dreams," he said, tracing his fingers lightly along the soft curve of her cheek. He didn't know exactly when the realization had taken shape in him, but he no longer believed that psychic power was the gift he had once perceived it to be. Aria had taught him it could also be a torment. He tucked her into his arms and stroked her back for a long while until he felt her muscles unknot. When he kissed her again, her mouth was warm and hungry on his, and he found himself wishing he could soothe her mind as easily as he could her body.

13

Heraklion: October 31

Nicodemus prowled back and forth through the apartment like a caged animal, moodily silent or growling responses to Philina's attempts at conversation. The high winds and rain that had kept him prisoner inside all week had virtually closed down the waterfront. A few daring men had taken their boats out. Two made it back to shore, barely alive. Another, less fortunate, drowned when his boat capsized in the turbulent waters. No other fishing boats went out. Many were smashed to pieces at their safe moorings. According to the newspaper accounts, not only the fishing industry was suffering. In the vineyards, the grapes, heavy and ripe for harvesting, had been torn from the vines by the wind and dashed to the ground, where the pounding rain reduced them to a muddy pulp.

Streets throughout Heraklion were said to be flooded, many impassable to all but emergency vehicles. Schools had to be closed and businesses had to deal with shortages of supplies and personnel.

Toward the end of the week when Philina announced that she was going out to do her marketing, Nicodemus flatly forbade her to leave the apartment. Philina stood her ground. In her bulky black coat and galoshes, with a black scarf wrapped securely around her head, she looked like a defiant penguin. Nicodemus told her so, breaking into an unexpected smile as he did.

Philina smiled back, glad for the small respite in tension. All week long she had tiptoed around, trying to stay out of

Nicodemus's way, fixing his favorite dishes, trying to engage him in light conversation, and all the time anticipating the sudden explosion, the inevitable bursting of the dam within him. He was no ordinary man—she had known that when she married him—and even in the best of times life with him was not easy. Now as she watched him, his fleeting smile was replaced by thin-lipped sternness.

"You're crazy, you know. You'll drown out there. They'll find you floating in one of those streets that have turned into a lake."

"We have to eat," she replied pragmatically. "Panakos's store is only a few blocks from here. I don't like shopping there—his nails are always dirty and he charges too much—but it can't be helped."

Nicodemus strode past her and pulled his coat from the closet. Philina was rarely stubborn, but when she made up her mind to do something, it was futile to try talking her out of it.

"If you insist on going, I'm going with you," he grumbled, setting his fisherman's cap squarely on his head.

The wind was at their backs, pushing them along so quickly they were forced into a running walk in order to keep their balance. Nicodemus had his arm linked firmly through Philina's, but it seemed as if the sudden gusts that billowed her skirts would wrench her from his grasp and carry her off like a giant black parasol.

Abandoned cars wallowed tire-deep in the middle of the street. Tattered awnings flapped against buildings like broken birds' wings. They passed no one else on their way, but glancing up they saw grim faces pressed against windowpanes observing their progress.

Although they tried to avoid the worst puddles, water spilled over the tops of Philina's boots and plastered Nicodemus's pants to his skin. He couldn't help wondering if starvation would be any worse than pneumonia. But he said nothing, unwilling to complain in the face of Philina's stoic silence.

By the time they reached Panakos's store, the rain had soaked through the backs of their coats, and puddles formed around them wherever they stood. Panakos was alone in the store, dozing in a chair tilted back behind the counter. He lived upstairs and had come down not because he expected any business on such a day, but to escape his wife's endless carping. He was a small man with dark hair slicked back from a low forehead. At the sound of the door he ran his fingers through the greasy strands of hair, then pushed himself out of the chair.

Philina grimaced and reminded herself to buy only packaged goods. Nodding an indifferent greeting, she moved off along the narrow, crowded aisles, selecting only essential items, since they would have to be carried home. While she shopped, Panakos chattered to Nicodemus, happy to have an audience.

"Business's been real bad. A handful of customers the whole week. But like I told my wife," he said philosophically, "it's got to improve. People got to eat, after all." Nicodemus nodded with pretended interest and let the proprietor ramble on.

"One of those archaeologists who dig out at Knossos came in earlier in the week."

Nicodemus was immediately alert.

"He was saying how this rain has really wrecked their excavations. Set things back months. He thinks there'll be a problem with funding. He was sure upset. But what can you do? He should have gone into groceries; they're a necessity. Excavations we can all live without." He chuckled at his cleverness.

Nicodemus's lips pulled up in a vacant smile while his thoughts raced on ahead. If Panakos had his information straight it would mean at least a temporary reprieve for their sanctuary. Could this awful weather simply be Zeus's attempt to protect his place of worship? Were the gods once again manifesting their presence on earth?

Philina had come up beside him. She set her basket on the counter, and Panakos left off talking in order to tally the amount. Philina paid him, rolling her eyes at some of the prices, then transferred everything to the net shopping bag she'd brought along in her purse. Nicodemus bought one of the newspapers that were stacked near the counter and tucked it inside his coat to keep it dry.

The trip home was, if anything, worse. Walking into the

wind was like trying to penetrate an invisible brick wall. At times they seemed to be marching in place. The rain coursed down their cheeks and into their mouths, and they had to stop every few yards to catch their breath. By the time they reached home, Nicodemus's one desire was to shed his soaked clothing and be dry again. But the phone was ringing when they opened the door. He rushed to answer it, his chilled body responding as if in slow motion.

Andreas's deep voice boomed over the line, clipped with tension. There were problems with the tunnel. Massive leakage. The sparse vegetation in the area couldn't hold back the amount of rain that was falling. He worried about a cave-in that might deny them access to the sanctuary.

Exhausted and troubled already, Nicodemus had to draw upon his last reserves of strength to keep his voice calm yet authoritative. He told Andreas to do what he could to save the tunnel but not to take any unnecessary risks. They would simply have to wait out the storm and deal with its consequences later.

He hung up the phone and slumped into a chair, oblivious to the water that seeped from his clothes. One disturbing question circled over and over in his brain. Why would Zeus save his sanctuary only to deny his followers use of it?

Philina found him still sitting there after she had put away her groceries. She tugged and coaxed him into the bathroom where she drew him a warm bath before going to change her own clothes.

Almost too tired to think anymore, Nicodemus lay back in the soothing water and closed his eyes. Philina's strength never failed to amaze him. It was not the sort that enabled her to lift heavy objects or knock out adversaries. It was just the sort that endured. He could use a little of that himself right now.

He stayed in the tub until his skin was puckered and the water had grown as cool as the air. He emerged from the bathroom refreshed and composed to find Philina bustling about the kitchen preparing lunch. He wrapped his arms around her and kissed the top of her head, which just reached his chin. Between them, words were sometimes difficult, even unnecessary. After several moments Philina drew away, insisting she had to check the soup that was simmering on the stove. But Nicodemus saw her brush away a tear as she turned from him. It had been too long since he had held her so. He must not let time slip away from them in the future. He kissed her gently on the cheek as she stirred the soup. Then he went into the living room to read the newspaper.

Although it had been protected by his coat, the paper was sodden and the newsprint reeked like stale ashes. Nicodemus skimmed through the first two pages, which were devoted entirely to the storm and the worsening conditions all over the island. They contained nothing he didn't already know. But his heart lurched painfully when he read the headline on page three. The words danced tauntingly before his eyes and he had to blink hard to refocus them so he could read the article. He read it a second time aloud, as if to better absorb the impact. Brutal tornadoes were ripping through Europe in places where none had ever been recorded before. Blizzards were paralyzing the southern United States and other subtropical regions. Meteorologists the world over were groping for answers. But there was only one answer, the one Nicodemus had tried to avoid confronting all week. He'd even allowed himself to believe that the explanation lay in the preservation of their altar at Knossos. But he couldn't comfort himself with that possibility any longer. The deviate weather patterns were too far-reaching. The gods were involved, but in a much more menacing way than he had been willing to imagine. And the reason was Thera. Yet she had gone to France. Nicodemus had taken the information straight from her mind. It had to be the truth. But, he wondered, with mounting disquiet, was it the truth in its entirety or just a fraction of it? Had she somehow learned to transfer thoughts to deeper levels of her mind where she could shield them from his scrutiny? He had never heard of such a thing before, but he couldn't discount the possibility. He had played the ostrich for too long already. It was time to pull his head out of the sand.

He went to the telephone and called the university in Athens. The secretary in the registrar's office refused to supply him with Arlette's home address or phone number, referring importantly to school policy as if it were religious dogma. After a long, frustrating exchange, Nicodemus was allowed to

plead his case to the registrar himself. He concocted a story of
dire family emergency that made it crucial for him to reach his
daughter who was visiting her former roommate. The registrar
—a brusque, efficient man—promptly suggested that he call
Arlette himself and ask her to contact Nicodemus. That way
no rule would be broken. Having little choice, Nicodemus
thanked the man and settled himself by the phone, certain it
would never ring.

Philina served him his lunch where he sat by the telephone.
He didn't tell her why he was waiting there and she didn't ask.
She assumed the calls had to do with his "pagan religion,"
and the less she knew about that the better she liked it.

Nicodemus ate the soup and pita without appetite. He was
nearly finished when the phone rang.

"Mr. Koraes?" a woman's voice inquired.

"*Ne*, this is Nicodemus Koraes."

"I am Arlette Marceau," she said in slow but impeccable
Greek. "I received a call from the registrar's office at the
university saying you needed to speak to me." She sounded
perplexed. Apparently whoever had called her had not explained the circumstances.

"Yes, and I appreciate your calling. It is of the utmost importance that I speak with my granddaughter, Thera."

There was a brief pause before Arlette replied. "Mr.
Koraes, Thera is not here."

That wasn't possible. "She said she was going to visit you,"
Nicodemus insisted politely.

"She did. But she was here for only a few days before she
went on."

Her words were not entirely unexpected, yet they howled
through Nicodemus's brain like an echo of the storm that
raged outside.

"Mr. Koraes?" Arlette's voice startled him; he'd forgotten
she was still on the line.

"Yes, yes, I'm here." He struggled to form his thoughts
into coherent words. "Did she say where she was going?"

"No. In fact it was rather peculiar how secretive she was."

"*Efharisto*, Arlette. Thank you anyway. Good-bye."

"I'm sorry to have been of so little help. *Herete*, Mr.
Koraes."

Nicodemus replaced the receiver and tried to think what to do next. There was no point in attempting to track Thera down through the airline's passenger lists. She was too clever to travel under her own name. Besides, he already knew where she was headed.

14

New York: October 31

The dreams had been prophetic. Each news update confirmed them. Sudden, inexplicable storms, floods, and cold waves were claiming lives all over the world. The death toll already hovered near a thousand; Aria knew it would go higher.

She listened to the radio as she added the final touches to her makeup. She wasn't in the mood for a party tonight, but Michael insisted it would do her good to have some fun. Besides, how could she disappoint Karen?

The six o'clock newscast went off, and the d.j.'s voice filled the room with carefree chatter that seemed irreverent. How could he listen to the world's miseries and then pick up right where he left off with that inane prattle? she wondered irritably. Maybe he didn't listen to the news anymore. Maybe he just flicked a switch and dozed while it was on. Aria wished she could flick such a switch in her mind.

She tossed down her eye shadow pencil and studied herself critically in the mirror. Her face was smooth, unlined; her eyes glowing with a soft light. But the dreams were taking their toll, even if she could find no outward sign of it. Inside, her nerves had turned to high-tension wires that vibrated with every breath she took.

The timer rang in the kitchen area. Aria jumped, then smiled sheepishly at her reflection. Halloween—what a night to be on edge. She turned off the bathroom light and went to take the quiche out of the oven.

The fluted crust had turned a golden brown, and the smells

of spinach, cheese, and mushrooms mingled appetizingly in the heated air of the tiny apartment. Aria placed the quiche on a cooling rack on the counter, wondering why she didn't feel hungry. She'd had only coffee and toast for breakfast and then another cup of coffee with Karen between classes. Karen had eaten a sandwich, talking rapidly between mouthfuls about the party and all that she still had to do. But her chatter was enthusiastic, not plaintive. She liked giving parties, liked being around people. Aria had sipped her coffee and listened inattentively, as if a part of her were listening somewhere else, preoccupied with more important matters, though she couldn't say what.

"You can tell me, you know," Karen was saying. "Everyone else will still be surprised." She chewed a wedge of tuna sandwich. "Aria, come on."

Aria looked up abruptly. "Is it time to go?"

"I think you've been gone awhile already," Karen replied with a good-natured frown. "Daydreaming?"

"Sorry, my mind must have wandered." She'd had trouble concentrating all day. She'd been so distracted in Dr. Fischer's class that her notes had made no sense when she reread them at the end of the hour.

"What was it you asked me?"

"What are you and Michael coming as tonight?"

Aria forced a smile. She had no intention of dampening Karen's spirits with her own peculiar mood. "You'll just have to wait until tonight," she said lightly.

"Oh, listen," said Karen, her mind already busy with other details, "you won't forget the quiche, will you?"

"No, I promise. Is there anything else I can do to help?"

"Yes—eat the other half of this sandwich." She pushed the plate across to Aria. "You can't live on love alone, and I won't be able to squeeze into my slinky costume if I go on this way. When I'm nervous I can't stop eating. Maybe I should go back to chewing on my fingernails. They aren't fattening."

The sandwich remained untouched in front of Aria. It occurred to her that unlike Karen, she lost her appetite when she was nervous. Yet she had no reason to be nervous—or none that she knew of.

Aria put down the pot holder and straightened the bodice of

her gown. It was a copy of a seventeenth century Spanish ball gown of emerald satin trimmed in lace, the kind of gown she had dreamed of wearing since her childhood. She had chosen the character of Dulcinea specifically because it would finally afford her the opportunity to wear such a dress. But somehow, even with the graceful skirts swirling around her as she walked, she didn't feel particularly regal or elegant. Her whole body tingled with apprehension, an anticipation stained with dread.

She tossed her head as if that simple motion might dispel her anxieties. Then she took up the *fontage* from the table and went to the mirror in the bathroom. Her hair was already pinned up to accommodate the three-tiered lace headpiece; she only had to position it and secure it in place. She was sliding in the last clip when the doorbell rang. The *fontage* still felt wobbly in spite of all the clips, and she nearly dislodged it completely when she forgot to duck as she went through the bathroom doorway. Holding the headpiece in place, she opened the door to Michael. He stood posing in the hallway—Don Quixote, carrying a spear that had been a broom handle a few hours earlier.

"Oh," she said, sucking in her breath. "That's fantastic. How did you ever do it?" With her free hand she reached out to touch the armor he'd fashioned from cardboard and then spray-painted bronze.

Michael pulled up his visor.

"And the helmet—you made the visor movable. You're really talented."

"Wonderful," he grinned, his mouth looking strange between the gray mustache and scraggly beard. "If I don't succeed as a parapsychologist I can always make my living designing clothes out of cardboard."

Aria laughed, a deep, loosening laugh that surprised even her. Ten minutes ago she'd have sworn she would not laugh tonight. Michael was admiring her costume, the low-cut bodice and cinched waistline, the flattering swell of the skirts.

"I'm glad we didn't try to make yours out of cardboard."

"You like it?" She pirouetted in front of him.

"Magnificent, except for one thing."

"What's that?"

"Are you going to have to hold that hat up all night?"

"No, I just have to remember to duck through doorways. They must have built them higher in those days."

"Or maybe they built their ladies lower," Michael said, trying to kiss her through the narrow slit in his helmet.

The party was well under way by the time Michael and Aria arrived. They'd been halfway there and had had to turn back when Aria remembered the quiche was still cooling on the counter. Although she felt more at ease now that she was with Michael, her mind was still disturbingly adrift.

Karen greeted them at the door, dressed like a huge butterfly in a slim black dress with brilliantly colored wings attached to her back and a pair of antennae bobbing above her head. Whenever she made a sudden turn, the ungainly wings flapped in someone's face or threatened to overturn lamps and vases. She took the quiche from Aria.

"You didn't forget. Great."

Aria and Michael exchanged a private smile.

Karen was rattling on, caught up in the excitement of her party. "I think you know almost everyone here. Fix yourselves a drink or have some of the rum punch on the table. I'll stick this in the oven."

Once she'd hurried off, wings flapping behind her, Michael and Aria stood in the entry for a minute trying to decide where to go and how to get there. The living room and dining room were filled with knots of people talking and laughing. Some had spilled over into the kitchen and bedroom. A few were even stationed just inside the bathroom doorway. The stereo was playing, but no one seemed to be listening and there was no room to dance in any case.

The doorbell rang and in order to make room for the new arrivals, Michael grabbed Aria's hand and started blazing a path through the crowd toward the rum punch.

They sipped drinks and nibbled on cheeses, quiche, and stuffed mushrooms. They talked about schools and careers, sports, fashions, politics, and love affairs, but the topic everyone eventually returned to was the weather: "Hasn't it been awful?" "If this is fall, can you imagine winter?" "Thank God it has finally calmed down." "But terrible things are still happening elsewhere in the world. Look at the newspapers.''

The groups shifted, formed, and reformed, and it was suddenly well past midnight. Someone had turned down the stereo so that it was a pulsing hum in the background. Karen had refilled the punch bowl and thrown some whole apples into it. A few of the guests were taking turns bobbing for the apples and succeeding only in swallowing mouthfuls of the punch. Everyone else had come to stand around them, laughing and applauding, giddy from the alcohol and the heat in the apartment. Most costumes were no longer intact. Aria had knocked off her *fontage* on a trip to the kitchen for ice. Michael had shed his helmet because the visor kept closing when he tried to drink, and Karen's wings were hanging like unhinged shutters. The guests, in general, appeared worn out but content.

Michael came up behind Aria and slid his hands around her waist. Had it been up to him, he would have left an hour ago. After a week of being apart, he longed to be alone with her. But he could see that the party was having a therapeutic effect, drawing her out of the introspective, troubled period she'd been going through. He hadn't heard her laugh like this in a long time.

Karen was taking her turn at the apples. She had one halfway out of the bowl when it slipped and fell back in with a splash that covered her face with punch. She came up giggling and licking her lips like a tipsy Saint Bernard. Everyone roared, doubled over with laughter. Aria leaned back against Michael's chest, wiping happy tears from her eyes. She didn't know exactly when it started. At first she thought someone had turned up the bass on the stereo. The vibration was a low rumble in the pit of her stomach. From there it seemed to radiate out along her limbs and up into her spine and her head. It was several moments before she realized that the floor itself was shaking beneath her feet, that the table and chair legs appeared to be dancing, and that the windows were rattling in their frames.

The laughter in the room turned to screams of panic. The happy party faces suddenly contorted with surprise, bewilderment, and fear. Aria herself trembled with fear, but she was not surprised. All day she had known this was coming, sensed it at some primal level.

Amid the terrified cries and confusion, someone dropped to the floor, and, wanting direction, everyone quickly followed. Before Aria could move, Michael caught her arm and pulled her toward the door. He threw the door open and pushed her down on the threshold, hunching his body over hers.

"Is it an earthquake?" she whispered, as if any loud sound might aggravate the situation.

"I don't know. It could be."

Aria heard other whispers passing among the prone figures in the room like lifelines of comfort. Then the shaking stopped as abruptly as it had started. No one moved for several minutes. Finally Michael sat up and drew Aria up beside him. The others rose, too, one after another as if it had all been an absurd game of follow-the-leader. Voices grew louder as confidence returned.

A man a few feet from Michael and Aria looked at them and shook his head. He was made up as a clown, but perspiration had etched jagged lines in his face paint, and the exaggerated corners of his mouth had leaked down to his chin.

"An earthquake? How can there be an earthquake? This isn't California; this is New York."

"There are fault lines here, too," someone across the room called back. "I saw them on a map once." Soon everyone was talking at once. Karen walked dazedly around the apartment, surveying the damage. A few glasses and pictures had fallen and broken, and a vase of flowers had toppled, spilling water onto the carpeting. Otherwise everything appeared to be intact.

Michael helped Aria to her feet. "I think we ought to try to get home." Aria nodded mutely.

They found Karen, thanked her, made her promise to call if she needed them, and then they left.

Out on the street, they saw that people were poking their heads out of windows or stepping hesitantly out onto the sidewalk, coats pulled on over nightgowns and pajamas. Faces drained of color, eyes wide, they gathered in impromptu groups while sirens screamed in the distance. Someone turned up the volume on a portable radio. Aria and Michael heard the studied calm of a newscaster's voice as they made their way to Michael's car. All indications pointed to an earthquake. A minor one. But even a minor earthquake in New York was major news.

Michael put his arm about Aria's shoulders, holding her tightly against his side, as if she needed comforting. Aria didn't protest, but in truth she felt more relieved than she had all day. It was the impending quake that had set her nerves on edge. Now it was over.

15

Heraklion: November 3

The horizon still bisected the sun when Nicodemus stepped outside. Although the rains had stopped two days earlier, puddles lingered everywhere, and a steamy moisture hovered in the air, transmuting the sharp daytime colors to soft pastels. He walked with his hands dug comfortably into the pockets of his old work pants. The air still had a snap of chill from the night before, but the sun was warm when it winked at him through the trees, promising a return to mild weather as the day wore on.

Birds twittered and chirped raucously, delighted to have the sun once again after the endless week of storms. But Nicodemus could not share their joy. His heart was a heavy stone that made his muscles ache with the effort of carrying it. And his mind was preoccupied with the events that lay beyond the brief respite of this cloudless day.

Up ahead he saw a bus approaching the stop where his side street intersected Avgoustou, the road leading to the waterfront, but he didn't increase his pace. When he was in a hurry or his back was troubling him, he took the bus. Most often he preferred the long, solitary walk, taking pleasure in the serenity of the early hours when few people were about and traffic was light. Today he walked so that he could think, as if perhaps he might find some remedy he had until now overlooked.

He turned north on Avgoustou. The bus had departed.

Behind it, keeping close to the curb, two middle-aged women in coarse black dresses and head scarves led donkeys slung with sacks of produce. It was a common enough sight on the island—this mixture of the ancient and the new—but it filled Nicodemus with an ominous sensation, and he couldn't help thinking that the world would soon witness a clash between the two such as it had never experienced before. Unless he could somehow prevent it.

As he neared the harbor, the traffic increased and other pedestrians appeared on the sidewalk. Young men and women with backpacks ate frugal breakfasts on the benches in the Park of El Greco, and the day assumed an ordinariness that lifted Nicodemus's spirits a small degree. It was hard indeed to conceive of a cataclysmic end to such mundane life.

Most of the independent fishermen had already set out for the day, but Petros's red boat was still tied up at the pier. Nicodemus picked out the stout figure of his friend bent over, repairing a fishing net. His two sons worked at the rear of the boat.

"*Kalimera sas*, Petros," he called out.

Petros looked up and waved. "Good morning," he said as Nicodemus came up beside him.

"You're late getting out today."

"I know. I know. Again we have trouble with the engine. My two engineers there are working on it," he said with a grunt. "I liked it better when we depended only on the wind." His lips hitched up in a nostalgic smile, showing off crooked yellow teeth. "When we were young men. Ah, it was good then, no?"

Nicodemus smiled and nodded. Good and less complicated.

"You want to go out with us? If we ever go out?" Petros asked, raising his voice so that his sons could hear. They looked up, waved to Nicodemus, and shrugged, used to their father's harassment.

Nicodemus clapped his friend on the shoulder. "*Ohi, efharisto*. Not today. I will see you tonight, though?"

"Of course," Petros said, all at once solemn. "I pick you and Thera up at seven, right?"

"Not Thera, just me."

Petros's eyebrows shot up. Since she was a child of seven Thera had not missed a convocation. He was about to ask what was wrong, but he could see by the rigid cast of Nicodemus's face that the question would not be well received. He let his mouth fall closed in silence.

"Tonight then," Nicodemus said and walked on.

He was sitting atop a stone breakwater a quarter of an hour later when he saw Petros's boat glide away from the dock. Tonight you will know, Petros, he said to himself. Tonight you will all know. Thinking of the meeting, he was filled with a strange combination of relief and dread. The problem would no longer be his alone. It would be shared by the assembly and resolved by them. What he dreaded was the inevitability of that solution. Once before he had argued for Thera's life, on the day she was born. He would argue for it again tonight. And this time his staunchest adversary would most likely be his nephew—his beloved Nikolas. Thera was already lost to him, and would remain lost even if he was successful in saving her life. Now he would lose Nikolas as well. It could not be helped. Bitter tears pricked at his eyelids and blurred the horizon. He could not recall the last time he had cried.

Nicodemus remained sitting there as the gleaming white cruise ships arrived and departed, the tourists ebbed and flowed, and the early fishing boats returned. The sun rode up to its zenith, beating fiercely on his back until his shirt was soaked through with perspiration. He was lost in thought and memory, oblivious to the discomfort. Where, he wondered, did the fault lie? Was the blame to be laid on Thera alone? Others might place it there. Yet he felt culpable as well. He had failed to instill in her a proper respect for her heritage and the responsibilities it conferred. As a result, she had turned away from their religion to worship the private cult of her own powers. He had seen the subtle changes, seen the sweet, naive child slowly, insidiously buried beneath an impenetrable shell of will and desire. He had seen it all and refused to acknowledge where it was leading. Yes, the guilt was his, too.

Petros arrived on time. After a brief greeting, he and Nicodemus rode in silence. Thera's absence was palpable. Petros had pondered the significance of it all day. He had even mentioned it to his sons, who'd listened tolerantly, then resumed their own conversation about women. Their lack of interest pained Petros, who regretted that they did not share his beliefs. But his wife had been adamant about raising them in the Greek Orthodox church and had doggedly dragged them to services with her every week. The indoctrination had not taken, in any case. Both young men spurned religion in general, contenting themselves with the more concrete pleasures of life.

Petros sighed, reminding himself that Nicodemus, too, had had his share of problems with children. His only son, on whom he had counted to continue the religious line of Koraes, had turned away from the ancient gods in his late teens. And now there appeared to be a problem with Thera as well. A serious problem if Petros were to judge by the set of his old friend's face as they drove through the darkened streets to the meeting. Nicodemus looked like a man traveling to his own execution.

The assembly that night was small. Nicodemus had called for it unexpectedly only two days earlier. Several people had be unable to change their schedules in order to attend; others were home in bed with flu after the unseasonably cold, wet weather of the previous week. It was just as well, Nicodemus decided, surveying Andreas's living room. With only nine of them present, the room was already overcrowded and stuffy.

He paused in the doorway beside Andreas while Petros sat on an arm of the faded couch.

"How is the tunnel coming?" he asked.

Andreas's face was haggard and dirt-streaked, his clothes and fingernails caked with mud.

"I'm sorry I didn't have time to change," he replied with a self-deprecating gesture. "I worked on it up to the last moment. I had hoped to have it finished enough for tonight." He shook his head apologetically. "The more I fix, the more damage I find. Too much. It will be a long time yet, I'm afraid."

Nicodemus put his hand on the big man's arm. "I want you to slow down. Exhaustion will only lead to mistakes. We can't afford to lose you. We will make do for as long as we must. The gods are not without understanding." His voice cracked, and the last words echoed mockingly in his head. Soon they would learn just how far that understanding could be stretched.

Andreas nodded toward the living room. "Is everyone here or do you expect more tonight?"

Nicodemus wondered if he was discreetly referring to Thera. He had seen the surprise on Andreas's face when he and Petros had entered without her. Nicodemus studied the faces of those ranged around the room. Only one was missing.

"Nikolas has not arrived?"

"No."

Nicodemus glanced at his watch. It was not like his nephew to be late for a meeting. He would never give Thera the satisfaction of finding him at fault. And he had no way of knowing she would not be here tonight. Was it possible that he intended to miss the meeting altogether? Without him, Nicodemus would have little trouble persuading the assembly to adopt his plan. His heart lifted hopefully.

"It is time," he said. "We will not wait any longer." He strode to one end of the room where Andreas had set a table with the customary two bowls, the water flask, and the crown of myrtle. The low hum of conversation stopped abruptly, and everyone rose. Nicodemus saw them all look around the room, surprise and curiosity passing like a live current from one face to the next. But no one dared ask what they wanted most to know—where was Thera?

"My granddaughter is not here tonight," Nicodemus told them in a tone that forbade further questions. "We will discuss this matter later." He nodded to Petros. "I would appreciate your assistance."

Petros was startled at first, but he collected himself quickly and made his way to Nicodemus's side.

"It would be an honor," he said, his rounded torso appearing to swell further with pride.

With a minimum of prompting, Petros assisted in the preparations for the ceremony. Then Nicodemus motioned for him to rejoin the congregation, and he alone led them through the prayers. The familiar words seemed thinner, diminished, without Thera's echoing chant. Nicodemus wondered if the others felt the void as keenly as he. Then he chastised himself for allowing his thoughts to roam during communion with the gods.

He was concluding the first sequence of prayers when there was a hard rap at the front door. Everyone turned toward the sound, then back to Nicodemus who had continued without hesitation as if he had heard nothing. He didn't pause until he reached the place where he would have ordinarily begun the prayers for the specific concerns of the evening.

The rapping had continued at short intervals, and now he looked in Andreas's direction and nodded, a single, brusque motion. The assembly waited in a hush of expectation as Andreas went to the door. Nicodemus alone knew who would enter.

A minute later Andreas returned, Nikolas behind him. Nicodemus frowned disapprovingly at his nephew, but the younger man stood his ground with thin-lipped determination. When he realized that Nicodemus stood alone at the makeshift altar, his mouth spread in a narrow, self-satisfied smile. He bowed his head in a gesture that appeared to be deferential, but in which Nicodemus read a challenge.

He knows, Nicodemus thought with a cold shudder of foreboding. The room was painfully silent. They were waiting for him to continue. He tried to marshal his thoughts. What was next? He had to ask the gods' blessings in their efforts to restore the passageway to Knossos. Then he was supposed to implore Zeus to moderate the weather, which was still wreaking havoc around the globe. When Nicodemus opened his mouth to begin the last prayer, there was a hectic moment during which his throat constricted and no words would emerge. When they finally did, they sounded raspy and unnatural to his ears. Could the others hear in them the hypocrisy he felt? He stole an oblique glance at Nikolas and thought he saw the younger man nod almost imperceptibly, acknowledging that sacred words and pleas would no longer help; they were well beyond that point now.

When the last responses of the congregation had faded into silence, Nicodemus invited everyone to take a seat. Nikolas remained standing, leaning back against a wall, his arms folded in front of him in a deceptively casual stance. But focusing on the dark-lashed eyes, Nicodemus saw the same implacable rage he had first discerned in them weeks ago, and he knew the object of that rage was still Thera.

There were a few nervous coughs. Nicodemus pulled his gaze away from Nikolas. He would have to begin.

"I'm afraid that what we must discuss here tonight is not a pleasant matter," he said evenly. "You already know that Thera is not here. What I must tell you now is why she is absent." He paused, not for effect, but because his mouth was dry. He swallowed with difficulty. "It is my opinion that she has gone off to find her sister."

There was an immediate babble of exclamations, punctuated finally by Andreas's deep voice. "But how can she even know where to begin looking?"

Nicodemus shook his head. "I don't know. Every precaution has always been taken. Still, I doubt she would have left without some idea of where to start."

"She has to be stopped," an elderly woman cried out.

"Yes," Nicodemus agreed with a calmness he didn't feel. "She has to be stopped. And we do have the advantage of being able to find out her destination probably before she does. All it will take is one phone call. With any luck we will find her before she finds her sister."

"And then what?" Petros inquired, his pleasant jowls taut with concern.

"We bring her home."

"And make her promise not to leave Crete again?" Nikolas asked mockingly from the side of the room. "Do we stand guard over her twenty-four hours a day? And which one of us is strong enough to stop her if she decides to break away?" He turned to face the assembly. "Do you know how strong she's become? Do you have any idea what she's capable of?" His voice had risen as he spoke, and Nicodemus could see the effect it was having on the others. Fear was rapidly replacing concern on their faces. They were looking from Nikolas back to him for rebuttal; they wanted to be told the danger could be averted, Thera could be handled. As much as he wanted to, Nicodemus knew he could give them no such guarantees.

"I will deal with her," he said, his voice steel-edged with authority.

"You have tried to deal with her before, and this is where it has brought us," Nikolas thundered, drawing himself away from the wall to confront his uncle. "This matter is no longer within your jurisdiction. She has broken a covenant with the gods. The punishment for that is very specific. And if we fail to carry it out, thousands if not millions of innocent people will continue to suffer and die."

Nicodemus did not reply immediately. Everything Nikolas had said was true. Yet he still harbored the reckless hope that he could find Thera in time and make her understand.

"Now that Zeus has made his presence manifest in the world again," he said, "Thera cannot fail to recognize his fury. She will accept and believe all that she has refused to believe in the past."

"She believes in nothing," cried Nikolas, "and she never will. She cares for nothing. Nothing but her power. She nurtures it, cultivates it; she intends to see its limits obliterated." He turned abruptly from Nicodemus to the one other young man there.

"Christo," he said, "will you come with me?"

Christo nodded soberly, averting his heavy-lidded eyes from Nicodemus.

Nikolas turned back to his uncle. "We will need the address."

"I forbid you to harm her," Nicodemus growled, his eyes like pistol bores beneath the dark, swooping brows.

"You cannot forbid what the gods demand!"

Nicodemus studied the troubled faces of the men and women around him. He had known them all his life, and he knew their respect for him ran deep. He was an integral part of their religion, their beliefs. But now fear was threatening their faith in him, and Nikolas was exploiting that fear. A bleak frustration washed over him. The air seemed heavy, charged, as if an electrical storm were about to break.

"Go ahead, tell him," Nikolas shouted, his voice exploding in the silence. "Tell him you want us to go after her. Tell him you won't stand by and watch the world torn apart because he refuses to admit to his mistake."

At first there were only tentative nods and murmurs of assent, but gradually the voices swelled with confidence and volume until a single, unified cry, reverberated in the room: "*Ne, ne,* yes, find her!"

They had made their decision and Nicodemus knew he had no right to deny them the information they needed. He was a religious leader, not a dictator. And in truth someone had to find Thera. Alone, he would probably not be strong enough to restrain her. He doubted that even Nikolas and Christo together would be able to.

He held up his arms and waited until the room was once again quiet. Nikolas was watching him warily, his mouth twisted into a smile of satisfaction that swept through Nicodemus like a cold wind. His nephew sought a private revenge, and he was using the gods to achieve it. Didn't he see the corruption and sacrilege in his motives? Well, he hadn't won yet. Not completely. Nicodemus knew he, too, could invoke the aid of the gods in achieving his ends. Did that make him equally corrupt? he wondered. Perhaps, but he was not after revenge, just life. It was a question he would have to deal with later. Now all eyes were on him.

"Yes, Nikolas," he said sharply. "You are right. It is the gods' will that you go after her. And with their blessings you will find her."

Nikolas's smile broadened triumphantly, lighting his black eyes from behind.

"But," Nicodemus continued, "if you intend to do the gods' bidding, you must comply in every way with the procedures prescribed by them."

Nikolas cocked his head. His jaw clenched, outlining the rugged bone structure beneath the olive skin. He was a fool to have thought the old man would surrender his precious Thera so easily. "And these procedures, just what are they?"

"That any sacrifice to the gods be performed at one of the sacred mountain shrines by means of the labrys and in the presence of this congregation."

"And how are we to bring her all the way back here?" he snapped petulantly.

"If it is the gods' will that she be sacrificed, they will provide the way."

"Sometimes, Uncle, I wonder if it is the gods' will or yours that we follow."

Andreas, who was seated closest to Nikolas, reached up and put his hand on the young man's arm. "Careful, Nikolas," he murmured, "you go too far."

Nikolas pulled away without taking his eyes off his uncle. "I know you think you've found a way to save her," he said, his words slicing the air like razors. "You don't believe us capable of bringing her back. But we will find her, and we will bring her back, and we will execute her according to every last rite and rule you can dredge up. I suggest you do your studying well while we are gone, because there is not one loophole that will keep us from succeeding in the end. This I promise you." Nikolas turned on his last words and stormed out of the room. A moment later the front door creaked open and then slammed shut, followed closely by the roar of a car's engine.

Nicodemus was inutterably weary, and his heart felt as if it had collapsed in upon itself like a dying star. Both Thera and Nikolas were lost to him forever. He looked at his tiny congregation. They were waiting for him. In spite of their decision, they had not abandoned him, nor would they leave without his consent, as Nikolas had. He took a deep breath, but the air was too heavy to pull into his lungs, and it was several moments before he could speak.

"We have done what we can," he said to them in a voice that rumbled with uncertainty and emotion. "It is time to go home. The outcome rests in other hands."

16

Heraklion: November 4

"What do you mean you don't have it?" Nikolas demanded. They were sitting at the dining room table in Nicodemus's apartment. Philina had served them coffee with a platter of freshly baked *kourambiedes* and then retired to her bedroom to finish mending a shirt.

Nicodemus tossed down the walnut cookie he had taken.

"In my house you don't raise your voice to me, *andhras neos*," he replied tightly. He felt brittle inside from the effort of keeping his own temper. But he didn't want Philina to hear them, to find out the danger confronting her granddaughter. If Thera could not be saved, then he would have to tell his wife. There would be more than enough time for grief.

Nikolas lowered his voice, but his words took on a slick, venomous coating. "What you mean is that you won't give it to me."

"No. I mean I don't have it," Nicodemus repeated. "I called my son, but he refused to give it to me."

"No doubt after you told him the reason. He doesn't want his daughter harmed any more than you do."

"Perhaps you are right in that, but then, we are a gentle family, Nikolas. Blood lust is not a passion of ours. I don't know how you come by it."

Nikolas smiled crookedly. "Mine is only a reaction, Uncle. Better to ask how Thera comes by it." The smile became a hard, angry line. "She is the cause."

125

Nicodemus shook his head. "Still you refuse to tell me what she did to earn your hatred."

Nikolas regarded him with eyes like shiny, hard obsidian that revealed nothing. "The telling would not change anything."

For a moment Nicodemus considered reaching into his nephew's mind for the answer, but he quickly discarded that idea. Such an intrusion would be an abuse of his own powers. And what Nikolas had said was true enough. Knowing would change nothing.

"In any case," he sighed, "I didn't have to tell him the reason. He knew the minute he heard my request. Don't forget—he is my son and her father. He has ways of knowing."

Nikolas took a swallow of his coffee. "Didn't you explain the necessity of finding her? With all his knowledge," he said bitterly, "can't he see what's happening?"

"He doesn't believe in the gods—you know that. He hasn't believed since he was a boy. So he sees what he prefers to see. Freakish weather, yes, but brought on by physical phenomena, experiments with nuclear devices, space probes, the coming of another ice age. To him it is coincidence. To him you are a mortal threat to his daughter, a madman from whom he must protect her. He already carries a burden of guilt concerning Thera. He will not add to it by helping you."

"Then I guess it is as you said last night—the gods will have to help us." Nikolas pushed back from the table, grating his chair across the wooden floor. "And they will," he added as he stood. "Do not doubt it."

Nicodemus stared into his untouched coffee where an oily scum had accumulated on the surface. There was nothing left to say, and he was tired of fencing with useless words.

"If you know anything at all that could help us, tell me now," Nikolas urged him. "We leave in a few hours." He paused, and when he spoke again his tone was gentler, more reasonable. "You love your granddaughter, but you cannot sacrifice the world for her, Nicodemus, because in the end she will perish with the rest of us."

These last words, spoken without rancor, but with simple

certainty, reached straight into Nicodemus's heart, and he wondered if the gods were not already helping his nephew.

He rose from the table and pulled the keys out of his pocket. Kneeling at the old desk by the door, he opened the center drawer and withdrew the packet of letters. He slipped the bottom one from the pile and handed it to Nikolas.

"All that I know is in there," he said, his voice a harsh whisper. "It isn't a lot, but it may provide a beginning." He kept his eyes on the floor, refusing to look at the triumph in Nikolas's face. He felt a hand grip his shoulder briefly.

"I know how much this cost you," Nikolas murmured. A moment later he was gone.

Philina appeared in the doorway holding the shirt she'd been sewing. "Nikolas has left?" she asked.

Nicodemus tried to compose himself as he took his seat again, but his facial muscles were limp and uncooperative, and no amount of effort could draw his lips into a smile.

Philina sat down on the chair to his left, the shirt bunched in her lap.

"Something is wrong," she said.

He turned to her. "So," he said, trying to keep his tone light and teasing, "now you, too, claim the power of mind reading."

"No. I only read your face. Powers are your domain—and Thera's. I have no wish for them. To me they are no gift."

"Nor are they to me."

"It's because of Thera, isn't it—your sadness?"

He nodded. Although he had wanted to spare her any extra days of anguish, he could not bring himself to lie to her.

"I knew when the week ended and she didn't return. I knew there would be trouble," Philina said.

"Nikolas is going after her."

Philina's small face grew pinched with concern, the lines around her eyes and mouth deepening as if a drawstring had been pulled.

"He will bring her back, though. He won't hurt her . . ." Her voice quivered with a plea. "They have had their differences, I know, but he . . ."

Nicodemus came out of his chair to stand behind her. He

drew her head back against his stomach and gently massaged her shoulders.

"He won't hurt her. He'll just bring her back, Philina *mou*. Don't worry." It wasn't the whole truth, but it was the closest he could come.

17

New York: November 4-5

Thera stood at the window of her hotel room. A white garbage truck with a snowplow attached was rumbling along the block again. It passed every ten minutes now, and except for a fine layer of windswept snow, the center of the street was finally clear. Mounds of gray-brown snow formed a miniature mountain range that jutted out three feet from both curbs, burying the cars that were parked there and making it impossible to cross from one side of the street to the other. Eventually, Thera reflected wryly, someone would carve out a walkway. She hoped it would be soon. She'd been stuck in the hotel for three days, and the novelty of her first snowfall had long since worn off.

The snow had started to fall as her plane touched down at Kennedy Airport, and she'd been fascinated, watching the tiny flakes sift down from the low white sky like powdered sugar. While waiting to pass through customs she'd strained for glimpses of the snowy landscape beyond the glass doors, but she could see little through the milling crowds. The line she was on moved sluggishly, then came to a complete stop. It turned out that an elderly man ahead of her had concealed three kinds of fruit and an entire wreath of garlic in a suitcase among his clothes. By the time it was Thera's turn, her mood had soured. Anyone who dared tamper with her belongings would regret it.

The inspector she drew was a pale young man with skin so soft it appeared incapable of sprouting a beard.

"Is this it?" he asked tonelessly, looking from Thera's one suitcase up to Thera herself. "Or is there . . ." His eyes widened and a soft whistle passed through his teeth.

Thera smiled and tossed her golden hair so it would catch the high fluorescent lights.

The inspector's mouth slid into a cocky smile as he continued to appraise her.

"That's all I have," she replied in the smooth, nearly accent-free English she had mastered at the university. She shrugged. "I know you have plenty of fruit here, and I don't believe in vampires."

The inspector's smile widened. "I'm glad to hear that," he said. "The place already smells like an Italian restaurant. Would you please open this for me?"

Thera felt a small pit of anger open up inside her. She had nothing to hide from him, but she disliked the idea of a stranger rummaging through her belongings, and she wanted to be outside in the snow. Still, it would be quicker to comply than to argue. She found the key in her purse and opened the suitcase.

The inspector ran his hands around the insides of the suitcase, then poked between the layers of clothing and toiletries. Thera regretted that in her haste she had simply thrown her nightgown in on top of everything else. She watched as he slid his open palm across the sheer, silky fabric. He looked up at her with a lascivious smile, fondling the gown as if she were still in it.

"Everything seems just fine," he said, his voice pitched low with intimacy.

"Good," said Thera, her own voice compressed between tightly clenched teeth. She knew she should just lock the suitcase and leave. But she couldn't. He had used his trivial position of authority to invade her privacy. She felt abused, insulted. She wanted to pick up the sullied nightgown and fling it in his face. She steadied herself with a deep breath. There were better ways. Since she had made an impression on him, she would make sure it was a lasting one. As if some internal switch had been thrown, a provocative smile lit her face, glazing her eyes, parting her full lips.

Encouraged, the inspector murmured something to her.

Thera paid no attention. She was concentrating deeply, focusing on his body. She visualized the network of muscles and nerves that traversed his groin. With powerful fingers of energy she reached into him, clawing at the soft tissue until she saw the pain explode like gunshots in his eyes. His mouth flew open, and he staggered backward, doubled over. Thera held on, wrenching and knotting the nerves and muscles around one another into a tangled mass. She felt his blood vessels bulge, straining against the pressure. Then one by one they began to burst. He fell onto the inspector who was working behind him, howling soundlessly, his face contorted and ashen. Sweat poured down his forehead and cheeks; runnels of blood spilled from his nostrils and the corners of his mouth. He screamed once, a tortured roar of pain, then sank to the floor in a heap. Thera let go.

She snapped her suitcase shut and slipped out into the rapidly converging crowd.

Outside was a dreamland sheathed in white. She stood on the sidewalk smelling the crisp freshness of the snow, intrigued by the way it muted sounds and softened angles, by its power to transform the world. She was watching the way the flakes melted on her hands when the blast of a car horn snapped her to attention. A garish yellow taxi had pulled up at the curb. The driver, a double-chinned man in a bomber jacket that was ripped under one arm, was leaning across the front seat yelling to her through the half-open passenger window.

"Well, lady, what's it gonna be? D'ya wanna ride or ya gonna stand there till ya turn into a drift?"

At first Thera had trouble deciphering his question; a lot of the words seemed to have been routed through his sinuses.

"Ya gettin' in?" he prodded.

"Will you take me into Manhattan?"

"That's what I get paid for," he said more amiably. "Hop in."

Except for a few graphic suggestions directed at other drivers, he kept up a continuous string of chatter for the hour it took them to reach midtown on that Friday evening. Thera, who usually had no patience with small talk, forced herself to listen carefully, hoping to soak up as much knowledge of the city as she could. It was the driver who suggested the hotel she wound up staying in, assuring her that it was reasonable and not located in an area clogged with tourists.

By the time he dropped her off, the snow was covering footprints and tire tracks as quickly as they were laid down, and so much ice had built up on the taxi's windshield that the driver had to get out and scrape it off.

"This here's gonna be one helluva storm," he grumbled, holding his jacket closed with one hand and working at the ice with the other.

He had been right. The storm broke all existing records. Between Friday evening and Sunday afternoon, it dumped three and a half feet of snow on New York before blowing out to sea. Blizzard-force winds piled the snow into drifts that soared as high as fifteen and twenty feet. Visibility deteriorated to zero in a matter of minutes that first night, and thousands of rush hour motorists were stranded in their cars while temperatures plummeted into the teens. Fifty-four deaths had already been attributed to the storm, and scores of people were still unaccounted for as the massive cleanup began. Shortages of staple food items were widespread. Life had come to a standstill. And no one felt it more acutely than Thera. She had limited funds and limited time. Now three precious days had been wasted. Nicodemus was sure to have figured out where she was and might already have sent someone after her. She slammed her fist down on the windowsill. She had to find her sister, and she had to find her soon.

Below her on the street several people had appeared, armed with snow shovels and bundled inside layers of coats, hats, scarves, boots, and gloves, some even sporting ghoulish-looking ski masks against the knifing winds. As they worked at the buried cars, they looked to Thera like exotically colored ants attacking Mount Everest. At another time she might have found the scene amusing, but now it only served to heighten her frustration, reminding her that she didn't even have suitable clothing. Without waterproof boots and gloves she wouldn't get too far before frostbite set in. A good chunk of day four would have to be sacrificed to properly outfitting herself, she realized, turning abruptly from the window.

By early afternoon Thera had purchased the necessary

clothing, including a warm scarf, which she wrapped around the lower half of her face to warm the frigid air that swept into her nose and mouth, cutting her breath to shallow, painful gasps. She stopped at a small coffee shop to rest and warm herself with coffee and a sandwich. Then she set out again with the list of law schools she'd compiled. She used buses whenever possible; they were cheaper than taxis and less apt to become mired in snowdrifts. She avoided the subways. The cab driver had advised her against them, and he had been right about everything else so far.

She hoped to visit all six schools that afternoon, but traffic was badly snarled by snow-removal vehicles and by the snow itself. Pedestrians seemed to be making better progress slogging along the slush-covered sidewalks. Only the concussive winds and numbing temperatures kept Thera's impatience in check. She sat on the molded plastic bus seat and grimly watched each traffic light turn red several times before they could move through another intersection.

In spite of the delays, when she walked into the first law school she was buoyed by a renewed surge of optimism. Not much longer, not much longer, a voice in her head chanted to the clacking tattoo of her bootheels.

She found the registrar's office easily, but she paused in the hallway before putting her hand on the doorknob. No one was around. She closed her eyes and concentrated, hoping to pick up a sense of her sister's presence nearby. It was something she'd never consciously tried to do before, but there had been times when she'd known with certainty that she would bump into a particular person around the next corner, or that she would find Nicodemus at home when he should have been at work. She even remembered, as a toddler, knowing moments before someone would walk into her room. It was an instinctive ability to distinguish between different individuals' energy fields, like being able to tell one snowflake from another without the aid of a microscope.

She stood there with her eyes closed for several moments, but either this was the wrong school or her instinct wasn't operating. She opened the door and walked into the office.

The registrar was unavailable, but Thera was helped at once by a Mrs. Clark. She was tall with tightly permed hair and blue eyeshadow that reached up to thinly penciled brows. She listened attentively as Thera explained that she was trying to locate her sister.

"I'm afraid I won't be able to help you, dear," she said with a narrow businesslike smile. "We're not at liberty to reveal anything about our students to anyone who walks in off the street. I'm sure you can appreciate the reasons behind the rule."

Thera could not. "I can prove I am who I am," she replied, unzipping her pocketbook to find her passport.

The woman held up a long, bony hand. "That wouldn't matter. Even if you had a picture of the two of you together, the rule would still stand."

Thera pulled the zipper closed with an angry tug. One thing she certainly didn't have was a photograph of herself with her sister. She looked into Mrs. Clark's eyes. They were brown, lapped with middle-aged folds of skin at the corners. She had managed Nikolas; she could manage a petty clerk. She drew her energy into a tight laserlike beam and projected it through her own eyes into the brown eyes across from her, straight back into the delicate convolutions of Mrs. Clark's brain. She saw the woman's face contort momentarily with confusion and fear as she fought the intrusion. She blinked rapidly as if trying to reorient herself and ward off a dizzy spell. Thera eased back; the woman would be of no help if she fainted. Then Thera instructed her to go to the files and look for her sister's name.

To Mrs. Clark the command seemed to have originated within her own mind, and although she had reservations about acting on it, she couldn't quite remember what they were. Thera sent the command again. By the third time she felt the familiar pulse of pain erupt between her eyes, but she also felt Mrs. Clark's defenses crumble. Five minutes later Thera was out in the hallway checking that law school off her list.

It was a murky, gray twilight by the time she crossed off the fourth name. She was standing at a bus stop, oblivious to the throngs of rush hour workers pressed around her. Even the cold seemed distant, muted. Only the pain in her head was real. All the law schools in New York seemed to have a uniform policy of not releasing student information, and

Thera had had to resort to the same method of securing that information. The individuals themselves had not been difficult to manipulate once she took hold of them, certainly not worth comparing with Nikolas. It was their numbers that had drained her. Four of them in only a few hours. There'd been no time to rest or recover. Her eyes burned, and a jackhammer of pain pounded relentlessly at her temples. The city's lights and noise were searing, like steam on a fresh, raw burn.

When the bus arrived, she was propelled aboard by a tide of people, and she fell into a seat beside a young man who clucked his tongue and leered openly at her. As the bus got under way, he made a few low remarks in a language Thera didn't understand. She ignored him. She couldn't fight back now anyway, and she had to keep track of their progress or she would miss her stop altogether in the dark.

By the time she stepped down from the bus, the sidewalk lay beneath a slick sheet of ice. Halfway to the hotel entrance her foot skidded and flew upward, throwing her to the hard pavement with a resounding smack. She sat sprawled there, stunned and bruised, while people picked their way around her as if she were just another inconvenient mound of snow. She pushed herself up, glad that no one had stopped to help her. She wanted no intimacy with this grueling city. All she wanted was her sister. And she would have her yet.

The morning sun set the room ablaze at six o'clock. Thera opened her eyes and saw that she'd forgotten to draw the curtains. She tried to sit up, but her head felt heavy, ungainly, her neck muscles too sore and weak to hold it up. Gingerly she lay back down. It would be days before she was completely "well" again. She pulled the covers up to her chin, shivering as the warmth of sleep left her. Last night she'd thrown off her clothes, not even bothering to find a nightgown before crawling into bed. Now she regretted her haste as she turned, pressing her bare skin against a chilly section of sheet. As much as she wanted to fall asleep again, her stomach kept clenching uncomfortably, a persistent reminder that she'd neglected to eat dinner as well.

Reluctantly she rose from the bed, and after showering, bundled herself into her outer clothing and left the hotel. It was just after seven. Traffic was already heavy, but few pedestrians were about.

She found a coffee shop a block away where she had a breakfast of eggs, ham, and toast. It was still too early to tackle the remaining schools on her list, so she lingered over a second cup of coffee while she tried to plan her day. After some consideration she decided there would be little point in visiting the registrars at these schools. They would refuse her the information she requested, and she could not force them to comply, not the way she was feeling. What remained for her to do? Thera smiled with satisfaction as a new idea began to take shape. Perhaps yesterday had not been as fruitless as she had assumed. If nothing else, it had narrowed the field of possibility. With only two schools left, logic and instinct might accomplish what sheer force had not. The one drawback to the new plan was that it would cut drastically into her funds. But the alternative was to give up, and that was not an option Thera could accept. She swallowed the last of the tepid coffee, wishing it were Philina's strong brew.

Finding a taxi wasn't difficult. The morning rush was still ahead. Thera slid into the back seat, the cold of the vinyl penetrating all the layers of clothing she wore. The driver looked at her in the rearview mirror, his jaw moving up and down on a wad of gum.

"Where to?" he asked.

She gave him the address of Fordham Law School. "But don't stop there."

The driver was already maneuvering the cab back into traffic. "You want to go there, but you don't want to stop there," he repeated as if he were mulling this over for his own clarification.

"That's right."

"Then what?"

"I'll let you know when we get there."

The streets were all clear now, though hubcap-deep in slush, and the drive crosstown and uptown took only fifteen minutes.

"There it is—Fordham Law," the cabbie informed her as they cruised past a modern glass and mortar building. He looked into his mirror. Thera's eyes were closed.

"Hey, lady, are you all right?"

"You mind your business and leave me to mine," she said.

The cabbie shook his head. "Lady, my business is driving, and since you're the one I'm driving, how about telling me where we're going?"

She opened her eyes. Nothing. "Take me through the neighborhoods near here where a student at that school might live."

The cabbie shrugged. "It's a big city. I've got the time if you've got the money."

Thera ground her teeth. She didn't have the money; she didn't even have the time. She leaned back and tried to relax with her eyes closed again as the taxi traveled in expanding squares around the school. They'd been driving for over an hour when she bolted forward.

"Stop. Stop here!" she commanded.

Her eyes flashed open. They were on a one-way street lined with parked cars. Apartment houses rose up like prison walls on either side of them. The driver pulled to the curb at a fire hydrant.

The sensation was magnetic, stronger than Thera had expected. She felt like a bloodhound who'd just picked up the scent of its quarry. And not a moment too soon.

The cabbie had turned around to look at her. He chewed his gum, while she paid him.

"Hope it was all worth it," he said, counting the bills.

Thera stepped out. "It will be," she said, and a smile spread across her face.

The cabbie spat out his gum and watched her walk into the building across the street. How was it that such a beautiful face could leave him feeling as if he'd just stepped out of a cold shower?

Thera stood in the small vestibule where the tenants' names were listed beside buzzers on one wall. Her eye dropped down the columns. She found what she needed at the bottom of the second row. Koraes: 4B. She tried the inner glass doors. Locked. She'd have to announce herself from down here. A pity. She would have preferred to see her sister's face at the moment they met. She pressed the button beside 4B.

No curious voice broke the silence. She pressed the button

again. Still no answer. She peered at her watch. It wasn't yet ten o'clock. Could she be in class? To have come this far and to have to wait now was almost unbearable. Maybe her sister had only gone to buy milk or to walk a dog. But she could also be out for the day.

Thera couldn't stand and wait in this vestibule. It was unheated, and her gloved hands were already aching with the cold. She'd have to go back to the hotel. By bus. She had to pack her things anyway. She'd return here in the evening. The decision, although practical and logical, did nothing to soothe her frustration. It was like a tar pit boiling so close to the surface that she could taste its bitterness. She wanted to strike out at someone, something. To shake the whole damned building until it collapsed into a pile of rubble at her feet. The locked doors taunted her. Her eyes flashed, fury shooting out of them like arrows to the heart of a target. The glass shattered, but remained in place, leaving the doors like enormous crystal jigsaw puzzles framed in metal.

Thera winced, immediately regretting her actions as the fading pain in her head roared to the surface once more. She heard the hum of the elevator inside the lobby. This was no time to be seen standing there. Pulling the scarf over her chin and mouth, she turned and left the building.

18

New York: November 5

Aria had been awake for some time. She'd watched the room slide from black to gray and finally to the pearly white of day. Sleep was becoming more and more difficult. Her senses were too well honed, too poised. For what she didn't know. After the earthquake on Halloween, she'd relaxed, but only for a few hours, like an intermission before the next event. When the freakish early November blizzard ripped through the city, she had accepted it with equanimity. More lay ahead.

Having Michael with her helped. She couldn't imagine coping with her dreams and nature's tirades alone. She turned her head to look at him. He was lying on his back, one arm flung above his head, shadows sculpting his cheekbones and deepening the cleft in his chin. His eyelids twitched as he turned onto his side facing her. Thank God she had decided to go home with him after the party. She would have gone crazy stranded alone in her studio the past four days. They had stopped off there just long enough for her to throw some clothes into an overnight bag and to check for damage from the quake. Two paintings had fallen onto the couch and a sheaf of notepaper was scattered across the floor, but nothing had been broken.

In Michael's loft the usual disarray made it difficult to tell if anything had even shifted out of place.

One of the advantages of being a clutter bug. Aria smiled to herself. She drew the quilt up over Michael's bare shoulder, then lay back, hoping to fall asleep again. After a few minutes she sat up. Her head was throbbing with the same miserable headache she'd had since yesterday. She slid out of bed and padded barefoot to the kitchen, the one room where she had insisted on establishing some order. The bottle of aspirin was on the counter. She took two of the tablets, though they did little to diminish the pain. Convinced the weather was to blame, Michael had suggested she try antihistamines. But they hadn't worked either. Aria yawned widely and wondered if lack of sleep was the problem.

After starting the coffee, she rummaged in the refrigerator for eggs and milk. Then, armed with flour, mixing bowl and muffin tin, she whipped up a batch of Michael's favorite popovers and put them into the oven. Since she'd begun spending weekends at the loft, she'd stocked the pantry and added more cookware. English muffins and peanut butter sandwiches got tiresome awfully fast.

While the popovers baked, Aria showered and washed her hair. She woke Michael when the oven timer rang. He opened one sleepy eye and looked at her. Her cheeks were flushed from the heat of the shower, her hair a shiny sweep of gold that framed her face.

"What right do you have to look so good at this time of the morning?" he murmured, grabbing her arm to pull her down beside him. "I'm just going to have to mess you up." His eyes were wide open now and dancing with light.

Aria landed on the bed with a soft thud, and Michael pinned her under him. She laughed, trying to wriggle away.

"Breakfast is ready. I made popovers, and they're no good if they get cold."

He lifted his head to sniff the air. "Smells great. We'll heat them up later."

She started to protest, but he covered her mouth with his, swallowing the words.

Breakfast turned into a late brunch, and Michael insisted the reheated popovers were the best he'd ever eaten. Even Aria's headache seemed improved. When she mentioned this to him, he proposed writing an article extolling the curative powers of sex.

"But what will become of all the women who have relied on the old headache excuse for years?" she teased.

Michael shrugged. "You have a point there. Maybe it's best not to upset the status quo."

"Speaking of which, it looks as if the city is finally back on its feet again. I guess I'll be having classes this afternoon."

Michael spread another popover with marmalade. "I ought to get back to work, too."

"Your enthusiasm is underwhelming. I seem to remember a time when your research was all-important."

Michael grinned around a mouthful of popover. "That was before I found and lost the best subject in the world."

"You'd like me to continue, wouldn't you?" she asked soberly.

"As Mr. Lansing, researcher, graduate student, and doctoral candidate, emphatically. As Michael, no way. At least not until we have a better fix on what we're messing with."

"You're beginning to sound ever so slightly like my father," she chided him, though privately she savored his concern.

"Now you've gone too far." He tossed a popover at her, bouncing it off her nose.

It was another hour before they were both dressed and ready to leave. But Aria wasn't in any hurry. She only had two classes, and they didn't begin until two o'clock. She would still have time to stop off at her apartment to pick up her books.

Michael planned on spending the afternoon collating data and setting up appointments with his volunteers. Neither prospect fired him with the old excitement anymore. His comment to Aria had been painfully true. It was hard to lose such an exciting subject and still be content with the more common ones. Maybe once he completed the preliminary work and actually started testing his hypothesis, he would once again feel that intense glow of total involvement.

Who was he kidding? Total involvement in his work was no longer possible, now that he had Aria. And he didn't regret the trade-off one bit.

She came out of the bedroom buttoned into her lavender quilted coat, with a matching knit cloche pulled down over her forehead. Her eyes, reflecting the color, sparkled like amethysts. Michael snuggled her into his arms.

"After having you all to myself for four days I'm really

going to miss you," he said, feeling a tugging emptiness as if she were already gone.

"I think we have to look at it this way," she said, her head tucked under his chin. "It's only two more days till the weekend."

Michael laughed. She could feel the vibrations of it where her temple touched his throat. She turned her head and put her lips to the spot. He groaned softly.

"How about I pick up a pizza and meet you at your place tonight?" he offered.

19

New York: November 5

Aria walked toward her building from one direction as Michael approached from the other. Although it was fully dark, she knew it was Michael by the large white pizza box in his hands as he passed beneath the glow of a street lamp. She waved, and he balanced the box on one hand in order to wave back. Aria had visions of it flipping off and landing on the wet pavement, but he made it to the door without mishap. She joined him there a few moments later.

"Just what I like," she said, pushing up on her toes to kiss him, "a man of his word."

"It was only to protect my honor that I didn't eat it on the way over here. I'm starving." He stamped his feet, and clumps of brown slush dropped off his boots. "You practically need hip boots to cross the street since it warmed up today."

Aria held the door for him and followed him into the vestibule. Michael whistled under his breath when he saw the shattered inner door. A large hand-printed sign had been taped to the metal frame where the glass doors met: Please Use Side Entrance.

"What the hell happened here?"

"Oh, I forgot," Aria said. "I saw it earlier when I came by for my books. Isn't it incredible the way the glass is completely shattered, but not a single piece of it has fallen out?" She glanced at Michael. He was studying the doors, a frown wedged between his eyebrows.

"What is it?" she asked.

He shook his head. "I just can't imagine what could possibly have done that. If the doors had been hit by something, there would be a center, and the cracks would radiate out from it like a web or a splash. This looks as if a force of some kind hit everywhere simultaneously. It doesn't make any sense."

Aria shrugged. "When I see the super, I'll ask him. Wouldn't want your curiosity to go unsatisfied." When she got no response, she tugged at his arm. "There's probably a simple explanation for it. Come on, that pizza smells like heaven."

They were near the side entrance when the first bolt of lightning tore through the sky. It was followed immediately by another, arcing slightly higher as if the first had lit the fuse of the second. Thunder rumbled, building to a powerful crescendo that pounded in their ears, Aria jumped and came to an abrupt stop. Michael crashed into her, juggling to keep the pizza box from toppling out of his hands.

"Another selection from nature's vast repertoire," she said grimly as she opened the door with her key. Once Michael was inside, she tugged it closed behind them.

"You're still thinking about Nostradamus," Michael said rhetorically. Of course she was. He was, too. After Aria had mentioned the French prophet that night two weeks ago, he had gone to the library and found a book of the man's prophecies. Over the centuries his predictions had proven uncannily accurate. And he had indeed foreseen disastrous natural upheavals for this decade.

Aria nodded. "That plus my own awful dreams." They were waiting for the elevator. She turned to Michael, her features locked in a tension that made her appear gaunt and waiflike, her eyes magnified by a fine sheen of tears.

"That's the second time I've seen a chain of lightning," she said, her voice a thready whisper. "The first time was in a dream last night."

The elevator arrived, and the door rumbled back on its track. Michael wanted to say something that would comfort her, but sometimes words were useless. If he hadn't been holding the pizza he would have taken her in his arms. When she was pressed against him, it seemed as if he could share the burden, lessen the pain. Now all he could do was follow her into the elevator.

Aria set out plates and glasses while Michael washed off the oil that had seeped through the pizza box onto his hands.

The pie had cooled, leaving the cheese thick and rubbery, but neither of them thought to reheat it. They ate in silence, while the storm raged outside. Lightning razored through the sky, bolt after bolt of it, continuously crossing the heavens then retracing its path to start over. It made Aria think of a series of whips being snapped out, recoiled, then snapped out again. The madly flashing light gave their movements the speeded-up jerkiness of an old movie. The thunder crackled and hissed like a massive fireworks display.

Michael slid his hand across the table and twined his fingers through Aria's, and her lips flickered in a smile of gratitude.

"Sounds like we're really in for it," he said. "I just might have to stay over."

"Sacrifices, always sacrifices," she laughed.

"The role of martyr suits me, don't you think?" Michael grinned.

Aria was about to reply when there was a sharp clattering against the windows as if someone had thrown a handful of pebbles up at them. They both swung their heads toward the sound; Aria's fingers tightened around Michael's, the brief laughter gone. They got up and went to the windows, hands still linked. Lightning blinded them for a moment like a camera flash. Then they saw the hailstones, as smooth as white marbles, glancing off the building and bouncing in the street below.

"What next?" Michael remarked.

Aria shuddered, and he felt the tremor pass from her hand to his. "That's a question I'm afraid to ask lately."

The doorbell rang then, its mechanical buzz jarring and out of place in the midst of the storm's brutal tones.

"Are you expecting someone?" Michael asked, releasing her.

"No. Unless Karen decided to stop by," she replied halfway to the door. "But I can't imagine why she'd be out in this weather." She released one of the locks. "Who's there?"

No answer, just the insistent ringing of the bell again. Aria put her eye to the peephole. Whoever was there was standing off to the side so that she could only make out one small section of a face. A woman's face. Maybe it was Karen after all.

Michael was beside her now. Had she been alone or had she seen a man out there, she would not have opened the door. When she did, she staggered backward as if she'd been knocked off balance by a strong gust of wind.

Before her stood her own mirror image. She blinked hard and tried to control her breath, which was coming in short, useless gasps. She felt as if she were living through one of her bizarre extended dreams. Words formed in her mind, but even though she moved her lips, no sound emerged. She stood there mute, her feet rooted stiffly to the floor. Yet in spite of the initial shock, a new understanding was whirling in her mind, taking shape like a coalescing chunk of planet. As incredible as it was that this mirror image should be standing there, it was also somehow right. Like the final piece of puzzle that appears too large, but fits exactly when pressed into its space.

The woman who might have been her reflection, smiled.

"Adriadne, hello."

Michael's eyes were darting back and forth between the two, wondering if this was just some optical illusion. But even as the thought crossed his mind, he dismissed it. While they were identical from the high sweep of cheekbone to the delicately bowed mouth, they were wearing different clothing, and the stranger's hair, although the same shade of sparkling gold, was several inches longer than Aria's and glistened with melting crystals of ice.

Thera could feel their confusion, the man's even more hectic than her sister's. But she had her own surprise to deal with. It had never occurred to her that Aria might be married or living with someone. Men were always getting in her way, it seemed. Her eyes rested briefly on Michael in his tight faded jeans and green sweater. Oh, he was attractive enough, but he would only complicate matters. Aria didn't need him. Not anymore. She would have to prove that to her. Thera felt the anger snaking through her mind. It took a wrenching effort to subdue it. Later it might serve her, but not now.

Michael thought he saw a darkness cross Thera's face. Perhaps just a trick of the lightning; it was gone before he could be sure, leaving him with an uneasiness he didn't understand.

The three of them stood frozen for a minute, like a tableau. Then Thera stepped inside. She had a suitcase in one hand, which she set down beside her.

"I'm Thera," she said simply.

"Thera?" Aria whispered, reaching for the association the name was meant to elicit. She shook her head vaguely. "I'm sorry, I . . ."

So, mused Thera, Aria didn't know anything.

"I guess I am quite a shock to you," she said gently. "They said you were never told, but I wasn't sure until just now. I'm your twin sister," she added with a laugh, "but I guess that much is pretty obvious."

Aria tried to laugh, too, but all that came out was a hoarse clicking deep in her throat.

Through the open door they could hear footsteps coming down the hallway. Thera wheeled and stiffened like a deer alert to an approaching predator. She reached behind her and flung the door closed as a couple of teenage boys shuffled by.

The sudden furtive action bothered Michael. Had it been triggered by a simple desire for privacy, or something more? He glanced at Aria to gauge her reaction, but she was too absorbed in other thoughts to bother with why or how a door had been closed.

"I don't understand," she was saying to Thera. "I mean, how could I have a sister, a twin sister, and not know about her?"

"That's the easiest part to explain," Thera replied with a rueful twist to her lips. "And I intend to explain it all."

"Why don't I take your coat?" Michael offered, needing to do something.

Thera shrugged it off and handed it to him. "Thank you, uh . . ."

"Michael," he supplied.

She extended her hand to him, and Michael shook it. He had never judged a person by a handshake before, but this one was patently different from most. It was polite, but at the same time cold and distancing as if a line were being drawn between them. He thought of two boxers shaking before a bout. He was relieved once they'd moved apart.

"I didn't know Ariadne had married," Thera said lightly.

Aria laughed, a nervous warble. "Michael and I aren't married. We were just having a quick dinner together." Even as she said it, she wondered why she felt the need to explain, to minimize their relationship. Why she felt, in fact, apologetic for Michael's presence during this strange reunion.

Thera's coat had begun to drip from the melting hail. Michael took it into the bathroom and hung it over the tub. When he returned, the women were sitting on the couch, turned toward each other, their profiles like two sides of an ink blot. He leaned against the accordion door that could hide the kitchen area from the rest of the apartment, thinking that he really ought to leave Aria and her newfound sister alone to get to know each other. But something made him stay where he was. Maybe it was curiosity, or maybe he stayed because the storm had intensified, the hailstones a pounding fusillade that seemed capable of smashing the windows at any moment. Neither Aria nor Thera appeared to notice the ominous barrage.

"I have so many questions," he heard Aria say. "How do I even begin?"

"Let me," Thera replied readily, preferring to guide the conversation. She had to be careful. If she overwhelmed Aria with too much information, she could frighten her off or make the unbelievable even harder to accept. Unfortunately, time was still a vital consideration. Aria would have to know everything before Nicodemus sent his men after her. And Thera had no doubt that he would send them or that they would eventually find her.

"You had no way of knowing about me, Aria," she began, "because we were separated at birth. I knew about you because I was told. And the reason for that I'll explain later. Our parents brought you here, and I was left with our grandparents to be raised on Crete." She paused and put her hand over Aria's, her voice suddenly brimming with emotion. "That's how it was meant to stay, but I needed to find you. I don't think I spent one day of my life not wondering where you were or what you were doing. You were like a part of me that was missing."

The last words resonated deeply within Aria, and she felt her eyes flood with tears, remembering all the times she'd known the same nameless ache. "You could be speaking for me. I went through it, too, I just never understood it before."

Thera fought back the smile that pulled at her mouth. She was playing it exactly right.

Michael was listening, trying not to interrupt, the question "why" forming more and more insistently just behind his lips until it took all his willpower not to blurt it out.

Finally Aria asked the question for him.

"But why—why separate us? Why keep you a secret from me and have you raised by your . . . our," she amended self-consciously, "grandparents?"

Thera sighed and looked pointedly in Michael's direction for the first time since he'd rejoined them.

"It's all right," Aria told her. "Michael and I are . . . really close." Again that queer sensation of doing wrong, of offending her sister. It nagged at her, but there were so many other thoughts vying for her attention that it was quickly swept beneath them.

"I'll make some coffee," Michael murmured, feeling uncomfortable and distinctly unwelcome. If Aria had asked him to leave then, he would have. But she didn't. It was only Thera who seemed to resent his presence. And her resentment was tangible, like a wave of water so cold it bruises the skin. He told himself he was being touchy and ridiculous. Even if Thera did want to be alone with Aria, it was completely understandable. They were twins, identical twins, who'd started life as two halves of a whole. Now, after twenty-four years, they were finally together again.

He bustled around the cramped kitchen area, ostensibly preoccupied with locating coffee pot, cups, and spoons. But he kept his ears tuned to the conversation that had resumed on the couch. Though Thera had lowered her voice, he could still hear her clearly enough. For once he was grateful for the close quarters of the studio apartment.

"You and I," said Thera, "are from an ancient line. One of

the oldest in Greece. Anyone who lives on Crete could tell you what the name Koraes means, though most consider the story only a legend now—fantasy, nothing more.'' She laughed, a low syrupy laugh like someone who was privy to a secret. ''But what they don't realize is that legends are always born of fact, and in this case very little was ever added or changed.''

Michael finished measuring the grounds and started the stovetop percolator that Aria preferred because it brewed the strongest coffee. He set the timer for six minutes, then turned his attention to the sisters again.

Thera turned to him. Since he insisted on staying, she would have to include him and convince him as well. She toyed with the idea of using her mind to manipulate him, but she dropped it immediately as being too risky. She didn't know how well developed her sister's abilities were. If Aria picked up on what she was trying to do to Michael, it might alienate her completely. As long as Aria was present, she would have to use a more conventional means of persuasion.

''Are you a religious man, Michael?'' she asked.

''Catholic by training, nothing much now. Why?'' he asked warily. What did this have to do with the legend? And why had she suddenly decided to include him?

''Wouldn't you say, then, that if man can turn away from God, God can also turn from man? Surely a divinity would have the same prerogatives and more.''

He shrugged. ''There are people who believe that's happened already.''

''Do you?''

''I've never given it much thought.''

''Consider this,'' she turned back to Aria. ''The gods of ancient Greece were not mythical. They were real. As real as the Christian God who is worshiped today. Perhaps more so. According to the legend I spoke of, the Koraes family is descended directly from one of the gods the ancients revered— Aphrodite. She fell in love with a mortal, a shepherd named Anchises. She took him as her lover and bore him a son.''

Michael tried to stifle the laughter that fizzled up in his throat like carbonation. He clamped his jaws shut on it, but a sputtering croak emerged anyway.

Thera whipped her head toward him, glowering fiercely.

"Why should that be harder to accept than the notion of Mary, a mortal virgin, bearing the son of your Christian God?" she demanded.

Michael no longer had any urge to laugh. He had just noticed the most remarkable difference of all between the sisters. While Aria's eyes were a soft, translucent gray, warmed by a hint of lavender, Thera's were as cold and opaque as gunmetal.

"I never thought of it in quite those terms," he admitted deferentially. "I didn't mean to offend you . . . I—"

"Never mind," she snapped, cutting him off, dismissing him. When she spoke again it was to Aria, and her tone was surprisingly sweet and mellow.

"I'd guess Damos raised you without any religion."

Aria nodded.

"I know. He turned his back on the gods when he was quite young. But why not? In truth they turned from us long ago. Still, he's a fool to ignore their legacy and a greater fool for trying to deny us ours."

Michael heard the bitter undertone that had crept into her last words. It brought to mind a chameleon sliding continuously back and forth from one protective color to another. Which color was the true one? The timer rang. He took the pot off the stove.

"Do you believe the legend?" Aria asked Thera as they joined him at the table. "Do you believe we're descended from a goddess? It's hard enough for me just to believe I actually have a twin sister."

"It doesn't require an act of faith—I know it's true," Thera replied with a gentle firmness that made it seem somehow possible. "And you will, too, before long."

Michael poured the coffee. Thera drank it black, the way Aria did.

"This is the first decent cup I've had since I got here," she said. "But you haven't had real coffee until you've had Philina's."

"Philina?" Aria repeated.

"Our grandmother."

Aria put her cup down, shaking her head. "I feel like someone who's awakened after a twenty-four-year coma.

Every answer seems to create more questions. I don't even see what this legend has to do with our having been separated."

Michael almost applauded. A similar question was pounding around his brain like a horse on a circular track.

"To understand that, you must first understand that Aphrodite, like all gods, had certain powers and that some of those powers were inherited by her half-mortal son Aeneas." She paused to take another swallow of coffee.

Michael and Aria exchanged glances, Aria's of amazement, Michael's of wry disbelief.

"The other gods were jealous," Thera resumed, "afraid that the mortal might use this power to usurp their place. For their own protection they decreed that no identical twins be permitted in Aeneas's line. You see, they believed that in such twins the power would be magnified, bounced back and forth between the two, almost like light in an endless series of mirrors."

"Were there ever twins before the two of you?" Michael asked, intrigued by the story, though he still regarded it as fiction.

Thera nodded. "At least three times, if the records can be trusted."

"And what was done about those twins?"

"In each instance, the second twin was sacrificed to the gods."

Aria shuddered. She wondered if Thera knew which of them was the elder, but she didn't ask.

Michael was frowning. "But you yourself said this religion is extinct today. So why should your being twins have any significance?"

"I may not believe the gods are still interested in us," Thera said with the studied patience of a teacher with a slow student, "but there is still a small sect on Crete that worships them and believes in the ancient precepts. Nicodemus, our grandfather, leads them."

"Come on, now," he shot back. "You're not seriously saying he was going to have one of you two murdered." Somehow that idea was harder to accept than all the other incredible things he'd already heard.

Thera nodded and drained her cup. "It was Damos who

came up with the solution—separating us. He didn't believe the gods were still around, but as long as the others did, he had to appease them, assure them there would be no divine retribution. They were skeptical of his plan at first, but as time passed and no cataclysm shook the world, they conceded that the gods had accepted his compromise."

"And now you're here," murmured Aria.

"Do they know?" Michael asked, thinking of the frantic way Thera had thrown the door closed.

"I didn't tell them my itinerary," she replied calmly, not wishing to add fear to her sister's already strained emotions.

"But eventually they will figure it out. And if you knew where to look for Aria, so will they."

Thera shook her head. "May I have more coffee?" She waited while Aria refilled their cups. "I didn't know where to look," she went on, neglecting to add that Nicodemus's men probably would.

Michael stirred sugar into his coffee. "Then how did you find her?"

"A lot of legwork and a little intuition."

Michael's head came up abruptly, and he dropped his spoon into the cup, splashing coffee over the rim.

"What do you mean, intuition?"

Aria looked across at him, puzzled by the intensity of his tone.

Thera arched one eyebrow and waited for him to say more, so that she would know just what he was after.

"You're psychic," he said, as much to himself as to them. "Of course you are. Aria is, and you're her identical twin." He fell silent, his mind speeding on ahead of his mouth. What an opportunity Aria and her sister presented. He could compare their psi abilities and determine to what extent heredity and environment had shaped them. He might even forget his original hypothesis if he could get his adviser to agree. He brought himself up short. He'd sworn to himself not to subject Aria to any more testing, but the scientist in him yearned to study the mysteries of these psychic twins. It was a chance of a lifetime. His eyes shifted to Aria. She was smiling at him in a mildly confused way, as if she'd just heard a joke she didn't quite understand.

"Michael, are you with us?"

He nodded as another thought skimmed through his mind.

"What exactly are the powers you say you inherited from this goddess?"

Now Thera understood where the questions were leading. Well, she had intended to explain something of the nature of their powers anyway. Certainly not the full extent of them. But why was Michael so fascinated with this particular aspect of her story?

"Precognition, telekinesis, thought transference?" he prodded.

"Yes, to some degree."

"In other words, psychic abilities."

"Labels are superfluous," she said tersely.

Michael glanced at Aria. She, too, had made the obvious connection. "Do you think that's why I scored so highly on your tests, Michael?"

"What I think," he replied evenly, "is that you and your sister are both psychic, that psychic ability may be inherited to a large degree, and that this goddess legend is irrelevant to an explanation of your abilities. It's a provocative story, but without any real substance." He looked squarely at Thera, challenging her to refute his assertions.

She was smiling, but her eyes were cold ash.

"Believe as you wish, Michael, but in time you will come to see, as others have, that you are wrong. Divinity cannot be measured in human terms. You speak with great conviction, but in truth you do not know what you are dealing with."

Michael raked his hand through his hair. Damos had used almost the same words when he'd tried to convince them to stop the experiments. Was there more involved than he was willing to acknowledge? He felt like a knight who has just discovered a potentially fatal chink in his armor.

In the momentary silence he became aware that the storm had stopped. It hadn't faded, grumbling off into the distance; it had simply ceased as abruptly as it had started.

Thera had noticed it, too. "The eye of the storm," she remarked. "This may be only an intermission."

Michael glanced at his watch. It was after nine. He had intended to spend the night with Aria, but Thera's suitcase, standing inside the doorway, was a mute reminder that he would have to go. He pushed back from the table, leaving his fresh coffee untouched. "I guess I'd better get on home in case you're right about the storm."

Thera nodded, and Michael caught a subtle mockery in her expression, as if he were performing as she'd intended him to.

"Nice meeting you," he said, but the words were jagged splinters on his tongue.

"It was a pleasure, Michael," she replied smoothly. "I'm sure we'll be seeing a lot of each other now that I'm here."

There was a finality to the statement that caused Michael to wonder just how long she intended to stay.

Aria walked him to the door. "I'll speak to you tomorrow," she said. She had always dreaded him leaving, but now all she felt was a sense of relief. There'd been a draining tension between Thera and him all evening. As if they were vying for a prize and that prize was she.

Michael kissed her, but she drew back after only a moment, glancing over her shoulder. Thera was facing the other direction, drinking her coffee. Yet Aria felt as if there'd been an entire audience watching them.

"I want to show you something," Thera said. It was an hour later, and she and Aria had cleared the table and washed the dishes.

Aria looked up from the convertible sofa she'd been about to open.

"Move aside a minute," Thera instructed. From the moment the door first opened, she had been fighting her desire to test her powers to see if they were actually magnified in her sister's presence. She suspected that she might have to work at incorporating and properly handling any new energy she derived from Aria, but she assumed she would feel the difference in intensity right away. She'd held herself back until now, worried that she might scare Aria off. But she'd reasoned that concern away by telling herself that such a demonstration would, if anything, increase her credibility. Once Aria witnessed some concrete evidence of her sister's claims, she would have no choice but to believe everything.

Aria had moved to one side of the couch. Thera focused on

it, thinking ruefully that the effort would no doubt worsen the pain she'd been burdened with all day. But it would be worth the discomfort to find out what she longed to know. She tugged. There was some resistance; then she felt the couch's mechanism begin to move. But it was no easier than it would have been if she'd tried it alone. She turned to Aria, and the couch settled back upon itself again.

Aria was staring at it in amazement. "My God, Thera, how on earth did you do that?"

Thera ignored the question. She funneled her energy out toward her sister, then began to draw it back. She had an anxious moment when she didn't know if she was strong enough to regain control. Then, with the suddenness of a rubber band stretched to its limit and released, a powerful jolt of energy slammed into her. Thera felt as if a spike had been driven between her eyes at high speed. The room upended, and a gray veil spun around her, pierced by cyclical flashes of light. She crumpled to the floor, struggling to hold on as consciousness veered away. She wasn't sure how long she lay there, but gradually her sight cleared and the room steadied. She locked on the couch immediately and willed it to unfold. This time it sprang open without hesitation, its legs lifted off the floor by the force of its movement.

Aria watched, too dazed to absorb the meaning of what she was seeing. She'd been awed by the way the couch had vibrated and started to move the first time Thera looked at it. But then her sister had turned to her, and she had been engulfed in a strange, brilliant sensation. It had lasted only a moment or two, leaving her feeling hollow, depleted. She'd seen Thera collapse, and though she'd tried to go to her, her limbs would not respond to her brain's command, as if there were a short circuit in her nervous system.

Thera pushed herself up, her smile wan but triumphant. "You see, Ariadne," she said, her voice shaking, "some things go beyond the realm of scientific explanations."

Aria's legs tingled, then started to buckle under her. She took a step toward the open couch and fell sideways onto it.

"What happened to me?" she asked, her voice catching with fear and confusion.

Thera dropped down beside her. She stroked back the hair

that had fallen over Aria's eye. It was peculiar. Like reaching into a mirror and touching her own reflection.

"Nothing to worry about," she soothed. "Nothing that a little practice won't fix."

Aria looked up at her sister, so familiar yet so unknown, and a glacial fear oozed over her.

20

New York: November 7

Karen threw the Styrofoam cup into the trash bin, though it was still half full. Without company, drinking the cafeteria's bitter coffee was no pleasure. She wondered if Aria would return to classes on Monday. She'd already missed two full days, and Dr. Fischer was known for basing his exams on his lectures, whether they covered prescribed material or not. Karen decided it was a good thing she wasn't the one whose long lost twin had shown up on her doorstep. She shook her head, remembering how she'd stopped by Aria's apartment yesterday to drop off some notes. She'd felt like someone who'd had a few too many drinks and was seeing double. Though twins were no rarity, it was startling to discover that someone you were close to was really part of a matched set.

Once the initial shock was past, Karen had been able to detect subtle differences between the sisters—their posture, their expressions, the thrust of a chin, the way they used their hands, and most notably their eyes. Maybe the light had been hitting them at different angles, but the gray of their eyes was not quite the same. By the time Karen left the apartment she had learned to tell them apart. For some reason that had made her feel distinctly better.

She glanced at the clock over the doorway as she left the cafeteria. Class breaks had always flown by before. Now here she was with another fifteen minutes to kill. She quickly discarded the idea of a stroll outside. Although clear skies had followed the terrible electrical storm, temperatures had dipped

158

below zero, barely struggling up to ten degrees at the height of the day. The city streets had buckled and cracked, and yawning pot holes had appeared overnight as if some huge nocturnal beast were feeding on the concrete and macadam.

Instead she decided to stop in at the registrar's office to pick up a copy of the spring course listings. That should leave her with just enough time to make it to class without rushing.

There were two men ahead of her. One of them was talking to a secretary. The other was leaning against the counter, possessively fingering the nylon travel bag that was slung over his shoulder.

Karen stood off to one side, waiting for them to finish. She pretended to be absorbed in the notices tacked to the bulletin board on the wall nearest her, but she couldn't help noticing the strong accent in the man's speech. She tried to place it without success. She turned back to them. Both had black hair and olive complexions. They could be Italian, she supposed, but the accent didn't sound right.

She didn't realize she was staring until the one with the bag glanced over at her. She felt herself redden, and she smiled a brief, apologetic smile. He didn't acknowledge it, and Karen caught a furtive, uneasy look in his eyes before he turned away. After her vacation in Spain, Karen knew how difficult it was to get along in a country where you didn't speak the language. Maybe the secretary had never known that feeling, because she was clearly losing her patience with the men.

"No, I'm sorry. There is just no way I can give you that information." Her lips were pursed, and she wore a weary, put-upon expression.

The man said something about an emergency and demanded to speak to whomever was in charge. His tone was authoritative, challenging.

The secretary's brow smoothed as she finally saw an end to the discussion. "Mr. Purcell is the one you'd want to speak to, then. He's not in at the moment. Let me have your name and a number where you can be reached, and I'll see to it that he gets in touch with you as soon as possible." She reached for a notepad.

"Koraes. Nikolas Koraes," he said. "Here, I write it for you."

The secretary pushed the pad across the counter to him and went back to sit down.

Karen's mouth dropped open. Could she have heard the name correctly? She moved toward the counter. The two men were conferring rapidly in their own language.

"Excuse me," she said.

They looked at her. For the first time she was able to clearly see the face of the one who had called himself Nikolas. He had sharp features dominated by smoldering black eyes that seemed to leap out of his face at her.

"I didn't mean to listen to your conversation," she said tentatively, "but I heard you say your name was Koraes."

It was obvious that the one with the bag didn't understand English. He cocked his head to one side, then to the other, as if that might help him make sense of her words.

"Yes, my name is Koraes," Nikolas replied warily.

"I know someone by that name. Maybe it's the person you're looking for."

The change in his expression was subtle but immediate. A new intensity glowed in his eyes, and a smile played at one side of his mouth.

"Who is it you know?"

"Her name is Aria, short for Ariadne. She's a friend of mine and—"

"Yes, yes," he interrupted excitedly. "It is Aria I look for. You know, then, where I find her?"

Karen nodded. "Are you a relative of hers?"

"Relative?" he repeated, stumbling over the word.

"You know, family."

His face brightened. "Ah, yes, family. I am cousin to her."

Karen laughed. "This is unbelievable. If anyone else turns up, I may just faint."

"Someone more comes for Aria?" he asked.

"Yeah. Her sister. But you must know Thera. She just came in from Greece, too."

Nikolas nodded. "Yes. I know Thera." He spoke briefly to his friend whose round face lit with comprehension. "You will tell me now where I find them," he said, looking back at Karen.

She hesitated for a moment, then decided it was only his

poor grasp of English that had turned the request into a demand.

"They're probably at Aria's apartment." She tore a piece of paper off the notepad and wrote down the address for them.

"Thank you." Nikolas took the paper and hurried off with his friend before Karen could say she'd been glad she could help them. As the door swung shut behind them, she realized she ought to let Aria know her cousin was on his way to see her. After all, how many surprises could one person be expected to handle in a week? She checked her watch. There were only three minutes left before class. The spring catalog could wait; she felt an obligation to call Aria. Even if it meant walking in late on Fischer's lecture.

Nikolas took the travel bag from Christo. He went into a bathroom stall and locked the door behind him. It took him only a moment to locate the small case that held the syringes and vials of sedative. Dr. Vodopia had been reluctant to give them to him, but as a member of the congregation he understood the importance of this mission. Nikolas opened the case and looked at the needles. Their silvery points shone even in the dim bathroom light. Excitement coursed through him. These were his only weapons, all he would need to overpower Thera and bring her home. The doctor had shown him how to introduce the sedative into the syringe and had explained how to administer the injection, admonishing him to be sure no air remained in the syringe. One air bubble could be lethal. Nikolas had assured the doctor that he understood. It was almost too tempting, though. Such a simple way to be done with her. He could say he'd been nervous, there'd been a struggle, in the confusion he'd neglected to clear all the air out of the syringe. Even Nicodemus would accept it as an accident. But the gods would not. Nikolas picked up one of the vials and filled a syringe. Then he snapped the case shut and slid it into one of the pockets of his jacket, where it would be close at hand. With the travel bag hanging from his shoulder, he left the stall and nodded to Christo.

Karen could hear the muffled voices in the background. She

pressed the receiver against her ear trying to pick up what they were saying. When she had told Aria about meeting Nikolas, her friend's response had been unexpectedly terse as if she were not so much surprised as disturbed by the news. She'd wanted to know where and how the meeting had taken place and at exactly what time. Then she'd asked Karen to hold on while she spoke to Thera. Now Karen could distinguish Thera's voice, strident and enraged, and Aria's, sober but placating. After a minute Aria was back on the line.

"Listen, Karen," she said urgently. "Nikolas mustn't find Thera. I can't explain it all to you right now. She's fairly safe as long as I'm with her, but it would be much better if we weren't here when they arrive. Do you think—"

"Don't even ask. I'll meet you at my apartment as soon as you can pack."

"Thanks, I'm sorry. I don't know what else to do."

"I should be the one who's sorry," Karen said grimly. "I'm the idiot with the big mouth who put you two in this situation. Besides," she added more brightly, "I have an extra bedroom, and I'd love the company."

Karen pulled on her coat and headed for the door, wondering whose class notes she and Aria could borrow.

"Did you stop by the apartment?" Thera asked before Michael had walked through the doorway.

He looked at her as he shrugged off his coat. There was a heightened tension about her. It pulled her skin tautly over her cheekbones and shadowed her eyes. Whatever it was she feared, it was real enough to her. He handed the coat to Karen.

"I drove by. Thanks, Karen."

Aria wandered in from the bedroom. Seeing her, Michael's heart lifted. It was amazing that the same face could trigger such different responses in him.

"Hi, I didn't hear you come in."

Michael crossed the room and kissed her. "Private Investigator Lansing reporting." He waited for a smile, but there was none. Aria, who'd always been so quick to smile, was as solemn as her sister.

"Who was there?" Thera asked.

Michael sat down on the couch and drew Aria down beside him. "Well, I don't know exactly who you have in mind, but I did see a couple of guys in the lobby across the street from Aria's place. For that matter they could have been anyone. There's one hell of a lot of people in this city."

"Were they dark? Was one dark and good-looking?"

"Yeah, they were dark. As for good-looking, I didn't pay attention. They weren't my type." He watched Thera's mouth curl with annoyance.

"Be serious," Aria chided, seeing her sister's disapproval and feeling in some way responsible for what he said and did.

"I'm trying," Michael replied. "It's not all that easy."

Karen had sat down across from them. Only Thera remained standing.

"You want proof," she said. "You want unimpeachable sources." She shifted her gaze to include her sister. Aria had seen her use her powers several times now. She seemed to accept their existence, if not their source. It wouldn't hurt to lay the truth out before her. And Thera knew just how to do that.

"Tomorrow we'll take a little trip," she said. "It's time I met my parents."

21

New York: November 8

The phone call had been difficult. Thera had made it clear that
Aria was not to reveal her presence ahead of time. She was
only to say that she and Michael wanted to come for a visit.
Helena was delighted and inquired if they would stay for dinner this time. Had she already forgotten the near disaster of
the last visit? Aria wondered. But of course even that would
pale beside the impact of this one. Unable to say more, she
suggested they wait and see. Before Helena could insist,
Damos took the phone from her. He listened to the little
prepared speech Aria had already recited to her mother. There
was a long silence before he replied.

"This is not just an ordinary visit, is it, Ariadne?" His voice
was calm, but there was a strain beneath it that made the
words almost too crisp and clear.

Aria wished she could tell him then, to ease the shock. But
perhaps in some way he already knew. She looked at Thera,
standing a few feet away. She couldn't disappoint her. After
all these years Thera had the right to set the stage for the
meeting.

"Not exactly," Aria said. Then, hoping to detour him, she
added quickly, "By the way, you'll be happy to know that
Michael and I have dropped the experiments."

"Yes. I am glad to hear that." But there was no joy in his
tone, only the same cool wariness.

"So we'll see you tomorrow," she had said, trying to end

the conversation before she lost control of it.

"Tomorrow," Damos repeated. "We'll expect you."

Now Aria sat wedged between Michael and Thera as they sped along the expressway. There was hardly any traffic, but Michael was frowning at the road, his fingers curled tightly around the steering wheel. He hadn't said a word since they'd left Karen's apartment. He'd advised against making the trip when the first hurricane warnings went out. But Thera was intractable, and in the end Aria had sided with her, saying that they could always stay the night with her parents if necessary.

The silence in the car was oppressive. Aria made a few half-hearted attempts at conversation, then gave up and tried to distract herself by listening to the radio. But after each song there was another report on the freak late-season hurricane that had been spawned two days ago in the Gulf and was cutting a swath of death and destruction across the coastal states as it tore up toward New York. It was advancing at tremendous speed with winds that came close to tornado force. It had ripped apart entire towns, flooding escape routes with walls of rain driven so savagely they bruised the skin.

With each news update Michael's expression darkened, his jaw clenching as if to hold back a rush of words. Aria reached up and ran her fingertips along the hard line of his cheek. He turned to her, his mouth softening into a smile. She smiled back and felt better. Things had become terribly strained between them since Thera's arrival. It was possible that Michael was jealous of all the time she was spending with her sister. But that couldn't be helped just yet. She would make it up to him soon, though. She let her hand drop to rest on his thigh. Michael took one hand off the wheel and put it over hers. For a moment she was filled with a sense of well-being and relief. Then she felt Thera's gaze on her. She drew her hand out from beneath Michael's before turning to her.

Thera was regarding her with one eyebrow arched, a pose she struck when she was annoyed. And for the first time it occurred to Aria that Michael might not be the only one who was jealous.

By the time they left the car in the parking area below the house, the sky was as rough as a choppy sea. Low gray-black clouds pitched and churned above them, and the wind slammed into them, stinging their eyes and pounding their ears. They were breathless by the time they'd climbed the steps to the house.

Without a moment's hesitation, Thera pressed the doorbell. Aria wished she'd had time to compose herself; her knees were as wobbly as gelatin, quivering uncontrollably. She stole a quick glance at her sister, who seemed remarkably poised and at ease. Aria was still marveling at Thera's self-control when the door opened and Damos stood before them. She tried to produce a smile, but only succeeded in swallowing loudly.

Damos's eyes traveled over the three of them. They didn't linger on Thera, nor did his expression change. He just nodded slightly as if confirming a private thought.

"Come in," he said evenly.

When he stepped aside, Aria saw her mother standing behind him. Damos reached out to steady Helena even as she faltered and drew back. He murmured something to her, and although she straightened up, she still clung desperately to his arm.

"Nice to see you both again," Michael murmured, feeling as if he were trespassing.

Damos nodded. "Michael."

There was an awkward moment of silence, broken finally by Thera.

"Is this all the greeting you extend to a daughter you thought never to see again?" she asked, her tone cool, baiting. Damos remained unruffled, but she could see the emotion working in her mother's face. Surprise and fear and pain glittered feverishly in Helena's eyes. She released her grip on Damos and slowly came forward. Her arms trembled as she held them out.

"Thera." The word was a hoarse sigh, and tears spilled onto her cheeks.

Thera's lips curved up as she moved into her mother's embrace. From Michael's perspective the smile seemed replete with satisfaction rather than happiness, and a new wave of uneasiness washed over him. He turned to Aria, who stood beside him. She was sniffling happily at the reunion. Michael was contrite. Did he just want to imagine the worst of Thera?

Damos's voice broke in on his thoughts. "Why are you here, Thera?"

Thera looked up at him, one arm still around Helena's waist. "To see you, of course. To see Aria and you."

Damos turned away abruptly and shut the door. "We can talk in the den."

"I thought you would be happy to see me," Thera said, once they were all seated and Damos had poured drinks for Michael, Helena, and himself. She watched Damos's hand quiver as he lifted the glass to his mouth. He was not as strong as he appeared. Emotion was already breaching the surface. Thera was filled with a pleasure she hadn't anticipated. Over the years she'd often thought about her parents. In the beginning it had been with curiosity and later with a calm indifference. She'd been staggered by the unexpected anger that had surged up in her when the door opened and Damos stood before her. These were her parents. And they had deserted her. They had taken her sister and left her behind. Suddenly she wanted more from them than a simple confirmation of her story. She wanted revenge.

Damos took a mouthful of the scotch and waited while it burned its way down his throat. His pulse was leaping in his veins like something trying to escape. All of his suspicions and premonitions had not prepared him for this moment.

"How can I be happy to see you, knowing the danger you have placed yourself in?" he asked.

Thera shrugged. "I am well able to take care of myself."

"Do you think it is simply talk, a game of words to them?" Damos demanded, incensed by her casual attitude. "Do you think your mother and I gave you up that easily? It was your life we traded for. Nothing has changed. It is still your life we are talking about."

"Which is precisely why I have come to you," Thera replied, glancing at her sister. "Aria must believe what I have told her. So that she, too, will understand the danger. Our safety lies in each other."

Damos's heart clenched painfully. All these years he had tried to keep Aria unaware of her background, innocent of the power and the danger. Now Thera had laid all his efforts to waste. He thought of Nicodemus and wondered, as he always did, if his father would actually have allowed the congregation to sacrifice one of the baby girls.

"Does your grandfather know where you are?" he asked heavily, draining his glass and going back to the bar to refill it.

"Yes."

"You know him better than I do now. Will he send men after you?"

"He already has."

Damos capped the bottle. "I see."

"Tell Aria and Michael," Thera demanded. "They need to hear it from you."

Damos sat down across from his daughters and smiled bitterly. "There is little else I can do." For the next quarter of an hour he explained the circumstances of the girls' birth and the necessity of separating them.

Michael listened carefully, finding it hard to believe that this acclaimed architect could speak of mythology as if it were fact.

"You really do believe, like Thera, that your family's psychic abilities originated with the goddess Aphrodite?" he asked, trying to mask his skepticism.

"You have tested Aria. Have you not seen for yourself how gifted she is? How far superior to anyone you have ever studied before?"

Grudgingly Michael had to admit this was so. "But that alone doesn't prove a divine connection," he argued.

Damos's gray eyes flashed with irritation. "I am not attempting to convert you to my beliefs," he snapped.

"You never spoke about religion at all," Aria said, to draw the conversation away from Michael. "I always assumed you were an atheist."

Damos shook his head ruefully. "Had you asked me two weeks ago if I was an atheist, my answer would have been an unqualified yes. Now I am not so certain." He pushed himself out of his chair and walked toward the plate-glass windows. They were rattling under the force of the wind. Below the house, the usually placid waters of the Sound were being whipped into a foaming fury. Yet the coming storm seemed no more than a reflection of his own inner turbulence. Conclusions that had once been as solid as bedrock were suddenly crumbling shale. He finished his second glass of scotch and turned back to the others.

"I thought I'd divested myself of religion when I was in my teens. And here I am doubting myself again. I seem to have lost the certainty of youth." He paused and gestured to the ominous scene outside. "We are suddenly plagued by inexplicable weather, horrible devastation. All over the world it's the same. And I find myself reconsidering many things, among them the possibility that Zeus and the other gods never left, but just fell silent for a while."

"Let us not go overboard, Father," Thera chided him with a sardonic smile. "The world today is of our own making."

"Or so you would prefer it to be."

"So I know it to be. You'd do better to blame the weather on nuclear tests or space probes or the coming of another ice age than on some jealous god who disappeared thousands of years ago."

Michael tried to remember what he'd learned about Greek mythology. Something in their exchange jarred him, but he couldn't put his finger on it.

The rain started then, not with a few warning drops, but all at once, driving into the windows with such force it seemed it might slice through the thick glass. Helena jumped in her seat. Thera patted her hand.

"It's all right, Mother. It really is just a storm." But Helena's eyes were locked on Damos with a fear that vibrated in the air.

Aria slid her hand across to Michael. She urgently needed his stability, his normalcy. Instead of finding pleasure and comfort in this reunion, she felt as though she were being plunged into one of her dark, forbidding nightmares.

Thera saw her sister reach out to Michael. She wanted to thrust him aside and reassure Aria herself. Prove to her that together they were strong enough to face anything. But she restrained herself. She had to wait for the right time.

Damos had returned to his seat. "It appears we'll be having

company tonight," he said, affecting a lighter tone. "Helena, why don't you see about fixing that dinner you were hoping to talk them into?"

Helena nodded and rose. He was right. She would feel better if she kept busy.

"Aria, why don't you and Michael see what you can do to help your mother?"

Once they were alone, Damos turned to Thera, his voice once again sober. "Do they know where to find you?"

"They know of Aria's apartment, but we left before they got there. We're staying with her friend Karen now."

"They'll find you there, too. They didn't come all this way to fail."

"Neither did I."

"What can you hope to accomplish?" Damos demanded in exasperation.

Thera glanced around the room, settling on the areca palm in its massive planter near the desk. A moment later she was moving it through the air toward her father.

Damos watched in grim silence as she set it down beside him. "Impressive."

"That's nothing compared to what Aria and I can do together."

"To what end, though?"

"Power. With power everything is possible."

Damos felt his skin go cold, as if the wind had punched a hole in the windows and begun to howl through the room.

"Does Aria know what you are planning for her?"

"I am planning nothing for her. I want only to give her what is hers by birth. To show her what lies open to her."

"She's satisfied with her life and with the career she's chosen. But now she isn't even safe leaving the apartment to go to her classes. You have no right to inflict your desires on her this way."

"She chose without knowing the choices!" Thera retorted. "You talk about rights. What gave you the right to deny her that knowledge?"

"We did it to protect her."

"To protect her from your superstitions."

"Those men who are after you are not a superstition.

They're dangerously real," Damos reminded her. "Do you intend to spend the rest of your life hiding from them?"

"Soon I'll be strong enough to take care of them."

"By which you mean . . ."

"By which I mean I do not intend to be hounded by their outdated fears. I will do what is necessary to ensure that."

Damos did not reply immediately. The lack of emotion in Thera's voice had chilled him more than her words. How could this woman be his daughter, Aria's twin? And what part of the blame rested with him for having deserted her?

"If you have any love for your sister, you will leave here, Thera, and go back to Crete," he said, his voice commanding and pleading all at once.

"It is for love of my sister that I will stay; we belong together. And if you are wise, you will not interfere." Her voice, low and ominous, was nearly swallowed by the shrieking wind that buffeted the house with increasing force. The lamp that had flickered uncertainly while they talked suddenly went out, plunging the room into a murky darkness.

Damos could hear Helena in the kitchen instructing Aria and Michael to stand still while she found candles and flashlights. In another minute she would come into the den to guide him and Thera out.

"You may be able to conquer mortal enemies, Thera," he whispered harshly. "But what about the others?"

Thera's eyes bore into him, cutting through the darkness with a luminosity all their own. "The others are only in your imagination."

The narrow beam of Helena's flashlight swung into the room.

"Damos, Thera, come into the kitchen with us. We have a kerosene lamp."

Damos rose reluctantly and followed the women out. He had more to say to Thera, but he didn't know when he would be alone with her again. Not that it mattered. She would never change her mind. Her determination was an inviolable fortress. The most he could hope to do was protect Aria.

"It's a good thing we have a gas stove," Helena said brightly as she set the veal piccata on the dining room table, "or we'd be eating cold sandwiches tonight." She sat down beside Thera. The risks might be enormous, but she was glad to have both her daughters with her. It was a dream she'd never thought to see fulfilled. A dream she'd never dared describe to Damos. Now that it had come to be, she wished he would allow himself to enjoy the moment. She passed the platters of food and tried to keep the conversation going. It wasn't easy. Damos sat at the other end of the table, remote and taciturn. Thera's mood seemed to have darkened as well.

"Would you like some veal?" Helena offered.

Thera didn't respond. She was watching the way her father would turn to look at Aria between each forkful. His precious Aria. The anger was a fire burning just beneath her skin. Her cheeks were flushed with it.

Helena repeated her question, extending the dish of meat toward her.

"No. No, thank you," Thera said, abruptly holding up her hand and deflecting the plate. It went flying out of Helena's grasp to shatter on the marble floor.

Helena immediately left her seat to clean up the mess. When Aria got up to help, she sent her back to her seat. "If we all try to do this in the dark we're going to wind up with a worse mess. You go on back and finish eating."

Damos was glaring at Thera. "I think you owe your mother an apology."

"It was an accident, just an accident," Helena assured him as she collected the shards of china, and mopped up the veal with a stack of napkins.

"An apology," Damos insisted.

"You are a fine one to talk of apologies," Thera snapped.

"It's all right, Damos, really it is." Helena had come to stand beside his chair. "Please."

Damos said nothing more, for Helena's sake. If this was to be her only night with both of her daughters, he would not spoil it.

Helena returned to her seat, trying to act as if nothing had happened. But the tension in the room was palpable, and the food stuck like straw in her dry throat. Michael and Aria exchanged uncomfortable glances, then concentrated on finishing their meal.

Thera ate, too, but without tasting what passed through her mouth. With her peripheral vision, she watched her father tear off a piece of bread. She wished she could augment her power with Aria's. But Aria would feel the energy surge and release as she had that first night in her apartment. No, Thera decided, she would have to manage this on her own.

Damos stuffed the bread into his mouth, grinding it between his teeth, punishing it the way he wanted to punish Thera. Feeling her eyes on him, he glanced at her and was surprised to find her staring straight ahead and not at him at all. He was letting emotion cloud his mind, he thought irritably. He swallowed and speared the last forkful of his salad. Then something went wrong. Horribly wrong. He tried to breathe, but no air filled his lungs. When he tried to cry out, no sound emerged. His fork dropped with a clatter onto the plate. He pushed away from the table, one hand clawing at his throat.

Helena was the first to realize what was wrong. She jumped up, shouting for help. Michael was behind Damos in an instant. Clamping his fists against the older man's diaphragm, he jerked sharply in and upward. After the second attempt, a soggy mass of bread flew out of Damos's mouth, and he took a noisy, wrenching gasp of air. Michael steadied him as he sank into his chair.

Then, while Aria tried to comfort her mother, who hovered at Damos's side close to hysteria, Michael took one of the flashlights and disappeared down the hallway toward the den. He returned a few minutes later with a bottle of brandy.

"You were magnificent, Michael," Thera said as he poured the brandy and handed the glasses around. "I can't think what might have happened if you hadn't been here."

Michael took a swig of the fiery liqueur and studied her over the rim of his glass. She was smiling, but her eyes were filled with bitter contempt. And Michael couldn't help thinking she had somehow played a part in the incident. And that she would have preferred Damos dead.

Michael was given the guest room. The sisters were to share the room that had been Aria's as a child. Michael trailed behind Aria on the stairs.

"Wait," he whispered, taking her hand and holding her

back. As soon as the others had disappeared into their rooms, he pulled her into the guest room with him. Aria started to protest, but Michael ignored her and closed the door. In the pitch darkness he reached out and drew her tightly against him.

After a moment Aria returned the embrace, wondering why she had hesitated, and how she could have forgotten the magic of being in Michael's arms.

"God, I've missed you," he murmured, his lips clinging to hers. "Stay here with me."

"I can't. My parents aren't that understanding." She was also thinking that Thera wouldn't approve. But she didn't say so.

"Wait until they're asleep; then come back here."

"What if Thera says something to them?"

"Thera," Michael sighed. "Then wait until you're sure she's asleep, too."

"If I can."

Michael kissed her again. "Promise."

"I'll try. That's the best I can do." She took a step toward the door.

Michael released her. "Aria?" he said as she fumbled for the knob.

"Yes?"

"Be careful of your sister."

"What on earth for?"

He wanted to tell her that he thought Thera had engineered Damos's choking episode, but suddenly the idea seemed preposterous. He would only sound like a fool and wind up alienating Aria as well as her sister.

"Just a gut feeling, that's all," he replied lamely.

"Oh, Michael," she laughed. Then she opened the door and walked out.

Thera set the flashlight on the dresser. "I was about to put my clothes back on and go looking for you."

"I was saying good night to Michael," Aria explained, feeling like a child who'd overstayed her curfew.

Thera was stripped down to her bra and panties. She pulled back the covers on one of the twin beds and lay down. Aria undressed, switched off the flashlight, and got into the other bed. Lying there in the dark room listening to the storm rage around them, she remembered how she'd wished for a sister all through her childhood. Someone to play with, someone to share her thoughts and secrets with, someone to occupy the other bed at night so she would never be alone during thunderstorms. Now here she was with her sister only a few feet away. Her wish had come true. She wondered what Thera was thinking. Was she comparing this room with the one in which she had grown up? Had she longed for a sister, too? But of course it had been different for her—she had always known she had one.

Which was worse, Aria mused, longing for something you knew you could never have or longing for something that was there but just out of reach? It was a question she couldn't answer, but of one thing she was certain: Now that she did have a sister, she wouldn't easily give her up. In spite of the dangers Damos foresaw.

"Thera," she whispered.

"Yes?" The disembodied voice floated back as it had so often in Aria's childhood games of let's-pretend.

"Those men who are after you, do they really believe your coming here has angered their gods?"

"Their gods and themselves," Thera replied scornfully.

"What do you mean?"

"They cannot bear to see such power in our hands—women's hands. They blame jealous gods, but it is truly they themselves who choke on jealousy."

Aria shuddered at the sudden reminder of Damos's brush with death. She was sure the remark had been unintentional, yet it left her with a peculiar discomfort.

Thera was still speaking, as if she were unaware of the impact of her last words. "It is no different anywhere. In every religion, in every nation, men wish at all costs to keep their position, their power."

"Not all men are like that," Aria protested, pushing the choking scene from her mind. "Michael isn't."

Thera laughed. "You see in him what you want to see. I am not so blind. I see only a man. A man with the same greed and insecurity as all men."

"No, you don't understand," Aria hurried to explain. "You don't really know Michael at all. He was thrilled with the level of psychic power he found in me. In fact, he wanted to try to help me expand it through hypnosis. It's part of the thesis he's working on."

"And what made him stop?"

"Some weird things started happening to me. He got scared, worried that he was pushing me over the edge into something he didn't understand."

"More likely, he was scared of losing his control over you."

Aria fell silent. She was hurt and angered by Thera's attack on Michael, but she was determined not to fight with her. It was to be expected that she and her sister would have some divergent views, she told herself. After all, they'd been raised on opposite sides of the world with completely different values and beliefs.

Thera stared into the darkness, chastising herself for having said too much too soon. She had felt Aria's anger spring up like a hot, impenetrable barrier between them. And all because of Michael. Yet Thera was no longer quite as eager to be rid of him. In trying to defend him, Aria had set an intriguing possibility before her, one Thera was determined not to ignore. She waited several minutes to give Aria time to calm down.

"I'm sorry, Aria," she said softly. "I'm afraid I judge all men by my own experience. I had no right to do that with Michael." She could feel the veil of anger disintegrate even before Aria replied.

"It's all right. I've misjudged plenty of people myself."

Thera paused long enough to appear to be changing subjects. "You know, Michael's experiment really does sound fascinating. Do you think he would consider trying it with me?"

"I'll ask," Aria said, hoping she had stumbled upon a way of bridging the gap between her sister and Michael. "I'll speak to him about it tomorrow."

Aria waited until Thera was asleep. Then she slipped out of bed and quietly pulled on her clothes. She padded across the room, relying on her memory to avoid bumping into the furniture. When she turned the doorknob she winced at the sound of the bolt disengaging. Thera didn't stir. She let herself out into the hall and made her way to Michael's room.

After the door clicked closed, Thera stretched and resettled herself. She disliked Aria's sneaking off to Michael, but certain trade-offs had to be made. And Michael would be more amenable to working with her if he didn't feel she was keeping Aria from his bed.

22

Damos was in his bathrobe drinking coffee when Michael came into the kitchen. The electricity was still out, and the heavily overcast sky cast a dismal light over the room.

"Good morning," Michael said. "How are you feeling?"

Damos looked up. "Good morning. Better. Much better. I'm afraid I never really thanked you properly last night. But I am grateful, truly."

"I'm glad I was there," Michael said, remembering the expression on Thera's face.

"There's hot water in the kettle on the stove if you'd like some coffee. Until the power is fixed, we have only instant."

"Thanks, instant's fine." Michael took one of the cups left in the drainboard after dinner. He made coffee and joined Damos at the table.

"I was listening to the portable radio before I came down this morning," Damos remarked. "It sounds as though we were very lucky. The storm devastated parts of the island. Killed at least ten people, injured a lot more."

"Where is it now?"

"Gone out to sea. They're hoping it won't rebuild itself and turn back up to New England." His pale eyes were bleak and weary.

"Unbelievable weather," Michael murmured, wondering if he dared mention the thought that had crossed his mind in the early hours of the morning.

He sipped the black coffee, hoping to bolster his courage. He might have saved this man's life last night, but he was still distinctly uneasy around him.

"Something you and Thera were discussing yesterday stuck in my mind," he began finally. "Zeus was the most powerful of the Greek gods, sort of the head of them all, wasn't he?"

Damos's brows drew together. "Yes," he replied carefully.

"But wasn't he also the god of weather?" Michael held his breath waiting for the reply.

Damos studied the young man before him. Could he possibly be his ally? His only ally? Helena and Aria were far too enchanted with Thera to pay attention to his warnings.

"Yes," he said. "Zeus was the god of weather." He watched for Michael's reaction. "Perhaps he still is."

Michael was chewing absently on his lower lip. Even if he couldn't quite believe in the reappearance of a Greek god, as a parapsychologist he should at least keep an open mind. "It worries you, doesn't it?" he asked after a moment.

"Yes, but there is something that worries me more."

Not wishing to pry, Michael waited.

"I'm afraid for Aria's sake," Damos continued.

"Why?"

"The men. The ones who were sent to find Thera. In principle it doesn't matter which of the girls they abduct, as long as they manage to keep the twins apart." Damos saw Michael's whole body tense as he spoke. "Even if you do not believe in lost gods, Michael, the danger to Aria is very real and very immediate. Watch out for her. Protect her if you can. I don't mean to put the entire burden on you, but there is no else who can help her." His voice was even, controlled, as if he had lived for a long time with this particular dread and was reacting by rote.

Michael nodded, not trusting his own voice to be as calm or assured.

Helena begged them to stay another day. Until there was no chance that the storm would turn back on them. Until electricity was restored and traffic lights were operating. Until the roads were cleared of tree limbs and other debris. She knew that once they left her house she would never have them together again. But Michael was determined to leave, and for once Thera was on his side.

"Be careful," Helena reiterated as she and Damos walked them to the front door. "Especially on that strip of road that runs between the inlet and the Sound. You know it might not even be passable," she added glancing hopefully at Damos for corroboration. "The water just washes over it whenever we have a big storm.

Damos made no comment. A dark premonition had stolen over him as she spoke. He wished he could grab Aria and lock her away until the danger had passed. But would it pass? He looked at Michael. A good man, but hardly a match for Thera. Her powers were already too well developed. He felt the aura of them like a crackling field of energy surrounding her. Though no one else suspected the truth, he knew how close she had come to killing him last night.

The sisters were kissing Helena good-bye. Aria came to him and pressed her cheek to his. He closed his eyes, and tears burned against his eyelids. Then Thera was before him.

"Father," she said, with a bitterness he could almost taste.

"Thera." He couldn't reach out to her. Even though Helena wanted him to. Even though it would make this parting more bearable for her.

Michael broke the tension of the moment by opening the front door. He thanked them again for their hospitality and ushered Aria and Thera outside. Before turning to follow them, he looked back at Damos and nodded. The older man nodded back, and Helena wondered what strange new alliance had been forged between them.

Helena had been right about the highways. Work crews were still busy trying to clear the main arteries. It would be days before they were free to start on the smaller roads. Every few yards Michael had to stop the car in order to lug tree limbs out of their way. In one spot where a birch had been uprooted and lay across the road, he asked Aria and Thera to help.

Thera stood to one side watching in disbelief as her sister bent and started tugging at the tree. She was like a sighted person closing her eyes and refusing to see.

"Move away," she commanded sharply.

Michael looked up at Thera, his arms still wrapped around the tree. "How about more muscle and less supervising?" he snapped back.

"Just move away."

Aria had already backed up, aware of what Thera had in mind. "Michael, come here," she urged.

Reluctantly Michael moved off to the side. "Now what?"

Thera didn't reply. She was staring at Aria. Then she turned toward the tree. Michael was about to demand an explanation when the birch shuddered, then flew off the ground and into the brush at the side of the road. Open-mouthed he whirled around to stare at the sisters. Thera was gazing at him with smug satisfaction, but Aria seemed pale, almost dazed.

"I believe you call it telekinesis," Thera said as he hurried up to them.

Michael put his arm around Aria's waist. She wobbled uncertainly and produced a weak smile.

"She'll be all right," Thera told him. "Soon we'll have it mastered."

Michael wasn't comforted by the statement. He held Aria more tightly to him. She seemed to be threatened on so many sides. How could he protect her from all of them?

It had taken them more than twice the usual time to drive from the Koraes house to the narrow roadway that Helena had warned them about. Michael slowed to a stop so he could determine the condition of the road. It appeared clear and dry, the water lapping placidly at the sandy shoulders on either side of it.

Aria looked out along the narrow half-mile strip of macadam and wished they would turn back. But she didn't say anything, because she could not explain why her stomach was twisting and the hair at the nape of her neck was standing out. The sky was a dark, mottled gray, sweeping into the water with no discerniable horizon. Sky and sea had become one continuous sphere around them. Aria felt like Jack in the palm of the giant.

Michael put the car into drive, and they started along the road. Almost at once there was a loud sucking noise like that of an inverted windstorm, and Aria saw that the water had drawn back from the sides of the road, revealing rocky shoals. Then the funnel of water out in the Sound caught her eye. It seemed to have sprung up spontaneously, drawing its force from both the clouds and the water in a furiously rotating column. And it was heading straight at them. She cried out to Michael, but he had already seen the danger. The car leaped forward as he pressed the accelerator to the floor. Aria glanced quickly back at the road. They were only at the halfway point. She doubted they could reach safety before the water spout was upon them. The car was already being buffeted by the outer winds. It weaved wildly across the road as Michael struggled for control.

"No, Michael," Thera shouted. "You have to stop."

"You're crazy," he yelled back at her, the roar of the wind so loud it seemed to be inside his head.

Aria saw the calm determination in her sister's eyes. She put her hand on Michael's thigh.

"Listen to her," she pleaded, fighting to be heard. "Michael, listen to her."

Michael put his foot on the brake, and the car skidded to a stop. He didn't know what Thera had in mind, but he could no longer see beyond the frantically spinning clouds that encircled them, and if he kept going he could easily drive straight into the water.

Thera shifted sideways in her seat and locked her eyes on Aria's.

"The power is ours. Don't be afraid. Don't let it overwhelm you."

The wind was rocking the car with such force it seemed it would flip it over at any moment. Water poured in through the window and door frames. Aria fought to block out her fear and concentrate, steeling herself for the surge of energy. When it came this time she was ready. It was no worse than riding the crest of a wave. Back and forth the energy surged between her and Thera, growing with each exchange until it was a visible glow of light joining them and surrounding them. The light expanded, enveloping Michael and then the car itself. Abruptly the shaking stopped. The car stood like a granite rock in the midst of the tempest.

Fear had passed from Aria, replaced by a feeling of well-being and satisfaction unlike anything she had ever experienced. And in that same instant she knew she could never explain it to Michael. He wouldn't understand. But Thera would. Already did. After all, they were two halves of a whole, weren't they?

Within a few minutes the storm was over. The deadly funnel of cloud, wind, and water dissolved as rapidly as it had formed. Almost sadly Aria felt the connection between her and Thera break, the level of power diminish until it was a gentle vibration within her.

"We can go forward now," Thera said when Michael made no move to start the engine.

Aria swiveled to face him. "Michael? Are you all right?"

"Yeah," he mumbled distantly, wading through the fear, awe, and relief that engulfed him. He turned the key in the ignition. As they started along the rain-slicked road, he couldn't help thinking that the water spout had not been a coincidence. They'd been lured onto the road, set up to be killed. But by what? He knew what Damos's answer would be.

23

Nikolas looked at his watch. Christo was late. He gnashed his teeth as much from anger as from the effort to fight the chill of the night wind. He ducked into the vestibule of the building across from Aria's. It was difficult to keep up this vigil and yet remain unobtrusive. Soon someone would become suspicious enough to call the police. But the sisters couldn't stay away forever, he reasoned. It was a question of what would happen first. Nikolas flexed his shoulders and knees, which were stiff with the cold. He didn't like leaving things to chance, even if the gods were on his side. By the time Christo appeared, his stomach was twisted with hunger and frustrated rage.

"*Sighnomi,*" Christo said sheepishly. "I missed my stop on the subway and—"

"Your apologies don't interest me," Nikolas retorted. "Just be on time from now on."

"From now on? How much longer can we continue this?"

The question was the same one that had plagued Nikolas all day. Having Christo echo it only served to irritate him more.

"Tomorrow I try something else. But for tonight nothing has changed."

Christo nodded and stifled a sigh, wishing he had never agreed to come along on this venture.

"Do not fall asleep," Nikolas reminded him sternly. Then he pulled up the collar of his coat and walked out into the night.

• • •

Michael was ticking off a list of items in his head as he swung through the glass doors and out into the street. He thought he had everything Aria had asked for. How much longer would this go on? Karen didn't seem to mind the arrangement, but how would Aria catch up on her schoolwork? She'd already missed too many classes. When he'd brought up the subject, she had coolly brushed his concerns aside. She would drop out if she had to and continue next year. What disturbed Michael the most was the careless way in which she seemed to have handed her life over to her sister. Karen agreed with him. He had seen it in her expression. But there was nothing either one of them could do about it. In fact there was little enough he could do to keep his promise to Damos, except to be with Aria whenever he could and to insist that she not leave Karen's apartment. She and Thera were virtually prisoners there, yet she didn't seem to mind, and Michael couldn't help feeling a little jealous of the pleasure she found in her sister's company. He didn't know how much longer he could bear to live on the periphery of her life.

He had almost reached his car when a figure slipped out of the darkness and stood blocking his way. Michael tensed, adrenaline shooting through his body. Without turning his head, he scanned the street. There was no one else around. He was debating the wisdom of smashing the suitcase into his assailant's head when the man spoke.

"Excuse me."

The unexpected words momentarily confused Michael. He squinted into the feeble light of the street lamp, wondering if he knew this person. But the face was as unfamiliar as the heavily accented voice.

"Yes?" he said guardedly.

"I am sorry to bother you, but I saw you come out of that building." He pointed behind Michael to Aria's apartment house. "And I was hoping that maybe you are acquainted with Ariadne Koraes."

Suddenly Michael realized that he had seen this man before, standing in the vestibule of the building across the street. He was one of the two who were after Thera. Or Aria. He remembered what Damos had told him, and an icy chill flashed along his spine. He willed himself to be calm and prayed the effort wouldn't show.

"I only know she's a tenant there."

"Ah," the dark-haired man shook his head in disappointment. "You see, I am her cousin. From Greece. I wished to visit her before I return home. But she has been away, and I thought perhaps you could tell me where I might find her."

This was not the brainless thug Michael had anticipated. He was a bright, appealing young man with a gentle voice. Michael understood now why Karen had so naively supplied him with Aria's address.

"I'm afraid I can't help you. She probably is away, now that I think of it. I haven't seen her lately."

"I thank you anyway."

"Sure." Michael started to walk around him. "Good luck."

Driving off down the street he glanced in his rearview mirror. Aria's cousin was walking away in the opposite direction. Just how determined was he? How much of a threat to Aria? A thought crossed Michael's mind then. It made him want to smile and frown simultaneously. He just might have found a way to keep Aria safe forever. But he wasn't sure he was capable of doing it.

24

Nikolas was worried that he wouldn't recognize her. She hadn't been particularly remarkable. And he was afraid to stand right at the doorway to the school for fear she would remember him. By now there was a good chance she'd been told who he was. Or at least that he presented a danger to Aria. So he wandered up and down the opposite side of the street, sipping cup after cup of coffee, watching the people pass by, and keeping an eye on the school as discreetly as possible.

Finally, through the homeward-bound crowds that kept obscuring his view, he saw her. She walked quickly, buttoning her coat as she went. Nikolas threw away his empty coffee cup and hurried along behind her, staying on the opposite side of the street, but keeping pace with her. After several blocks she disappeared down the steps to the subway. Nikolas snapped his head around. There was no entrance on his side of the street. He ran out into the heavy traffic, weaving between the cars, oblivious of the obscenities shouted at him. She was out of sight by the time he reached the subway entrance. He dashed down the steps, losing his footing and grabbing the handrail to keep from falling. His arm wrenched sharply, feeling for a moment as if it would disconnect from his shoulder. He staggered over to the turnstile, disoriented with the pain, and dug around in his pockets for a token. Someone asked if he was okay. He didn't answer. He could see the young woman standing on the platform, and a train was coming. He could hear its swelling grumble, smell the stale column of air that preceded it. He found a token and pushed through the turnstile, holding the throbbing arm tightly to his side. The train's metal wheels screamed against the rails. He edged through the crowd, the pain soaring from his fingertips up through his neck and head whenever someone jostled against his arm. He entered the crowded car through the same door she did, but stood as far away as he dared.

Holding on to the overhead strap with his good arm, he glanced obliquely at her. He had never tailed anyone before, but he didn't think she had spotted him. She was standing halfway down the car, staring out at the black tunnel as if she were preoccupied with other things. She never turned to look behind her, not even when she left the train. Nikolas waited until the doors started to close, then followed her off. By the time they reached the street, night had fallen and although the darkness concealed him, it also made her more difficult to keep in view. Finally she turned into an old apartment house and, using a key, let herself into the lobby.

Nikolas waited for a quarter of an hour to make sure she was staying there. Then he found a public phone and called Christo to tell him he might have found the place where the twins had taken refuge.

"That was Karen," Aria said, as she hung up the phone.

Thera looked up from her armchair across the room. "What's wrong?" she asked, seeing how pale her sister had grown. "Where is she?"

"In Brooklyn, at her parents' apartment."

"I thought she was coming straight home after school," Thera said, losing interest.

"She was afraid to. Someone was following her. That guy she gave my address to."

Thera jumped up. "What happened?" she demanded, more agitated than Aria had ever seen her.

"She spotted him as she was leaving the school. She didn't want to lead him to us, so she went to her parents' place."

Thera paced the room. Thank goodness Karen had some sense. She wasn't ready to confront Nikolas yet. As long as Aria was with her, the encounter wouldn't be a problem. But they couldn't spend the rest of their lives constantly together. Somehow she had to strengthen herself, to draw enough energy from Aria to last through the times when they were separated.

"What are we going to do?" Aria asked, frightened for her sister and miserable because they had dragged poor Karen into their problem and now she couldn't even come home.

Thera stopped in front of the couch where Aria was sitting. "Can Karen stay where she is for a few days?"

Aria shrugged. "She said she could. Apparently her parents are thrilled to have her home, and she has some clothes there. She said not to worry—but I do, Thera. She shouldn't be involved in this at all."

Aria's voice had taken on a plaintive quality that irked Thera. Here was a woman with the potential to be a living goddess, and she was moaning over a trivial inconvenience. Would she never come to understand just who she was?

"Karen is not important," she said in exasperation.

Aria looked at her incredulously.

A smile broke across Thera's face. "She is not in any danger. What is important is making ourselves impervious to Nikolas so that he is no longer a threat."

Aria nodded, but she felt strangely unsettled, as if she'd just lifted up a rock and seen something repugnant slither out of view.

"Michael might be our only answer," Thera was saying.

"I told you he wouldn't even discuss it when I brought it up the other day. He's worried about getting in over his head."

"Then you'll have to convince him there's nothing to worry about." Thera's voice was sweet, coaxing, but there was a hard determination in her eyes. If Aria couldn't get Michael to change his mind, Thera would have to convince him her own way.

"It's out of the question."

"Michael, at least listen to me." Aria didn't know why she was whispering. Thera was in the bedroom watching television, and besides, she knew exactly what this discussion was about.

Michael was sitting on the couch, pulling his fingers through his hair the way he did when he was nervous.

"Don't you remember what happened during those simple experiments I put you through? And what about that one time I did hypnotize you? For God's sake, Aria, I'm not willing to risk it."

Aria caught his hand in hers and held on to it. "There's one thing you haven't taken into consideration. Since Thera's been here I haven't had any of those weird dreams or feelings." She gave him a moment to absorb that before going on. "It's as if one part of me always knew about her and was searching for her, reaching out to her. And I don't have to anymore."

Michael was silent. Maybe she was right. There hadn't been any strange incidents since Thera's arrival . . . The experiments with his other subjects had been less than exciting and only marginally productive. Having Aria in the program again would certainly give it a needed boost.

"I don't see how this would help Karen," he said, still unwilling to commit himself.

"Once Thera and I are strong enough, Nikolas won't be a threat to any of us. Everyone's life will return to normal."

Michael's lips curved in a wry, lopsided smile, and the gold flecks glittered in his eyes. "Everyone's?" He leaned toward Aria and kissed her. Then he turned solemn again.

"I don't know. I don't know. I have so many reservations. And to attempt it with both of you simultaneously . . ." His voice faded, and he shook his head. If he was really that set against the idea, why didn't he simply say no and stick to it? But he couldn't silence the part of his mind that wanted him to try it, that was tugging at him to agree. It was as if his brain were at war with itself.

Aria sensed the conflict in him, like two fields of energy pulling him in opposite directions. She wished she could make it easier for him.

Michael stood abruptly, too restless with indecision to remain seated any longer. It was then that he saw Thera in the doorway. She was staring at him, her face expressionless. He tried to turn away, but it was as if he were moving in slow motion, as if he were trapped within the pathways of her eyes. And within those few elongated moments his mind cleared, and the decision became so obvious he was amazed it had eluded him. There was such a vast amount of knowledge within his grasp and the risks were incredibly small. He would be careful, and everything would be all right.

Aria glanced up to see what had caught Michael's attention.

Thera smiled at her. "I'm going to make some coffee," she said. "Anyone interested?"

25

Aria and Thera were seated in the only two chairs. The blinds had been lowered, cutting the bright afternoon sunshine into thin ribbons of light that played against the office wall facing them. Michael rummaged through his files until he found his notes on Aria's previous tests. Then he rearranged the teetering stacks of books and papers on his desk so that there was enough space for him to perch on one edge. Setting his tape recorder beside him, he picked up a pad and pen. He was ready. But the powerful thrust of certainty that had led him to acquiesce last night had evaporated as if it had never been his at all. A growing apprehension had taken root in its place.

He looked at the sisters. They were angled away from him, their profiles identical, Thera's hair dipping just a few inches farther down her back. They appeared relaxed and comfortable. This was the best he could do under the circumstances. Thera had wanted to perform the experiment in Karen's apartment. But Michael had been adamant about using the office. As long as Nikolas was keeping his futile vigil in Brooklyn, the twins could safely leave the apartment. Besides, he'd argued, his notes, books, and tape recorder were at the office. What he didn't add was that he thought he would have more control in the small, familiar office where, in spite of the clutter, the atmosphere was scientific. Ironically, he knew his reasoning smacked of the superstitious. What had become of the objective clinical researcher he had once been? He felt like a lemming rushing full speed toward the cliff's edge.

"Will you be ready soon?" Thera asked impatiently.

Michael suppressed a sigh. With such an indomitable will, she might prove difficult to handle even in a hypnotic state. She had bluntly refused to have her psychic levels tested before undergoing hypnosis, claiming it was a patent waste of time. She'd pointed out that Michael had Aria's preliminary test results if he needed comparisons for his study. Then Aria had sent him a pleading let-it-drop look, and he had grudgingly backed off.

Michael clicked on the tape recorder, and with its soft hum filling the room, he initiated the process of hypnosis. Within a few minutes the two women were slouched in their seats, their heads lolling gently to one side as if they were napping. He instructed them to sit up, then led them through some simple commands to ascertain the depth of their trance. They responded quickly and well. They were in the first, light stage. He had to take them deeper, to the core of their subconscious, to the place where he believed psychic power originated and where in most individuals it was still kept under absolute lock and key.

As Michael drew them into the intermediary level, perspiration beaded on his forehead and wove wet threads from his temples down to his chin. It was at this stage that he had almost lost Aria the last time.

"Aria, are you all right?" he asked, angry with himself for the way his voice quavered. There was a moment before she responded, and in that time his pulse leaped frantically and it took all of his control not to jump off the desk and try to shake her out of it.

"Yes, I'm okay," she said finally, her voice clear but preoccupied.

"Where are you?" he asked.

"With Thera."

"Where with Thera?"

"Together."

Michael would have liked more information, but at least her responses were rational. And in English, he thought, swallowing the nervous laugh that bubbled in his throat.

"Thera, are you all right?"

"Yes." The reply was curt, almost angry, as if he were a

child who'd interrupted an adult conversation.

"Where are you?"

"Almost there."

"Almost where?"

"Let me be."

Michael was nonplussed. Never before had a subject under hypnosis given him a command. He could pursue it, try to dominate her, but he suspected that she was too strong-willed, that such a confrontation would prove futile. In any case he had enough to occupy him for now.

Slowly he continued to deepen their trance. Thera obeyed his commands without balking. Apparently she would be obedient if it suited her.

"Aria, Thera, I want you to open your eyes." He saw their lashes flutter open. "There's a basket of flowers in front of you. Do you see it?"

"Yes," they replied in unison.

"If you take a deep breath you will smell the flowers." In the silence of the room he heard them drawing in their breath.

Aria sighed with pleasure.

"What do they smell like?"

"Roses." She inhaled again. "And lilacs. They're magnificent."

"Thera?"

"Flowers." If she had said "Let's get on with it," the message would not have been clearer.

"Good. All right, I'm going to take the flowers away now. We have some work to do. I want you to listen to me very carefully and do just as I tell you. You are going to reach within yourselves, seek out the place where your psychic powers arise. Find the source." As Michael instructed them, his own mind was racing through the possibilities he had so often debated. Did this so-called sixth sense have a specific locus in the brain like the other five senses? Or was it instead a matter of information and energy being drawn from many areas and refocused?

"Aria," he prodded, when a few minutes had elapsed. "Have you located the source?"

"I think so."

"Can you describe it to me?" The old excitement was building in him.

"Energy. Like . . . like the core of a reactor. So much energy. But it's shielded, it's safe. I can't explain it any better."

"That's okay. You're doing well. Very well," Michael assured her. Then it did have one distinct, specific source. At least it did in Aria's case, he cautioned himself. He'd have to be careful not to extrapolate too much from this. If Aria's powers were derived from some ancient race of immortals or supermortals, they might be only loosely related to the common variety other people possessed. He jotted some notations on his pad and turned to question Thera. The pen dropped from his hand.

A pale halo of light pulsed around her, outlining her entire body. He'd seen that light twice before. The first time had been before Thera's arrival when it had glowed around Aria in his car. The second had been just days ago when the water spout had threatened their lives.

"Thera." He had to call her name sternly several times before she responded. "Have you found the source?"

"Yes."

"Describe it to me."

"It is beyond description. Beyond you."

Michael felt the emphasis on the word *you* as if it were a physical slap. He had to clench his jaw to contain the anger that welled up in him.

"The source, the energy, is it open to you? Can you reach it at will?"

"I have."

It was the answer he had anticipated. It accounted for the light. She already knew how to tap into the energy source. Had it always been available to her or had she learned to reach it through some form of self-hypnosis? And why had she been so eager to have him hypnotize her? What more did she hope to gain? He didn't have the answer, and he wasn't entirely sure he wanted it.

"Aria"— his tone softened as he said her name—"try to reach the energy. Remove the shield. It will not overwhelm you. You will control it. It belongs to you."

Michael forced himself to wait then, to give her time. He played absently with the buttons on his shirt until one twisted off in his hand. His mouth was dry, his tongue a rough stone that would choke him if he dared swallow. Would access to such power change Aria? Was it perhaps the only difference between the sisters? He should have considered that possibility before. Now, he realized with a sudden tightening in his chest, it was too late. Aria was bathed in the light, too. She had found her way inside.

"Are you there?" he asked, the words sticking in his mouth.

"Yes."

"How does it feel?"

"Like being born on a new plane." There was a mystical, almost spiritual note in her voice. Michael decided it was just a product of his own fertile imagination. If not for their sake, then for his own, it was time to end this session.

"Aria, Thera, I am going to count, and when I get to three, you will both awaken. You will feel well and rested." He hesitated a moment before adding, "And you will remember how to tap your psychic powers." He was about to begin counting when the light around the sisters intensified abruptly, brightening and expanding until it had encapsulated both women in a large double orb. For one strange moment they looked to Michael like twin fetuses in their placental sacks.

He shook his head to dispel the image. The light was growing brighter, as if it were feeding on an endless supply of energy. If he wanted to maintain what little control he had, he'd have to bring them out of the trance immediately. He counted to three. Neither Aria nor Thera moved. The entire office was illuminated by the light.

Michael jumped off the desk and swung around the chairs to face them. "Aria?"

Her eyes were open, but there was no sign that she saw him. He looked at Thera. She, too, was still lost in the trance. This was what Michael had feared. An old nightmare come to reality. He tried to think rationally. The energy field around them might be acting like a barrier, insulating them against his commands. If it was, he didn't know how to penetrate it. Maybe if he tried to bring one of them out at a time . . .

"Aria," he said, "you are going to withdraw now. You are going to shield the energy again. You will be able to go back to it at will. But for now you must withdraw from it. Do you understand me?"

"I can't." She sounded as if she were a long way off or submerged in water.

"Do you mean you won't?"

"I can't."

"Do you want to?"

"I don't know."

"Aria, listen to me," he said with all the strength and authority he could summon. "You must let it go and awaken when I count to three. You have no choice." Michael took a deep breath and prayed for the help of whatever gods there were.

"One, two"—he kept his voice slow and measured—"three." A muffled cry slipped from his lips when he saw that it hadn't worked.

Frantically he turned to Thera and tried to bring her out. But he couldn't elicit any response from her at all. One part of his mind was running desperately through everything he'd ever learned about hypnosis while another part was trying to decide whom he could call on for help. Then he noticed that the light had changed. It was weaker around Aria, more brilliant around Thera. His heart buoyed with hope. Maybe Aria was pulling out of it.

"That's it, Aria," he coaxed her. "Let it go. Wake up." Under his breath he added, "Come back to me."

Aria's eyelids closed. She slumped slightly in her seat. The light around her diminished to a dull glow. Michael kept talking to her, alternately encouraging and ordering her to awaken.

She was mumbling like someone deep in a dream, her facial muscles moving in response to stimuli only she could perceive. The light around Thera had grown so radiant that it hurt Michael's eyes to look at it for more than a moment. But he could see that it still encircled and connected the sisters. He might not be able to awaken Aria fully unless the connection was severed.

His head pounded with tension; reason was eluding him. Thoughts like dust motes swirled randomly through his mind.

Aria began to thrash around in her chair like a restless sleeper. Her outbursts grew louder but were still garbled except for a forlorn cry of "No."

Michael dropped to his knees before her and took her hand in his. It was cool and moist. He squeezed it tightly.

"Squeeze my hand, Aria," he demanded.

Feebly her fingers curled around his. In the glow of Thera's aura, Aria's skin was chalky, and the hollows beneath her eyes looked like purple bruises. Michael stroked her hand, tears of fear and frustration burning his eyes.

He was still in that position when a crack like an invisible bolt of lightning shook the room. Michael was thrown against the wall by the force of it. He pulled himself to his knees, his head aching and the world tilting dizzily around him. He tried to inch his way back to Aria, but he was repelled by a rippling series of shock waves. When the force subsided, he crawled over to her. She'd fallen from her chair and lay sprawled on the floor like a forgotten rag doll. The light around her was gone.

As Michael drew her up into his arms, she groaned softly and her eyes fluttered open.

"Michael," she whispered, as if to reassure herself that he was really there. "Michael."

"Thank God you're all right." He hugged her to him, his arms trembling, tears washing over his lashes and down his face. He wasn't sure how long he'd been sitting there cradling her in his arms and rocking back and forth when he noticed that the room was nearly dark again and Thera was watching them.

"How is she?" Thera asked.

"All right, I think. Just exhausted."

Thera stood up and stretched luxuriously. "You're a success, Michael," she remarked in a dry, ironic tone. "Aren't you pleased?"

Michael didn't answer. He didn't feel like a success. He felt manipulated and abused, and too weary even for anger.

• • •

The anger came later. Aria had gone straight to bed when they returned to Karen's apartment. Michael had had to support her during the trip back. But aside from a profound weariness, she seemed to be all right. He left her to sleep and sat down in the living room while Thera busied herself in the kitchen fixing dinner. She had assured Michael that he could go home, that she would care for her sister. But Michael had no intention of leaving just yet.

He tried to concentrate on a television program, then on a magazine, but he was too agitated and restless to stay focused on anything. Finally he wandered down the hall to the room where Aria lay asleep. He stood in the doorway, needing to be near her, yet not wanting to disturb her rest. He was about to turn back to the living room when he heard her say his name.

"Michael . . . is that you?"

He crossed the darkened room and sat down on the edge of the bed. "I'm here. Don't you want to sleep?"

"No. Don't go," she said urgently. She reached for his hand and gripped it tightly.

"You seem to be stronger. Feeling better?"

"Yes. Physcially."

"That's an answer with a built-in question. In what way aren't you better?"

Aria pushed herself up and leaned into him, nestling her head beneath his chin. "I don't know." Her voice was fragile, as vulnerable as a child's.

Michael wrapped his arms around her carefully, as if she might break under too much pressure.

"I think maybe you do know," he whispered.

Aria shook her head against his chest, not trusting her voice to make the lie convincing. She wished she could explain it to him. But it was too complex to put into words. Michael wouldn't understand. He would turn it all upside down and come to conclusions that were false and frightening.

"I'm not blind, and I'm no fool," he said. "I don't know what happened today while you two were under, but I know it scared you. For God's sake, it scared the hell out of me, and I was only an observer." His voice had grown louder as he spoke, and he had to make an effort to subdue it. "If you really want to sort things out, you're going to have to talk about it.''

So many new and contradictory feelings were involved that Aria didn't think she would ever be able to sort them out. She had been in possession of a power more remarkable than she had ever dreamed of. And she had come close to actually being one with another person. She'd been deluged with her own reactions and with others that came from outside her. The experience had been unique and tremendously fulfilling. But as pain and pleasure are two ends of one spectrum, so she had also encountered something strange and threatening, an insatiable hunger, a greed so ravenous it had taken all her strength to resist it. She couldn't even say where it had originated. Within the power itself? Within her? Or Thera? Michael was right. It had scared her. And it scared her now.

Michael felt her shudder. In that instant, all the fear and anger he had suppressed boiled to the surface with implacable force.

"Dammit," he exploded, "if you won't say it, I will: She almost destroyed you today. And she would have if it had suited her purposes."

Startled, Aria drew back and looked at him. By the dim light filtering in from the hall she could see the rage and love struggling across his features.

"Michael, no. She wouldn't hurt me."

"She already has. You know better than I do exactly what happened today. She drained you in order to strengthen herself. She'd see you dead to save her own life."

"I don't believe that," Aria replied staunchly, thinking of what Thera had told her, that men cannot bear to see power in women's hands. Michael was a man, after all. "Thera has spent almost all of her time trying to teach me to use and increase my powers."

"Only so that she can make use of them herself," he said savagely.

"Michael, maybe we'd better not talk about this anymore now. I'd like to get some sleep."

Michael didn't argue. He let his arms drop from around her. If he didn't ease up, he'd force her to choose between him and Thera, and he might lose her forever. It saddened him to think that their relationship had grown so precarious. But Thera wasn't going to win that easily. He wouldn't give up without a fight.

He kissed her gently and helped her lie back on the pillows. "You're right," he said. "You need to sleep."

Thera turned quickly and made her way back to the kitchen. She had to get rid of Michael before he turned Aria against her. She'd gained all she could from him. From now on he would only be in the way. Disposing of him would be a simple matter. She smiled. He might even choke on a piece of bread. No, she realized immediately, that wouldn't do. If Michael were to die he would only assume heroic proportions in Aria's memory. Aria would have to choose voluntarily to throw him aside. And Thera knew just how to arrange that. Her smile broadened. The arrangement might even prove enjoyable.

26

New York: November 15

Aria stepped out of the shower, pulled on her robe, and wrapped her hair in a towel. It felt good to be back home again. With her powers strengthened through hypnosis, Thera had deemed it safe for them to leave Karen's apartment. If Nikolas found her now, she would be ready.

Everything was finally getting back to normal. Aria even hoped to resume classes in another week. With a lot of cramming and effort she might be able to squeak by at the end of the semester. The only thing that remained unresolved was her relationship with Michael. Since his outburst against Thera, she'd heard from him only once. The conversation had been painfully subdued. The Michael who used to make her laugh so easily, who could brighten her day with the sound of his voice, was cloaked in the reserve of a stranger. He said he wanted to make sure she had recovered from the hypnosis. But he was remote and seemed only objectively concerned, as he might be about any volunteer in his research program. Aria had been close to tears by the time she hung up the phone.

Most of the time Thera kept her too busy to dwell on the problem, but in odd moments and when she lay in bed at night, she felt a gnawing ache for Michael, as if she had already lost him.

He was on her mind as she stepped out of the bathroom. Would he and her sister ever accept each other's presence in her life?

Thera was sitting on the couch, replacing the phone on its cradle.

"Oh, I didn't know you were out of the shower," she said. "That was Michael."

"What did he want?" Aria tried not to sound too eager, but constantly having to mask her feelings was wearing on her.

"He wanted to know if you'd come over to see him tonight."

"Oh."

"I told him you would. I hope you don't mind. I just think maybe you two could use some time together."

Aria stared at her sister for a moment in mute disbelief.

"You wouldn't mind if I went?" she asked finally.

Thera stood up and shrugged. "Why should I? I'm not in any danger now. In fact, I was thinking of going to a movie tonight." She started to walk into the bathroom, but turned back at the doorway. "He said to be there at nine. He has to run out and won't be back till then." She left Aria standing in the middle of the room.

The towel had come undone, and Aria's wet hair lay against her neck, trickling water under the collar of her robe and down her back. But she was too stunned by Thera's sudden change of attitude to notice. And just when she'd begun to fear she'd spend the rest of her life like a tennis ball, being batted back and forth between two opponents . . .

Michael switched on the television set to hear the news while he was changing. No one smiled on the newscasts these days. Even the most cheerful commentators had grown morose. All the major stories concerned weather conditions around the globe. Unrelenting droughts in some areas, unprecedented floods in others. The world food supply was beginning to dwindle. There was widespread fear of famine in even the most highly developed countries. And natural disasters were occurring with alarming regularity, like frightening surprises in a well-paced horror film.

Michael pulled a maroon sweater on over his jeans. The anchorman was describing the eruption of a long extinct volcano beneath the island of Santorini in Greece. Reports were still unconfirmed, but thousands of residents and tourists were believed to have been killed when more than half of the exotic vacationland sank into the sea under a devastating explosion of lava. Cruise ships, anchored in the bay directly over the crater, were tossed into the air like toys, then crushed beneath tidal waves that swept over the harbors of Crete, some seventy-five miles away.

"What next?" Michael muttered, tugging on a sock. He got up to look for the matching one, but jerked his head back to the screen as the newsman went on.

"Santorini, known as Thera to the ancient Greeks, was partially destroyed by volcanic action in 1400 B.C. And although there have been smaller eruptions since then, today's may well signal the island's demise. Looking elsewhere now, temperatures . . ."

Michael turned off the set and stood looking at the blank screen as if it might provide him with answers to some of the appalling questions that had invaded his mind. The island was Thera's namesake, and it had been destroyed. Was it a coincidence or something more? The scientific investigator in him balked at the idea of jealous gods. But at what point did coincidences stop being coincidental?

After he'd spent a quarter of an hour wrestling with the problem and becoming only more confused, he forced himself to finish dressing. He went through all his drawers searching for his sock. He'd have to make some effort to clean the place up before Aria arrived. During her weekends there she had begun to bring some order to his chaos. But in her absence, the loft had reverted to the wild. In exasperation Michael gave up on the sock and put on one that almost matched. If Aria mentioned his uncoordinated hose, he'd remove them. A good beginning, anyway. He grinned, cheered by the realization that she would be there with him in a couple of hours.

He'd been determined to keep his distance, give her space and time to miss him. But he hadn't slept all week, afraid she would discover instead that she didn't want him, didn't need him. When he answered the phone this afternoon and heard her voice, he'd stumbled over his words like a teenager with a crush. And when she suggested they spend the night together, he was sure she could hear the relief in his voice as he said yes.

The doorbell rang before he'd had a chance to do more than throw his dirty clothes into the hamper. He ran to answer it, tripping over the typewriter case he'd left near the door. He picked himself up and combed his hair back with his fingers.

Aria stood in the doorway in a red sweater dress, looking radiant but somehow different. Michael realized it was because of her hair. He'd never seen her wear it swept up that way in a loose bun with short tendrils of gold falling around her face. The style emphasized the angle of her cheekbones and made her look less sweet, more exotic. Desire and anticipation rippled through him.

She walked inside, and although Michael longed to pull her into his arms, he restrained himself, still not certain where he stood with her. He took her coat and threw it over the back of a chair.

"You're early." He tilted his head apologetically to the clutter surrounding them. "I didn't even have time to put the white wine in the refrigerator. Is red okay?"

Aria pushed aside the newspapers that littered the couch and sat down. "I'm surprised you're able to find either one," she laughed.

Michael went into the kitchen and returned with the wine, a corkscrew, and glasses.

"Yeah, well I guess this place has really missed your touch," he said.

"I know I've missed yours."

The cork came out of the bottle with a pop, and Michael looked at her with a smile that was half amused, half perplexed. Although Aria wasn't easily embarrassed, she also wasn't given to making remarks with sexual undertones.

She accepted the glass of wine he held out to her.

"I'm glad you're here." He sat beside her on the couch and clinked his glass gently against hers. "To understanding?"

Aria nodded and brought the wine to her lips, then set it down on the table.

Michael drained his immediately, hoping it would quell the anxiety that kept expanding in him like a balloon about to burst. He refilled the glass. Aria's remained on the table untouched.

"Don't you like it?"

"Yes, it's fine. But after having so much trouble coming out of the hypnosis, I'm nervous about anything that can affect my mind."

Michael felt a sharp pang of guilt, but he told himself it was unreasonable. After all, she and Thera were the ones who'd insisted on the session, not he. He drank more of the wine and was soon listening contentedly as Aria chattered about Karen and about her plans to go back to school. Then she asked about his work. And although she was looking at him with her old intensity, Michael had the vague sensation that none of his answers mattered to her. Just how much had the unfolding of her powers changed her? The question swam desultorily in and out of his mind, struggling with the effects of the wine until it was suddenly brushed away as if by the flick of a finger. Michael sat there trying without success to remember what he'd been thinking.

"Is something wrong?" Aria asked.

He massaged his forehead as if that might help to clear his mind. "No. I think I might have had too much wine." He looked at the bottle. It was empty. He didn't remember having finished it.

He saw Aria glance at her watch. He wanted to tease her about having another date to run off to, but the words never completed the circuit from his mind to his mouth.

She moved closer to him so that their thighs touched and he could feel the warmth of her through their clothes. He tilted his head and kissed her. Her tongue was moist and hot as it slid between his lips and into his mouth. Her fingers played through his hair, then down along the muscles of his neck and back. He drew away and, holding on to her hand, stood up.

"Come on inside."

"No, let's stay here," she said, tugging back on his hand. But before he could sit down again, she unbuckled his belt and opened his jeans. Startled and excited by her sudden aggressiveness, Michael didn't argue. He maneuvered out of the jeans and was about to take off his sweater, but Aria pulled him down next to her before he could do so. As he watched, she slowly undid the buttons that ran the length of her dress. She didn't remove the dress, but left it gaping open seductively. Beneath it she was naked.

She tucked up her feet and lay back on the couch, holding her arms out to him. Michael stretched out beside her, his body angled over hers on the narrow cushion. He saw her look at her watch again as he bent to kiss her.

"Timing me?" he whispered with a laugh.

Aria didn't answer. She drew him down hard against her, opening her mouth to his and writhing slowly beneath him until the question was routed from his mind.

They made love with such furious energy that Michael was breathless, but he couldn't seem to get his fill of her. It was as if he were caught up in a whirlwind from which he couldn't escape and didn't want to. Somewhere in the background he heard a clicking sound like a key working the tumblers in a lock. He dismissed it; Aria had the only other key to his loft, and she was here with him. But at that moment she started screaming, pushing him away, and shouting at him to stop. Bloodcurdling screams as if she were being raped. Stunned, he jumped away from her at the moment the door to the loft opened. She bolted off the couch, crying hysterically and holding her dress together.

Michael stared toward the door, his heart thudding with shock and confusion. Aria stood just inside the loft. Her face was a ghastly white, her eyes wide and unblinking as she took in the scene.

For a moment they were all immobile like stone figures in a grotesque frieze. Michael looked frantically back and forth between the two women. The one he'd thought was Aria stood huddled in the far corner, still clutching her dress. Her hair, unloosed from its bun, hung around her face. It was long, longer than Aria's. And with an escalating sense of incredulity and horror, Michael realized what had happened.

The frozen moment ended as Thera rushed to her sister's side and clung to her, blurting out phrases between tortured sobs.

"Thank God . . . just came by to tell you something . . . He said to wait for you . . . tried to make me drunk . . . attacked me."

Before Aria could make sense of what she had witnessed,

she was engulfed in the turmoil of her sister's emotions. Thera's distress and outrage flooded her mind and heart as if they were her own. And in that instant, Aria knew without question that Michael was guilty.

Aria stroked her sister's back and glared at Michael. How could she have misjudged him so thoroughly? How could he have done this to Thera? To her? She grabbed Thera's coat from the chair and, with her arm around her sister's waist, turned to run from the apartment.

Michael wanted to explain, to get up and run after her, but he was wearing only the maroon sweater and his mismatched socks. Thera had planned it all very carefully indeed.

As Aria swept her out into the hall, Thera turned back to Michael for an instant. She smiled at him, her gray eyes stained dark like tarnished metal. Michael felt his skin crawl, and he started to retch.

27

"Is that really you?" Aria repeated, squinting through the peephole. "What's your middle name?"

"Beatrice." Karen grimaced. "Does that satisfy you?"

Aria slid back the bolt and opened the door just enough for Karen to squeeze through. In spite of Thera's assurance that they were strong enough to handle Nikolas, she preferred avoiding such an encounter, especially when she was alone. She slammed the door shut quickly and stared at her friend.

Karen plucked off the blue wool ski cap and with it the black, curly wig that covered her own straight brown hair. Then she removed the mirrored sunglasses and the overcoat she'd borrowed from her neighbor.

"Did you really have to go through all this just to visit me?"

"Unless you wanted some cute but foreign company," Karen replied, flopping down in an armchair. "Whither I goest, they go."

"I'm sorry. It must be awful for you."

"Not to worry. I'm sure they have no intention of hurting me. And I don't think they'll outmaneuver me either. I grew up on Robert Ludlum thrillers."

"I guess it'll resolve itself when I come out in the open to start classes again next week," Aria said with a nervous hitch of her shoulders. "How about some coffee?"

"Sounds good." Karen leaned against the counter while Aria started the percolator. Now that she was here, she was afraid to open the conversation. Too much was riding on it.

Aria set the timer and turned to her. "So . . . what is this important subject you had to speak to me about in person?" She said it lightly, but her stomach was churning. She wasn't sure she could handle any more bad news or surprises after Saturday night. She'd barely eaten anything since, and whatever she had managed to get down had quickly come back up.

"Where's Thera?" Karen asked, stalling and wishing she could think of some way to ease into the subject.

"She went off to the museum." They were both silent for a moment. "I think you'd better just say it," Aria suggested finally.

Karen nodded. "I spoke to Michael yesterday."

Aria busied herself with finding cups, saucers, and spoons and putting them on the table. Karen waited for her to stop fussing.

"He told me what happened the other night. He wants to explain to you, but you hang up whenever he calls or else you take the phone off the hook."

"There's no need for explanations. The scene was self-explanatory," Aria said sharply.

"The old seeing-is-believing theory?" Karen retorted, trying to break through the wall that Aria was building around herself.

"You have a better one?" She didn't want to fight with Karen, too. Why couldn't she just mind her own business? But they had made this whole thing Karen's business, she realized contritely. Dammit! Why did everything have to be so complicated? She bit her lower lip, determined not to start crying again. Her eyelids were still swollen from yesterday. Even Thera, the true victim of the incident, was losing patience with her.

"Scenes can be staged," Karen said simply. "Some of the most magnificent buildings you see in the movies are only facades that look like the real thing."

The timer rang, giving Aria a few minutes to think while she filled their cups. She and Karen sat opposite each other.

"You're telling me I shouldn't necessarily believe what I saw. But by the same token, why should you believe whatever Michael has told you?"

"Because I know Michael. I sat with him the way I'm sitting

here with you. I watched him and I listened to him with as open a mind as possible. Now I may not be psychic, but on a pure gut level I know he wasn't lying."

"Then what did I see?"

"Did you ever have twins as friends when you were a kid?"

"There were some in school, why?"

"Didn't they ever try to fool you or the teachers by pretending to be each other?"

"Yeah, I suppose so. Are you trying to tell me that Thera posed as me and tricked Michael?"

"That's exactly what happened."

"Come on, Karen, why on earth would she do something like that?"

"To separate you and Michael." Karen paused to sip her coffee. "It worked pretty well, didn't it?"

Aria opened her mouth to refute Karen's theory, but she closed it again without saying anything. Her mind was busily turning the evidence over and studying it from this new angle. Hadn't she sensed Thera's displeasure with Michael from the very beginning? Hadn't Thera tried many times to talk her out of seeing him? But if she accepted Karen's contention, what kind of person did that make her sister? Aria felt as if she were racing through a maze filled with dead ends. No matter whom she believed, she wound up the loser. Her hand shook as she brought her coffee cup to her mouth. The cup tilted, splashing coffee over the rim and onto her blouse.

Karen grabbed a handful of napkins and began mopping up the spill. "Are you okay?"

"Yes," Aria mumbled, making ineffectual dabs at the spreading stain on her blouse.

Karen poured her another cup of coffee.

"What does Michael want?" Aria asked, sipping carefully.

"He wants to see you, to have the opportunity to plead his case in person." When Aria didn't reply, Karen went on. "If you could have seen him yesterday you wouldn't even hesitate. The man is being torn apart by what he did and because he thinks he's lost you."

Aria's heart twisted. She was suffering with the same kind of pain.

"Even if you don't think you owe it to Michael, don't you

owe it to yourself to make sure?''

She was on the verge of agreeing when the front door swung open and Thera walked in. Her hair was blown out around her, and her cheeks were rouged by the wind. She'd been smiling, but when she saw Karen at the table her lips straightened into a thin line.

"Karen, I didn't know you were coming over," she said, shrugging off her coat and pulling the scarf from around her neck.

Karen stood up. "Actually I was just about to leave."

"Nothing's wrong, I hope?"

Karen picked up the wig and tugged it on over her hair.

"Not that I'm aware of," she replied, imitating Thera's brisk tone. She put on the rest of her disguise, and Aria walked her to the door.

"Take care. I'll be in touch."

Aria pressed her hand as she started to leave. "Thanks." She closed the door behind Karen and turned to her sister.

"How was the museum?"

"Interesting. What was that all about?"

Aria started clearing the table. "Karen just stopped in to say hello. Do you want coffee? I think there's one cup left."

Thera shook her head impatiently. "That thank-you was not for the social call."

Aria found her sister's interrogatory tone unsettling. If she told her the reason for Karen's visit, what would her reaction be?

"All right," she said, stopping with her hands full of dishes. "Karen wanted to talk to me about Michael."

"That's not her affair!" Thera's voice was as cold and brittle as ice.

"Michael went to see her. In one way or another we've all made it her affair." Aria walked to the sink and put the dishes down with a clatter.

Thera followed her. "And exactly what does Michael want?" she demanded.

Aria had expected to hear fear or pain in her sister's voice at the mention of Michael. But all she heard was a haughty irritation.

Aria stepped past her and removed the coffee pot from the

table. "He wants a chance to speak to me, to explain what happened from his side."

Thera grabbed her arm as she passed her again. "You were there. You saw what happened. What could he possibly say to you that could change the truth or the magnitude of it?"

Aria pulled herself free. "I don't know. But if all he's asking for is a little of my time, I guess I can be generous. Then if I don't feel any differently about it, at least I had no part in ending it." She emptied the coffee grounds into the garbage and looked up at Thera. "Why does it bother you so much that I want to see him?"

"You're a fool," Thera sputtered and stalked off to the bathroom. Aria stood looking after her, wondering just how much of a fool she had been. She'd been so lost in her own misery that she'd hadn't given any thought to her sister's instantaneous recovery from her alleged ordeal at Michael's hands.

Thera appeared a few minutes later, brushing her hair vigorously.

"Are you afraid he'll say you pretended to be me?" she asked without preface.

Thera spun around, the arm with the brush raised over her head. "He'll say whatever he has to in order to trap you and turn you against me. A man who's been cornered will stoop to anything. He resents what you and I can be together. Raping me was his way of proving that he will always be superior."

The conviction in Thera's voice was unshakable. Aria felt herself starting to vacillate again. But she knew she'd have to be strong in dealing with both of them or she'd never know the truth.

"I only said I would listen," she said firmly. "I never said I'd be gullible enough to be taken in by lies."

Thera tossed down the brush and came to stand before her.

"You aren't going to see him." Her eyes were as dark and opaque as thunderclouds. Aria wanted to look away, but she forced herself to maintain her posture.

"Yes, I am."

"I refuse to allow it."

"You're strong enough to have refused Michael, too, aren't you?" she blurted out with sudden insight.

"Not drunk, I'm not."

"You didn't seem the least bit drunk that night."

Thera was silent for a moment. Aria waited, feeling as if she were on the brink of some horrible discovery. The air in the room was charged, threatening. It seemed to be closing in on her, and she felt the same cold, prickly fear she'd known when they'd been under hypnosis together.

"All right," Thera said, her words raking the stillness like sharpened claws. "Since you seem so determined to have the truth—I wasn't drunk. And Michael did think I was you. In fact, relieving the few doubts in his mind was child's play. Hardly worth my talents." She smiled with the memory of it.

Aria gasped, the admission slamming into her like a wooden board against her back, leaving her breathless.

"What's the matter now? I thought you wanted the truth?"

"Why? Why would you hurt me like that?"

"I didn't do it to hurt you; I did it to wake you up."

Aria shook her head in disbelief.

"Michael is beneath you. He's just a man. Good enough for a little pleasure, nothing more. You'll never reach your full potential if you're a slave to emotions for such a pathetic creature."

Aria's thoughts were colliding in her head with the impact of a meteor storm. She turned and walked away from her sister.

"Come back here." Thera called after her.

Aria felt herself being drawn to her sister like a piece of iron to a magnet. She reached deep within herself for the strength to resist. Grabbing her purse and a coat from the closet, she fled the apartment.

Michael had convinced himself that his relationship with Aria was over. In spite of Karen's willingness to take his part, it was still a matter of his word against Thera's. And his story sounded ridiculous even to himself. There was no point in hoping that Aria would turn her back on her sister.

He poured himself another tumbler of scotch. He preferred wine, but the scotch made him feel numb and comfortably detached from his feelings, as if they belonged to an actor in a movie he was watching. When the doorbell rang, he didn't answer it. There was no one he wished to see. But the bell kept ringing, tearing away at the pleasant veil that clouded his mind, and finally it occurred to him that the only one who might come to his loft on a Monday evening was Aria. A sudden rush of adrenaline propelled him off the couch. He took an extra moment to steady his wobbly legs before he pulled open the door.

Aria, unsure of her welcome, smiled at him sheepishly, but didn't cross the threshold. Michael started to reach out for her, then stopped, his arms suspended awkwardly in midair. What if this wasn't Aria? Her hair was loose, and it seemed to be the right length. But he wouldn't put it past Thera to have cut hers for an encore performance. How was he to tell? He studied her face, wishing he hadn't indulged quite so freely in the scotch.

Aria's brow furrowed. "Michael, are you all right?"

He sighed and spoke slowly, taking care not to slur his words. "I can't be sure who you are."

"Oh, Michael," she whispered, coming toward him. He appeared every bit as tormented as Karen had claimed. He hadn't shaved all weekend, and his hair was a tousled thatch that had fallen over his eyes. He seemed too preoccupied even to brush it away. He looked childlike and desperately in need of comfort. She stroked his stubbled cheek and had to bite her lip to keep from crying.

Michael tensed at her touch. Then he noticed her eyes. They were flooded with emotion and softened with the same gentle tint of lilac that had entranced him the first time he saw her. He remembered meeting Thera and how the difference in the sisters' eyes had struck him even then. Why hadn't he seen that on Saturday night? Had Thera used some kind of mind control on him? The thought made his stomach pitch. But it didn't matter just now. He opened his arms to Aria and hugged her tightly to him.

He held her that way, without moving, without talking, until he was able to absorb the fact that this was no drink-induced dream. Aria felt his body shake with muted sobs, and she couldn't hold back her own tears any longer. Their cheeks were wet against each other, Michael's mouth salty when he kissed her.

When they were calm enough to speak, Michael loosened his hold on her.

"Can I get you something?" he asked, walking her toward the couch.

"A box of tissues," Aria sniffled and laughed.

Michael came back with the tissues and handed them to her.

"That must be an all-time record for finding something in this place," she said, feeling better than she had in days.

"It's all a matter of incentive." He paused, afraid to ask the question that was uppermost in his mind, afraid of disturbing the tenuous peace between them.

"Does this mean you believe me?" he asked cautiously, sitting beside her.

Aria nodded. "I'm ashamed to admit that I might not have, if Thera hadn't confessed."

Michael's eyebrows shot up in surprise. "Why would she do that?"

"I have a feeling she's wondering the same thing right about now. Her anger got the better of her. She honestly believes that what she tried to do was in my own best interests."

"Doesn't that worry you? Frighten you?"

"Yes, it does. Somehow I'm going to have to make her understand that I don't want to live by her values or her rules."

"You can't mean after all this you still want her around?"

"Look, I know it doesn't make any sense. All the way over here I kept telling myself the same thing. But I can't bring myself to push her out of my life." She sighed. "Michael, what if I had been the twin who remained in Crete all those years to be raised by those people and indoctrinated in that strange religion? Maybe I would have turned out the way she has."

Michael's mouth curled with bitter humor. "Isn't guilt a wonderful invention?"

Aria put her hand over his. "Let's not fight about it. Not now anyway."

"Only if you promise to stay with me tonight."

"I can't. I'm starting classes tomorrow, and I need to catch up on a whole lot of sleep I didn't get this weekend."

"You're not serious about going back," Michael said, his face pinched with renewed concern.

"Of course I am."

"You can't."

"Now you're beginning to sound like Thera. And that's not like you."

"Aria, don't you see what will happen?" His voice was rising in spite of all his efforts to restrain it.

She didn't reply. She knew that Nikolas might find her, follow her home, but she'd managed to shunt that fear aside. Thera was strong enough to deal with him now. In any case, why should Michael be worried about Thera's safety?

Michael felt like shaking her to make her understand.

"It doesn't matter to those men whether they capture Thera or you," he said, hoping to shock her into seeing the danger. "All they care about is keeping you two apart, permanently!"

Aria fell back against the cushions as if the force of his words had thrown her. Thera had never raised that possibility, though she had said she was confident Aria could hold her own against anyone. Was that what she had meant? Aria struggled to compose herself. Either way she couldn't spend the rest of her life in hiding. She'd just have to hope that Michael was wrong and Thera was right.

She kissed Michael quickly and stood up. "Don't worry. I'll be fine. You don't realize just how strong I've become."

Michael followed her to the door, trying to think of an argument that might change her mind. But she was gone before he could. He stood staring at the place where she'd been, remembering Damos's plea and his own promise to protect Aria. There was only one way left now.

28

Heraklion: November 17

The chamber was dank and cold, the kind of cold that seeped slowly into the bones and left them aching. But there was a peaceful familiarity there as well. Nicodemus stood on the stepped altar for the first time in several weeks. Andreas had finally restored the underground passageway to safety, and the archaeologists had not yet resumed their excavations. For now at least the sanctuary was theirs.

He looked down at a dozen faces, all drawn in upon themselves with the same pervasive fear. He knew and loved every one of these people, and each, in his or her own way, had come to him with a similar request. That he lead them in a prayer for mercy and for Nikolas's success. Nicodemus had held out for as long as he dared. But the eruption of the volcano at Santorini had left him no choice but to comply. Here on Crete they had heard the hellish blast, and the sky was still dulled by its ashen debris. A fifty-foot tidal wave, unheard of since the extinction of the Minoans, had demolished Heraklion's harbor, submerging huge sections of the city and pushing the hideous death toll even higher. The message was as clear to the other congregants as it was to Nicodemus: Nikolas had not yet located Thera. The gods were growing implacable. Soon there would be no salvation for anyone, least of all for Thera.

The candle before Nicodemus sputtered with the same hesitancy he felt. It was one thing to know what had to be done and quite another to actually do it. With the initial offerings and prayers out of the way, the silence pounded in his ears, filled with the unspoken pleas of his people. In his heart he apologized to Thera. In spite of everything, he hadn't been able to excise his love for her. He cleared his throat and invoked first Minos and then his father Zeus.

"We beseech you, O Zeus, wise and puissant lord, help your servants Christo and Nikolas to find Thera so they may bring her back to us and we may deal with her according to your will. We know your wrath is just; she has broken our covenant with you. But will you not show mercy upon the poor suffering populations who had no hand in her misdeeds? Make manifest your great power and compassion by guiding us to her and by calming the elements, which you have thrown into upheaval and which you alone can tame."

Nicodemus's voice reverberated within the stone walls, fading gradually into the darkened corners. In the period of silent meditation and prayer that followed, the old man called upon Aphrodite to intercede in Thera's behalf or to furnish him with the strength to perform as Zeus decreed.

29

New York: November 18

Aria adjusted the shoulder strap of her pocketbook and smiled at the elderly woman who was riding down in the elevator with her. The woman smiled back. When they stepped out into the lobby, Aria almost asked her to see if any strange dark-haired men were waiting outside. She chided herself for even thinking of asking someone's innocent grandmother to run interference for her. Setting her jaw determinedly, she strode through the outer doors into the street.

It was a cold morning with a glaring white sky and the smell of snow in the air. A sporadic wind swung down between the buildings, numbing Aria's nose and sweeping her hair into a golden scarf behind her. She walked quickly to the corner, then turned toward the subway entrance, telling herself she wasn't hurrying out of fear, but because she had to be on time this first day back.

The morning rush hour was over, but the street was still busy. Aria found the striking of other footsteps on the pavement alternately comforting and frightening. She kept glancing over her shoulder until one fair-haired young man, assuming she was flirting, grinned back at her. After that, Aria looked only ahead and to the sides.

As she hurried down the subway stairs, she could hear him directly behind her. She hoped he wouldn't try to start a conversation. She wasn't up to fielding passes this morning. She tilted her chin up and tried to look aloof and unapproachable. As she turned toward the token booth, she caught him in the edge of her vision. But it wasn't the fair-haired man at all. This man had straight, dark hair and an olive complexion like her own. Her heart bounced up to her throat where it seemed to lodge. She stood before the booth unable to speak until the woman inside prodded her impatiently. In a shrill whisper she asked for two tokens. Then, not knowing what else to do, she moved to the turnstile. The man was ahead of her, already waiting on the platform. He wasn't even watching her. It had all been a silly mistake.

She passed through the turnstile and took up a position several yards from him, near a small knot of women who appeared to be out for a day's shopping. Although he seemed to pose no threat to her, she was still feeling skittish. She'd seen too many movies where the victim was pushed in front of an oncoming train.

It took all her restraint to keep from checking on him, but as the rumble of the train filled the air, she stole one surreptitious glance. He was staring straight at her. Before logic could intervene, she turned and fled through the gate and up the steps to the street. Her legs were pumping as fast as they could, but her efforts had the eerie quality of a nightmare, as if she were running in thick mud that sucked at her, holding her back. She strained to hear the sound of him pursuing her, but the train had entered the station, obliterating every noise except the pounding of her heart.

Once outside, she ran into the street, gesturing wildly for a taxi. One veered in to her, screeching its brakes as she dashed out to meet it. She pulled open the back door and jumped in, ignoring the driver's grumbling. She gave him the address of the school and told him it would be worth a big tip if he got her there quickly.

The driver shrugged and spun the wheel, plowing back into traffic and venting his anger on the cars that got in his way. Aria sat sideways, watching out of both the front and back windows. Apparently she had surprised the dark man with her unexpected flight. She didn't see him anywhere. And no car seemed to be following them. After several blocks she relaxed enough to worry about the insane way the cab driver was weaving in and out of traffic, pitching her back and forth with sudden stops and bursts of speed.

She was grateful when the law school loomed up ahead of them, thinking that even the imposing Dr. Fischer would seem friendly at this point. She paid the driver, got out, and turned away from the taxi, nearly crashing into Karen as she hurried toward the building.

"Hi, did you just get here?" Aria asked, as they fell into step together.

"A little while ago. I couldn't stand waiting inside. I had to make sure you got here okay."

"Well, I'm here," Aria said, hoping Karen wouldn't detect the forced brightness in her tone.

Karen was looking at her queerly. "You sound out of breath. Did you have to pedal that taxi or what?" She reached the door and held it open.

Aria considered telling her about the incident in the subway, but decided it had probably only been her imagination. If she made a habit of running from every dark-haired man in New York City, she'd have very little time for anything else.

"I got up late this morning," she said, "and I was afraid of having to face Fischer with yet another demerit to my name."

Karen nodded and followed her inside. "Does that also account for your interesting green color?"

Aria couldn't help laughing, and in the end she found herself explaining what had really happened. They were standing in the hall outside their first class. Aria was about to go in, but Karen put a hand on her arm and held her back.

"I don't know how you have the courage to go through this," she said soberly. "But don't be afraid of crying wolf. We all know there's really one out there, and no one's going to call you paranoid."

Aria smiled, feeling less burdened. Leave it to Karen to know just what was on her mind.

Thera stayed in bed after Aria left, luxuriating in the silence and solitude. Since moving in with her sister she'd had no time alone, and she'd begun to feel starved for it. She stretched and thought back to the previous night. She'd almost gone too far. She needed to remember that Aria was still tied to the reality in which she'd been raised. It would take some time yet before she would relinquish those narrow views. But Thera was impatient, eager to reach for the position of power and wealth she had foreseen for herself even as a child. Lying within the warm comfort of the quilt, she considered various avenues that might lead to the desired end. Suddenly she bolted up, a broad smile stretching her lips. The answer was so obvious she was amazed it hadn't occurred to her sooner. Religious cults were a growing trend in this country of free thinkers. Everyone was looking for a new set of fashionable answers. With powers as concrete and visible as hers, it should be ridiculously easy to build the largest cult following ever. She would, in fact, be a goddess—revered and obeyed as she deserved to be by virtue of her heritage. If mankind insisted on having gods to worship, she would willingly volunteer.

She threw back the covers, too flooded with enthusiasm and ideas to sit still. Of course she would still need periodic boosts of energy from Aria. But that should be no problem. Though she hadn't found her sister's weakness yet, surely the offer of divine status would be too compelling for even Aria to refuse.

Thera pulled on her bathrobe and padded barefoot across to the kitchen area to make coffee. With a steaming mug in her hand she leaned against the counter, refining her plans. First and foremost, she would need exposure. And the way to get that was to do something sensational. She never heard the muted squoosh of rubber soles on tile or the faint rattle of the doorknob.

When the front door was smashed open, slamming into the entry wall, she barely had time to drop the coffee cup and focus her mind on the imminent battle. For several moments no one moved. Thera made no effort to hide. If this confrontation was inevitable, she preferred to see it done with now so she could concentrate on her future.

She heard their cautious footsteps as they entered the apartment. She sensed their tension in pulsing waves and felt her own calm assurance like a soft cushion around her. They were approaching cautiously. Thera stood there and waited.

Nikolas appeared first, his lips curled into a mocking smile, Christo immediately behind him.

"So, we have found you."

"As I have allowed it," Thera replied. "I am weary of this doomed quest of yours."

Nikolas took a few steps toward her, Christo imitating each move like a mismatched shadow. "We have yet to see who or what is doomed," Nikolas said, resting his hand on his hip.

Thera laughed disparagingly. "I played with you at my whim when I was only a fraction of what I am now. Do you really think that having Christo along will even the odds?"

"No," he growled, shame and anger like a white-hot branding iron pressed against his memory. He lunged at her, pulling the syringe free of his pocket. Christo rushed forward to grab her from the other side.

Thera saw the glint of the needle in the light, and felt an instant's panic. She hadn't imagined Nikolas was clever enough to think of tranquilizing her. The two men grabbed her. Nikolas swung the needle down toward her arm. It penetrated the thick fabric of the robe. She riveted her eyes on it.

Nikolas's arm flew up and back, shattering at the shoulder, the same shoulder that had so recently been hurt. The pain careened through him, knocking the wind from his lungs and dropping him into a dark, violent whirlpool. His knees buckled beneath him. Clutching the syringe as if it were a lifeline, he fought savagely to hang on to consciousness. He was only vaguely aware of Christo's massive bulk sailing through the air and landing with a bone-cracking impact against the cabinets. With his last reserves of strength, Nikolas dragged himself up and scuttled across the room.

Christo lay immobile where he had landed. Thera checked to be sure he was unconscious. There was no need to kill the poor fool. Once Nikolas was dead, Christo would count himself lucky to live out his days on Crete.

She peered cautiously across the living area. Then with the exquisite languor of a cat toying with its prey, she focused on the couch and upended it, tossing it aside as easily as if it were made of cardboard. She did the same with each of the chairs and tables, until there was no piece of furniture behind which Nikolas could hide. She swept the draperies off the windows and flung open the door to the bathroom. Satisfied now that she knew where he was, she channeled a beam of energy toward the entry closet. It exploded outward in a cloud of wood and fabric, the concussion knocking Nikolas out into the center of the floor.

He struggled to his feet, dazed by the blast and by the pain that had spread like a flaming torch from his shoulder throughout his upper body. He transferred the syringe to his left hand, and started toward her, grunting with the agony of each movement.

"Look at you," Thera crowed. "You can hardly walk, let alone try to capture me."

Nikolas didn't respond. He came at her doggedly, past all rational thought.

Thera waited until he was a few feet away; then she reached for his neck with iron claws of energy. She found the hard, knob of cartilage there and slowly pressed in on it. She savored the frantic look on his face as he struggled. She increased the pressure. His eyes were bulging, his skin growing dusky. In another moment she would hear the satisfying crunch . . .

She crumpled to the floor. Choking and sputtering, Nikolas fell upon her, pushed up her sleeve, and jabbed the needle deep into her arm. With a rattling sigh he looked up and nodded.

Christo leaned back against the wall, blood running freely from his nose and ear, the cast-iron skillet dangling from his hand.

30

New York: November 18

"It's been looking like snow all day," Karen remarked as she and Aria stepped out of the elevator. "I wonder what it's waiting for?"

"Don't worry, we'll send out for a quick pizza and you'll be on your way before it starts."

"Are you sure your sister won't mind the company?"

"That's only the third time you've asked."

"Yeah, I guess it is," Karen murmured, knowing she would never feel comfortable around Thera again, and utterly confounded by Aria's steadfast loyalty to her twin.

They were only halfway down the hall when Aria let out a terrified cry. Before Karen could ask what had happened, she was racing madly toward her apartment, books falling from her arms and thudding across the floor. Karen took off after her.

"What is it?" she demanded breathlessly, as she came up beside her.

Without answering, Aria nodded toward the door. The lower third was caved in, and long, splintering cracks radiated in every direction.

When Aria started to reach for the knob, Karen tugged her arm away.

"Don't," she hissed, her teeth chattering. "They may still be in there."

Aria jerked her hand free. The same thought had occurred to her. But what if Thera were hurt or needed her? She closed her trembling fingers around the doorknob again. It wobbled as if it might fall off in her hand. She pushed, but the door just groaned and stayed where it was. Dropping the rest of her books, she leaned her shoulder against it and shoved. With a harsh scraping sound, it shuddered inward a few feet, tilting as if it were about to come off its hinges.

"Thera?" she called, her voice hoarse with fear.

There was no answer, no sound of any kind. She squeezed through the opening.

"Oh, my God," she said, momentarily frozen by the sight. "Thera." Then she was running blindly around the studio, tripping over furniture and crying out to her sister.

Karen remained just inside the doorway. Aria appeared like a child facing the enormity of the world for the first time, her face crumpled with bewilderment and dismay.

"She's not here," she whimpered. "And there's blood all over the place." She shook her head, tears cascading down her cheeks.

Karen went to her and held her while she cried. Once her sobs had faded to fitful hiccups, Karen righted a chair and made her sit down. Then she found the telephone lying beside a shattered table and dialed Michael's number.

"He's coming, Michael's coming," she said, kneeling next to Aria's chair. "He'll be here as soon as he can. Are you all right? Can I get you some water or maybe some tea?"

"No, nothing," Aria replied in a thin, strangled voice. Nothing would help. Nothing would bring Thera back.

While they waited, Karen tried to bring some order to the room. She gathered up the curtains, folding and stacking them neatly, and she righted most of the toppled furniture. The couch would have to wait for Michael. Then she brewed some tea in case Aria changed her mind. She was still at work when she heard Aria's voice raised vehemently. She turned to see her sitting on the floor with the telephone.

"Yes, I'm sure," she was saying. "If you could see this place you wouldn't be asking that question." She listened for a minute, tapping her fingernails nervously on a piece of the broken table.

"I'm not so sure you *are* upset. Yes, I can hear my mother crying. Is she crying your tears, too? Well, I can't accept that it's for the best. For whose best anyway? She's your daughter, for God's sake. Doesn't that count for something more than a handful of stupid platitudes?''

Aria's tone softened. ''No, I haven't forgotten whom I'm talking to. Please, if you won't help her, then help me. I've got to find her. Don't you have any idea where they might have taken her? Just a minute.'' She looked up at Karen. ''I need a pencil and paper. Look in my pocketbook.''

Aria jotted down an address. ''I can't promise that,'' she said. ''I have to go now.'' She hung up the phone and jumped to her feet.

''Your father?'' Karen asked.

''Yes, do you remember where I left my coat?''

''In the corner near the window, why?''

''He says he doesn't think they'll do anything to her. At least not until they get her back to Crete.'' She picked the coat up off the floor and pushed her arms into it.

''Aria, stop and think. What can you do against them if Thera wasn't strong enough to resist them?''

''I can be there for her; that may be all she needs.'' Aria grabbed her pocketbook and was almost to the door when Michael stepped in.

Snow covered his head and shoulders and the toes of his sneakers. It was caught in his eyelashes and in the day's stubble on his cheeks. His face was haggard, as if he hadn't slept well.

Seeing him, Aria felt herself weaken. Tears blurred her eyes again, and she desperately wanted the comfort of his arms.

''Talk about timing,'' Karen sighed.

Michael looked from her to Aria. ''Where do you think you're off to?'' he demanded. ''Do you have any idea what it's like out there?''

Aria stiffened. He had no right to talk to her that way. Didn't he understand what had happened?

''I'd say it's snowing,'' she replied brusquely, moving around him.

Michael stepped in front of her. ''Hey, I'm sorry. I was worried about you, and I had a hell of a time getting here. The streets are a disaster. The snow's coming down like a solid wall out there. The damned windshield wipers couldn't even keep up with it."

"Apology accepted, Michael, but I've got to go."

"Where?"

"To the airport. I have to try to find her before they . . ." She shook her head, unable to finish the thought.

Michael reached for her hands and clasped them between his. "Aria, there is no way you can make it there tonight. And even if you could, the planes can't take off under these conditions."

"I have to try," she said, her voice cracking. "I have to do something." She tried to pull her hands away, but Michael held them firmly.

"Let go of me!" she demanded.

"No, because if you get hurt it will be my fault."

"Don't be ridiculous, Michael. How on earth could it be your fault?" She stopped struggling, surprised to see tears shining in his soft brown eyes. He seemed to be growing paler as she watched.

Michael dropped her hands, and a deep, rattling sigh shook his body.

"I told them where to find her," he said quietly. "I went looking for them at Karen's place, at her parents'. And I told them I would help them if they promised to take Thera and not you. I even told them what time to come, so you wouldn't be home." He lowered his head, like a penitent awaiting punishment.

Aria's mouth went slack. She wanted to scream at him, to ask why, to pretend he hadn't said it at all, but no words came. She was outraged by what he had done, yet incapable of hating him. It had been the same with her sister. They both had the best of intentions, but they couldn't both be right. Aria stumbled backward and sank onto a chair, too mired in emotion to sort it out.

A glass was thrust at her. She looked up.

"It's scotch," said Karen. "Take a little."

She sipped it, coughing as it burned its way past the knotted muscles of her throat.

Michael was sitting on another chair, still huddled in his wet coat. Karen handed him a glass, too.

"I'm going to close the folding door to the kitchen so you guys can talk," she said. "If you want me just yell."

Michael drained the scotch in two mouthfuls. Then he turned to Aria.

"I don't know if you'll ever forgive me," he began. "The truth is, I'm not even sure anymore if I did the right thing. It seemed to be the only thing at the time. But that's not the point now. I can't let you get hurt. If you insist on flying to Crete to try to save Thera, I want to go with you. There's just so much guilt I can live with."

Aria put down her glass and went to the window. Through the steady curtain of snow the cars appeared to be moving in slow motion like her thoughts.

"I don't know if I want you with me," she said finally.

31

November 19

The cabin was dark, the window shades drawn to simulate night, though they had long since crossed through dawn into full daylight.

Michael stretched his arms above his head and tried to find a comfortable postion. He'd been sitting for so many hours that his long legs were cramped and sore. He pressed the button for the overhead light and checked his watch. Two more hours before they would land in Athens.

He switched off the light and looked at Aria. She had sworn she wouldn't sleep, but sheer exhaustion had overcome her. She lay with her head on a pillow she'd propped against the cabin wall, her legs curled beneath her. Her face was smooth and untroubled, as if nothing were wrong. Michael sighed, wishing it were more than just an illusion of sleep. By trying to protect her, he might have thrust her into more danger than ever. He stood up and rummaged in one of the overhead compartments unitl he found a blanket. Then he draped it gently over her, hoping he could be of some help during whatever lay ahead in Crete.

At first Aria wouldn't agree to his accompanying her, though he tried every argument he could think of. Karen had even lent her support, pointing out that Aria might need all the help she could find. Aria had simply shaken her head and refused to discuss the issue. In the end they had waited out the storm in heavy silence, taking turns staring out the window and listening to weather reports on the radio. Sometime after dark they made a pot of coffee and a platter of sandwiches, which sat on the table, untouched and growing stale.

It was nearly midnight when the snow stopped. It didn't taper off; it stopped as abruptly as it had started. One minute a veil of snow reached from sky to ground, the next, the night was startlingly black, without even a random flake swirling in it.

Aria was standing at the window when it ended. She walked over to the couch and picked up her coat and purse.

"The snow's stopped," she said calmly. "I'm going."

Michael jumped up. "I'll drive you to the airport," he said, still hoping she'd change her mind and let him come along.

"The streets won't be cleared yet; I'm going to take the subway."

He stopped, his jacket dangling from one arm, at a loss for anything else to try. Aria saw his face droop with defeat. A part of her wanted to reach out to him, but too much pain stood in the way, too much uncertainty about what lay ahead.

"All right, Michael," she said. "I don't see what good it can do, but you can come if you want to."

Michael nodded with an audible sigh.

She turned to Karen who seemed as relieved as Michael that Aria wasn't going alone. She held her keys out to her friend.

"Please stay here, at least for tonight."

Karen took the keys and put her arms around Aria. "Be careful," she whispered, too flooded with emotion to say all the things she wanted to.

On the way to the airport and for the hours they waited there, Aria said nothing unless Michael asked her a direct question. And then she responded with the careful neutrality of a sequestered juror. Michael knew he shouldn't expect things to be any different, but the cold unbreachable space between them was hard for him to bear.

He blinked and squinted as the main cabin lights came on. Beside him Aria shifted, snuggling deeper under the blanket, but she didn't awaken. Bleary-eyed passengers shambled down the aisles to the lavatories. The aroma of hot coffee filled the air, and the attendants began distributing breakfast trays.

Michael took a tray for himself, but refused one for Aria.

They could always find someplace for her to eat, but there was little chance of her getting any more sleep before this trip was over.

They landed in Athens a little before 7:00 P.M. Greek time and, although they were early, almost missed the connecting flight to Heraklion. Their passports were valid, but the customs officials wouldn't allow them through without first inspecting their luggage. Aria and Michael insisted that they had none, but all the officials would say was "Must wait, not to worry." And while they waited, the plane for Heraklion was readied for takeoff. Finally, out of desperation, Aria found another traveler who spoke both English and Greek. With his help she was able to explain that they had to get to Crete to see her sister who was dying. The words were difficult to say, and she saw Michael flinch, but the point was made. They were hurried onto the plane for the flight to Crete.

The airport in Heraklion was nearly deserted when their plane landed after eleven that night. Aria, feeling disoriented from lack of sleep and the changing time zones, willingly sank into a chair while Michael tried to rent a car. She was soon alone in the arrival area; the other passengers seemed to know where they were going and how to get there.

She saw Michael walking toward her, his familiar face comforting in this strange, empty building. And she realized how glad she was that she'd let him come along. It wasn't until he was standing beside her that she noticed his shoulders were sagging and his mouth was twisted into a grim line.

"I got ahold of one guy. A janitor, I think. From what I could understand, we won't be able to rent a car until morning."

"No, we can't wait that long," Aria groaned, sitting up rigidly. "That snowstorm already cost us too much time."

"I know. Listen, let's see if there's a taxi outside that can at least get us to your grandparents' place. We need more information from them anyway, and maybe they'll have a car we can borrow."

Aria stood up, teetering uncertainly for a moment before gaining her balance. Michael grasped her arm to steady her.

"Thank you, I'm all right," she said softly, but in a tone that invited no further contact. Michael drew his hand away and walked beside her toward the doors.

"I'm not sure my grandparents will give us any information," Aria remarked once they'd settled into the back seat of a taxi and told the driver the address that Damos had given her. "According to my father, Nicodemus was probably the one who sent the men after Thera to begin with."

"We'll try," Michael replied evenly. "We're here and we'll try."

They said no more until the taxi stopped in front of a row of small, dingy apartment houses. Michael paid the driver with drachmas they'd bought before boarding the plane in New York. Aria waited for him on the sidewalk, staring up at the dark building where only one light burned behind thin, faded draperies in a second-floor window. This was where her sister had grown up while Aria had lived in the luxury of Long Island and the security of her parents' love. What must it have been like for Thera, she wondered, to know she was the one who'd been left behind?

Aria heard the taxi's engine rev and fade away. Michael came up beside her. Although she had been in a hurry to get here, she entered the building hesitantly. The small vestibule was lit by a dusty, naked bulb hanging from the center of the ceiling. The air was dense with stale cooking odors and the acrid smell of mildew and age. Unpleasant yet familiar odors that reminded her of certain dreams. There had always been a link between her and Thera that even distance couldn't sever.

She started up the narrow, creaking staircase, comforted by the echo of Michael's footsteps close behind her. On the second floor she found the number Damos had given her. Before knocking, she listened for voices. But the building was so quiet she could hear the shallow, nervous rhythm of Michael's breathing.

She rapped firmly on the door. Almost immediately there was the sound of a chair scraping on the floor and then the soft padding of feet approaching the door.

"*Pios eine eki*?" a tearful, high pitched voice called out.

"Philina?" Aria said, hoping her grandmother spoke some English.

"*Ti thelis*?"

"Philina," she repeated, louder. She heard a lock being

turned, and the door opened revealing a tiny woman in a worn
bathrobe and slippers, squinting back at them. Suddenly the
old woman's eyes widened and she gasped. Latching on to
Aria's wrist, she pulled her into the apartment.

"Thera, Thera *mou*," she cried, embracing her.

Michael followed them in. Philina looked from him to Aria
and began chattering in Greek.

By the cadence of her voice she seemed to be asking questions, but beyond that Aria was lost. She shook her head.

"Philina, do you speak English?"

The old lady backed away a few steps, her eyes shining
feverishly out of a web of lines as she studied Aria.

"Thera?" she said, cocking her head uncertainly.

"No," Aria replied. "Ariadne."

Philina's mouth opened, and she crossed herself as auto-
matically as if she were blinking.

"Ariadne, Ariadne," she murmured over and over.

"I have to find Thera," Aria interrupted, emphasizing her
sister's name.

Philina nodded. "Thera." She thought for a moment, then
held up her finger and hurried past Aria and Michael into the
hallway, disappearing up the staircase.

She returned a few minutes later with a scrawny young man
in tow. He was still pulling his bathrobe closed as she dragged
him into the apartment and shut the door behind them. He
nodded sleepily at Aria and Michael and extended his hand.

"Hello, I am Hector," he said in passable English. "I
maybe can help."

Aria shook his hand warmly, hoping for the first time that
she might be able to locate her sister.

"Thank you for coming. Would you please ask Philina if
she knows where Thera is?"

Aria waited impatiently while Hector translated her question for Philina and then listened to the response.

He turned back to her. "Mrs. Koraes say her husband not
tell her. But she believe they take Thera to one of the mountain"—he chewed thoughtfully on the inner wall of his
cheek—"shrines," he added brightly, satisfied with the word.

"How many of these shrines are there?" Michael asked.

"They are most in caves. And caves there are many of here

on Crete." He spoke to Philina, then turned back to Aria.

"Mrs. Koraes say there are two they would go to. Idean Cave and Diktean."

Aria wanted to ask him how far away these two caves were, but he was listening to her grandmother, who had broken into an emotional stream of Greek, tears pooling in her worried eyes. Hector's face grew pale, his Adam's apple bobbing up and down vigorously.

"She says they kill her. They kill Thera at dawn."

"Are the caves near each other?" Aria asked, trying to keep the desperation out of her voice.

Hector shook his head.

Aria felt Michael's hand on her arm. She turned to him.

"I have an idea," he said. "I don't know if it'll work, but it's worth a shot if you're willing."

"Michael, anything. What is it?"

"If there really is some kind of permanent psychic connection between you and Thera, maybe you could tap into her subconscious—find out from her where she is."

"How? I wouldn't even know how to go about it. Unless" —she paused and looked at him—"unless you hypnotize me. That's what you meant, isn't it?"

Michael nodded. "With practice I think you could probably do it on your own. But it would take a lot of concentration, and the circumstances just aren't right now."

"Okay, let's try hypnosis," she said, pushing away the memory of the dark, ghastly hunger she had encountered there before.

While Michael readied the room, Aria explained to Hector what they were about to do and asked him to translate it for her grandmother. Philina pulled a rosary from the pocket of her robe and sat in one of the dining room chairs noiselessly mouthing prayers. Hector stood beside her in silent fascination.

Aria was seated in a deep-cushioned chair. All the lights were off except one lamp, which Michael had positioned at eye level in front of her. He took his place on the adjacent couch, the terrifying memory of the last session building around him like a dense fog. He should never have suggested this. Yet he

owed her the chance to find her sister even if he believed she
was wrong for wanting to.

Within a matter of minutes Michael had placed her in a deep
trance. Each time it grew easier, as if she were learning to find
her way through a maze by rote. Out of the corner of his eye
he could see Hector motionless, staring at him, and Philina
making the sign of the cross. He chastised himself for being
distracted and focused his attention wholly on Aria.

"I want you to look for Thera," he told her. "Tap into the
power if you need to. Find Thera."

Aria had already opened a channel into her energy core and
begun to probe for the pathway, the link, to her sister. It was
like navigating through a new, uncharted dimension. She
could sense Thera nearby; the gap between them was closing.
Soon they would be one. But at the moment of union Aria felt
the focus of her energy slip suddenly, losing traction like a
wheel mired in a ditch. Images floated before her, too blurry
to recognize or describe. Michael's voice dissolved to an indistinct hum, yet the very sound of it was reassuring to her.
With one tendril of her mind she clung to it as if it were a
lifeline. There was a quaking all around her, like a seething
anger barely restrained. The brutal force of it kept building,
and Aria realized with a sickening revulsion that it was siphon-
ing power from her. She was unnerved and about to back off
when the vague images began to clarify and come into sharper
focus. She had to hang on; the answers she needed might be
seconds away.

With a final wrenching, the anger sprung free, exploding
around her and within her so violently that she felt like a
rowboat being ripped apart in heavy seas. She would have
retreated then, flown back to the safe harbor of Michael's
voice, but the images had crystallized. She was in a cave. The
only illumination came from lanterns that etched hard circles
of light out of the darkness. The air was moist with the smell
of water, and everywhere she looked fine stalagmites and
stalactites reached for one another in a frozen dance. People
walked past her, moving in and out of the light like appari-
tions. A man was coming toward her. She felt a tremendous
surge of energy and saw him fly backward, smashing head

first into the cave wall. All at once she seemed to be in the middle of a bitter struggle, her power being sapped at an incredible rate. Then the scene before her dulled, obscured once more behind a hazy veil. She could hear Michael's voice calling to her like the plaintive moan of a foghorn in a storm. Homing in on it she dragged herself back to him.

When she opened her eyes, Michael was kneeling in front of her. His head flopped forward into her lap, his body quivering with exhaustion and relief.

"I'm all right, Michael," she whispered, stroking his head for a moment. "I can describe the place where they have taken her."

He straightened up and beckoned for Hector and Philina to join them. Hector's eyes were bulging, and he seemed unaware that his bathrobe had come untied, revealing his undershorts. Philina scuffled along beside him, the rosary clutched to her breast.

"She's in a cave. A large cave with water in it, I think," said Aria in a voice measured more by fatigue than calmness.

Hector began translating to Philina, and Aria wondered if she should mention the stalagmites. Would Hector understand the word? Before she could decide, she heard her grandmother speak briefly and triumphantly.

"The Diktean Cave," Hector said quickly. "Mrs. Koraes say must be Diktean. There inside is a lake."

"What time is it?" Aria asked, coming out of the chair with the renewed vigor of hope.

"Half past two." Michael looked at Hector. "Do you know of any place we could rent a car now?"

Hector shook his head. Then his mouth widened into a toothy grin. "I have car. I borrow it to you."

Aria threw her arms around him with impulsive gratitude, making the young man flush and stammer.

"I sh-sh-show map for y-y-you, too."

Twenty minutes later they were driving through the quiet streets of Heraklion to the Diktean Cave forty miles away.

32

Heraklion: November 20

"Hold him! Hold him tightly!" Dr. Vodopia instructed.

Andreas grasped Nikolas's left side. Petros braced him from behind. Between them, Nikolas stood motionless, too weak with exhaustion and pain to protest.

Vodopia seized the dislocated right arm, and with one quick, practiced jerk, popped it back into the shoulder joint. Nikolas fell unconscious before he could scream.

Andreas lowered him gently to the ground while Vodopia withdrew a syringe from his medical bag and injected him with a drug to deaden the pain.

Nicodemus viewed the procedure from a few feet away. When they had finished, he picked up the jacket that the doctor had had to cut off Nikolas, bunched it into a pillow, and eased it beneath his nephew's head. Pulling off his own coat, he spread it over him to keep out the damp chill. Then he sat down on an outcropping of rock nearby and watched him sleep.

The gods must indeed have been with you, he thought. How else could you have withstood such agony and come so far? According to Nikolas's own account, they had been traveling for two full days. Unable to arrange for an immediate flight out of New York to Athens and with the possibility of a snowstorm closing down the airports, they had decided to take the first available flight to a European city. The trip had taken them to Brussels, Paris, and finally Athens, with long delays between flights.

Nikolas himself wondered how he had hung on to consciousness or rational thought. But he knew that losing either would have meant losing Thera. They were walking a tightrope with her, having to keep her sedated enough to be harmless and yet aware enough to discourage curiosity. Even so, in each country they entered, a passport control agent had demanded to know why she appeared to be drugged. Nikolas concocted a story about being involved in an automobile accident on the very day they were ending their vacation and preparing to go home. A doctor in New York had sedated Thera to ease the pain of a fractured rib. Seeing the contusions on Christo's face and the pale haggard expression on Nikolas's, the officals were inclined to accept the story as truth.

When they arrived at last in Athens and it seemed they might actually make it all the way back to Heraklion, Nikolas realized with numbing horror that there wouldn't be enough of the sedative. The trip had taken longer than either he or Vodopia had anticipated. Hoping to stretch out the meager supply that remained, he waited longer between injections and decreased the dosage. He kept a constant watch on her, afraid to doze off for even a minute for fear that Christo would not be able detect subtle changes in her behavior quickly enough. They had arrived at Nicodemus's apartment with only minutes to spare. Vodopia had come at once, and when the emergency was past, the others had been notified that Thera was home.

Nicodemus had pleaded with his nephew to rest and let the doctor see to his arm before they attempted the long drive and the climb to the Diktean Cave. But Nikolas had stubbornly refused to consider such a delay, insisting that Thera be taken at once to the site of her execution. There, he said, he would rest in the hours before dawn.

Nicodemus had acquiesced. How could he argue? The gods were with Nikolas; he was acting on their commands. The old man had looked across the room at Thera, who was lying in peaceful sleep on the couch. Philina was kneeling beside her, stroking back the hair that fell across her face and making soothing, maternal sounds. He sighed tremulously. Nikolas's agony would soon be ending, and his own was about to begin. During the weeks that Thera had been gone, Philina had extracted his promise to do all he could to save their grand-daughter. Nicodemus had spoken the meaningless words to comfort his wife and help her through the waiting. But he had no delusions. The promise was a fraudulent one. He could do nothing to prevent what would happen.

Nikolas groaned in his sleep and kicked off the jacket. Nicodemus went to replace it, then took up his vigil on the rock again. The others paced around the cave or sat in small groups talking in muted tones. He had no desire to join them. He no longer felt like a part of this congregation that looked to him for leadership. He felt no pride in the divine spark that linked him to Aphrodite. He was nothing more than the carrier of a lethal gene, a gene that was destroying the grandchild he loved.

Nikolas didn't sleep long. With sunrise still hours away he sat up, shaking with cold in spite of the jacket he found draped around him. He was in one of the small recesses off the main area where no light penetrated. At first he didn't notice Nicodemus only an arm's reach away. But he could see Thera. She was seated, propped up against the wall on the other side of the cave where the lanterns had been positioned to form a spotlight around her. He couldn't tell if her eyes were open or closed, but it relieved him to know that her every move could be easily monitored.

"So, it seems you have won." Nicodemus's voice was so unexpectedly close that Nikolas jumped, causing a wave of pain to crash over him.

"You watch over me like a vulture, Uncle," he said once the pain eased enough for him to catch his breath.

"Not like a guardian?"

"I suffer too much to laugh," Nikolas retorted.

"Out of jealousy you misjudge me as you have all along. Loving Thera has never taken away from my love for you."

"That may be true. But it is long past mattering. What must happen here at dawn has nothing to do with my feelings or yours."

"I am not trying to bargain for her life. That is not up to you in any case. I only thought it was something you should know."

Nikolas pushed himself to his feet. Slipping the jacket from his shoulders, he held it out to his uncle.

"Take this now. Your back must be knotted from the cold." He started to walk away, then paused. "Tell me again of your love for me once the night is gone and Thera is no more."

Thera knew where she was. At times the world was a confusing melange of color and shape whirling past her. But occasionally she could see quite clearly. Although she understood that she was in grave danger, the possible consequences didn't register in her mind. It was as if she'd been cut off from her emotions, rendered incapable of reacting. She pressed her back against the cold stone wall and welcomed the chill that shot through her body. Even discomfort was preferable to feeling nothing at all.

She opened her eyes, wincing at the way the light made them sting. Struggling to ignore the pain, she tried to absorb as much about her surroundings and her captors as she could before they drugged her again. She felt the ropes that bound her wrists and ankles. She heard whispered conversations coming from several directions. With a sense of triumph she felt the swelling of fear and anger within her. Either they were late in medicating her or all the drug-induced sleep had somehow strengthened her. If she was careful not to let them know she was beginning to neutralize the sedative, she might still be able to save herself. She closed her eyes again. Let them think she still slept.

A moment later she felt Aria's presence, and her eyes flew open. As the images before her focused more sharply, she realized that Aria was nearby, not on a physical plane but on a psychic one. The presence was strong, though, so the physical distance between them wasn't great. She was coming to help. A new confidence filled Thera. Together she and her sister would effortlessly see to the destruction of their enemies. She opened herself up to her sister's hesitant probing. Keeping her eyes focused as best she could, she scanned the cave, sending the sensory information to Aria so she would know just where to find her.

Off to one side Andreas was talking to Petros. She saw Petros point in her direction and the taller man swing around to look. His brows jutted into a frown as he cautiously approached her. Thera averted her eyes and slumped, feigning sleep, but it was too late. Andreas was retreating, calling out to Dr. Vodopia, apprehension making his deep voice boom harshly across the cave.

Thera saw the doctor running toward her. Rough hands reached for her. She couldn't wait for Aria to find her. She wouldn't be drugged again. She would escape now. The doctor was nearly upon her, the hated needle poised in the air. She summoned all her strength and centered it on him. He flew backward with tremendous speed, striking the stone wall with a dull thud. Blood spread out like a halo around his head, and he crumpled to the floor.

While Thera concentrated on Vodopia, Nikolas scooped the syringe off the ground where it had fallen and plunged it into her arm. She shrieked with murderous rage and fought to free herself of the ropes, but she was growing lost once more in a maze of disconnected thoughts and actions. She felt Aria retreating and could find no way of holding on to her. But even as she slipped into unconsciousness, her last coherent thought was that she would win. Aria would find her in time.

Nicodemus was the first to reach the doctor, but there was nothing to be done. His head lay in a darkening pool of blood that seeped down around his body like a scarlet shadow.

The women had gathered into a shocked and silent group behind Nicodemus. After Thera had been subdued, the men joined them.

No one moved or spoke. Paralyzed with grief and anguish, they waited for someone to tell them what to do. Nicodemus wished he could abdicate the role of leader, turn his back on the whole of it, and walk away. But responsibility and faith were too deeply ingrained in him to disavow. He passed through the semicircle of men and returned with one of the cloths meant to cover the altar. Choking back tears, he spread it over the slain doctor.

"Andreas," he mumbled. "The labrys—it is ready?"

"Sharpened and ready," Andreas replied soberly. "Who will make the sacrifice?"

"I must," the old man said, his voice trembling. "It is my duty." He turned to his nephew. Nikolas's face was stony as he looked up from the shrouded form on the ground. But Nicodemus was glad to see no sign of triumph in his eyes.

33

Crete: November 20

The car was small and smelled of oil and refuse; greasy food wrappers littered the floor. Aria rolled her window all the way down, inhaling the cool sea air as they left Heraklion behind. Hector's map fluttered in her hand. They had found their way onto the coastal highway without trouble, and it was time now, not direction, that troubled her most. As the car hurtled through the dark, unfamiliar countryside with its steep hills and cliffs that plunged straight down into the water, she felt caged and helpless. They had a long distance to go, and dawn was only a few hours away.

Michael kept his foot pressed against the accelerator, weaving in tight arcs around slower-moving vehicles that got in his way. He had to wrench the wheel hard at sudden turns, and more than once the rear tires skidded onto the gravel shoulder of the road. Rigid with tension, he maintained his speed, grateful that they were traveling east, hugging the mountains and not the edge that fell away into the sea.

He had passed beyond exhaustion. His eyes felt as if they'd been glued open and might never close properly again. Adrenaline pumped through his body, depleting his last reservoir of strength. He glanced at Aria, her profile perfectly outlined in the harsh glare of oncoming headlights, and he wondered what awaited them at the Diktean Cave and if he would be able to help her. He didn't allow himself to think beyond that.

The highway cut through the tiny cluster of houses that was Gournia, and four miles farther ahead, just as Hector had told them, they found the turnoff for the Lassithi Plateau. The road was uphill and narrower, the climb steeper once they passed the village of Kera. They'd seen no other vehicles since leaving the coastal highway, and the dim, scattered lights of the villages seemed no more than primitive campfires, barely penetrating the vast darkness around them. Michael was caught up in the eerie sensation of having driven back in time to a place where technology hadn't yet been born and ancient gods still ruled. His pulse quickened, the hair on the nape of his neck stood out, and it took the grinding of the car's engine, as it strained up the final yards to the plateau, to reorient him.

"Is this thing going to make it?' Aria asked, breaking the silence between them for the first time in over an hour.

"Yeah," he replied, his voice sounding taut and unnatural to his ears. "I think the road has leveled out now."

"What's that?" she gasped as they swung around a sharp curve and an army of monstrous shapes sprung up suddenly in the beam of the headlights.

Michael slammed on the brakes, jolting them forward and back in their seats, before they realized that the monsters surrounding them were thousands of windmills, most disintegrating with age and disuse.

Aria laughed a short, grim cough of a laugh, and Michael jerked the car into first gear again, swearing at his own stupidity.

By the time the road had taken them around the edge of the Lassithi Plateau, the eastern sky was beginning to lighten with the teasing rays that precede dawn. Aria groaned, hope twisting and shriveling inside her. Then, in the midst of the cultivated fields, the fifteenth-century village of Psychron came into view. And, rising six hundred and fifty feet above it, Mount Dikte.

Michael parked the car on a shoulder of the road just outside the village. Aria opened her door and jumped out. The street was deserted except for a few dogs who studied them warily before continuing on their rounds. But Aria noticed smoke spiraling into the sky from several of the houses. It wouldn't be long before the men who farmed the plain would be out to begin the day's work. She wanted to be well away from prying eyes by that time.

Michael had come around the car and was standing beside her, holding the flashlight Philina had given them. The air was clear and brisk with a nighttime chill. He could tell by the way Aria was standing with her arms hugging her chest that she was cold. Under other circumstances he would have drawn her against him to warm her, but such times were gone, perhaps forever.

"Let's go," she said, "before we're noticed. The last thing we need is a crowd of curiosity seekers following us." With the help of the flashlight they found the dirt path, carved out over the centuries, that led up the gentlest slope of the mountain. Hector had told them that although the ascent wasn't difficult it would take them at least half an hour. Aria resolved to make it in less.

She walked quickly, her calf muscles tightening into hard knots from the unaccustomed strain, glancing up at the sky every few minutes to gauge the progress of their race against the sun. Though Michael directed the flashlight steadily ahead of them, they kept tripping over rocks and other debris. Halfway to the cave entrance Aria choked back a cry of pain and tumbled to the ground.

Michael hunkered down beside her. "What is it?"

"My ankle," she groaned. "I twisted it in one of those damn ruts. It felt as if it was going to snap off."

Michael lifted her hand away and gently rotated her foot. She grimaced with pain, but the ankle had full mobility and didn't appear to be broken. In any case there was no point in suggesting that they turn back.

Studying her ankle, Aria could see that it had already begun to swell. Her heart lurched—she wasn't using the flashlight, but she could see. She looked up. The sky was a dusty pink; any minute the sun would breach the mountaintop. She pushed herself to her feet and took a tentative step. The injured ankle buckled, refusing to support her weight. Without a word Michael put one arm around her waist, and she leaned against him. He could feel her body tense with each step, and in the brightening sky he could see her jaw clenched with pain and determination.

They were both perspiring and breathing raggedly by the time they found the cave. They came up to it from the side, so they wouldn't be seen by someone guarding the entrance.

"What now?" Michael asked. It was a question that had occurred to him often during the past forty-eight hours, one that he had carefully deferred until now for fear that Aria would have no answer.

Aria dropped her hand from his shoulder and leaned back against the rough face of the mountain.

"I'm not sure," she said, gulping at the air. "All I know is that I have to get to Thera. If she can share my strength, she'll be all right." She paused and her voice dipped so that it was barely audible. "Unless we're too late."

Michael nodded, too weary to know what he hoped for anymore. If they were late, Aria would be out of danger, but any thread of love that still bound her to him would be irrevocably torn away.

"Let's go, then," he said, holding his arm out to her.

They moved cautiously toward the entrance, expecting to be surprised at any moment by one of Thera's captors. But no one came. They stepped inside and waited for their eyes to adjust from the pale glow of dawn to the blackness of the cave. Aria felt her lungs laboring to draw oxygen from the thick, humid air. Michael pressed his mouth to her ear.

"We're going to have to use the flashlight."

"Okay, but keep it pointed straight down so it doesn't give us away too soon."

"Hang on tight," he whispered as his feet slid precariously along the slippery passage. According to Hector they had another half-hour's walk inside before they reached the first of the two levels of the cave. And with the ground this wet they didn't dare walk any faster.

Aria clung to Michael, her fingers pressing deeper into his flesh with every step as she was overcome by the slow but certain realization that she'd been here before. In a dream. Yet it was less a memory than a premonition. She sensed the cave crumbling around her, the awesome rumbling of the mountain vibrating through her body. And although she knew it wasn't real, she couldn't resist the fear that caught her in its iron grasp. She froze. Michael tugged gently at her, but she couldn't respond. She never even heard the two men steal out of the darkness behind them.

Thera had learned her lesson. She didn't open her eyes. The arm that lay beneath her was numb from the pressure of her body, but she didn't move. This time they wouldn't be aware that the sedative had worn off too soon. Relying on sounds and energy patterns, she was able to keep track of what was going on around her, and she knew immediately when someone was approaching to check on her. Nikolas. She knew just by the musky, male scent of him. It was a simple act of will to slow her heart rate and breathing. He seized her wrist. She went limp, though she yearned to fight back. Satisfied with her slow pulse rate, Nikolas dropped her hand, letting it slam onto the cave floor. Patience, Thera cautioned herself. Patience and you will do with him whatever you please. Aria was moving closer every minute. Thera had known it since she'd awakened, even as she'd known that her sister was not alone. Michael was with her, like a weak satellite orbiting a star. Thera wasn't pleased, but Michael was a minor problem, one she could deal with easily enough once she was safe. She carefully monitored their progress and with bitter frustration knew even before Aria did that the two men waited in the shadows.

Their sudden capture shook Aria out of the fear that had paralyzed her. She and Michael were shoved along the passageway by two men wielding knives and speaking rapidly in Greek. At least they were still moving in the right direction, she reassured herself, biting her lip against the pain that flashed like electricity from her ankle up through her body. Michael saw the tears streaming uncontrollably down her cheeks. He tried to fight off the men and help her, but the more he struggled, the more roughly they were both treated. In deference to Aria, he yielded.

The tunnel they were following led eventually to a large

open area in which they were made to stop. Although the flashlight had been knocked out of Michael's hands during the first skirmish, one of the men had a lantern. By its light Michael could see the vaulted ceiling high overhead. It fit Hector's description of the upper cave. But there was no one here. If they were holding Thera, she had to be on the lower level.

Aria was pushed to the floor, Michael beside her. Through the clouds of pain that billowed around her, she could hear the conversation between the two men change in tenor and grow heated. They appeared to be arguing, perhaps over what to do next. If she and Michael had any chance of escaping them, it would be now. All she had to do was reach Thera; then no one could harm them. She didn't allow herself to think about how she would manage to run. Somehow she would. She slid her hand across to touch Michael's and nodded toward the men.

Michael had come to the same conclusion. "Use your power," he whispered.

Before she could ask how, one of the men had yanked Michael upright, slicing his knife toward Michael's throat. Michael kicked out, catching his attacker in the knees. As the man's legs buckled, Michael smashed a fist into his nose, feeling it splinter under the impact. When the second man lunged, Aria focused all her fury on him and, with a bolt of energy that surprised even her, sent him flying through the air to land in a dazed heap twenty yards away.

Michael helped her to her feet. Then he grabbed the lantern and swung it in an arc around the cave until he found the passageway that would take them down to the lower level.

The altar had been reconsecrated and readied for the sacrifice. Nicodemus stood behind it lost in thought. Andreas approached quietly, reluctant to disturb him. He was saddened to see that Nicodemus, a tower of strength and faith to them all, suddenly appeared shrunken, as if gravity were whittling away at him. Andreas would have preferred to leave him in peace a while longer, but by his watch dawn had broken, and it was time to begin. Before he could say a word, Nicodemus turned to him.

"Yes, I know, Andreas. Will you gather everyone before

the altar?'' Andreas walked off, and Nikolas immediately took his place.

"She is still asleep. I couldn't rouse her," he said.

"Perhaps it is better that way. More merciful."

"Was she merciful to Vodopia?" Nikolas glared. "Or to the thousands who have died around the world because of her?"

"We discuss the quality of our mercy, not hers." Nicodemus spoke softly so that his voice wouldn't carry to the others who were congregating. Nikolas didn't respond.

"I see," Nicodemus said. "You wish her to suffer. That would be a source of satisfaction to you."

Nikolas's lips twitched with anger. "I want only what is right."

"Call it by its proper name," Nicodemus whispered sharply. "Call it revenge."

He turned to the congregation and held up his arms in prayer. Dismissed, Nikolas stalked off to wait beside Thera. His uncle would never understand that justice and revenge were sometimes one and the same.

Nicodemus recited the necessary words in a monotone devoid of feeling. If he allowed himself to think about what he was saying, he would never make it through to the end. Without turning around he knew that Andreas stood off to one side, the labrys in his hands, its double blade finely honed and gleaming in the lantern light.

"We bow to your will, mighty Zeus, as we return to you what is yours. In our frailty we sought to circumvent your commandment. Now we are come to this sacred place of your birth to beg your forgiveness and vow never again to break our covenant with you." Nicodemus bowed his head, and Nikolas stepped up to the altar with Thera in his arms.

Thera waited, calculating each second that passed. Aria was free once more. She would be there in minutes. The uneven stone scraped Thera's back as Nikolas laid her roughly on the altar. The cave was hushed, even breathing seemed suspended with a peculiar mixture of eagerness and dread. She could hear the rustling of the cloth that would be spread over her, Andreas's footsteps as he carried the labrys to her grandfather. If

Aria didn't arrive in another moment, she would have to open her eyes and try to defend herself alone.

The light behind her closed lids dimmed, and she felt the cloth touch her arm. She had to act now. Her eyes flashed open, immobilizing Nicodemus, who stood with the cloth poised above her. Before he could react, a woman in the congregation screamed. Within seconds the scream was echoed by others, and everyone ran, scattering into the far corners of the cave.

The three men at the altar spun around to see what had caused the sudden panic. Thera sprang to her feet, locking her eyes on her sister, who stood in the entrance with Michael.

Nikolas was the first to recover. "Get her out of here!" he cried, racing across the cave toward Aria. "They can't be together."

Andreas sped after him, still clutching the deadly ax. But it was already too late. Andreas let out a strangled cry, and his hands flew to his throat, the labrys clattering to the ground beside him. His eyes bulged as he pried frantically at the invisible fingers that were choking him. There was the unmistakable sound of bones snapping. His face went a lurid, dusky blue, and blood oozed from the corners of his mouth. With an expression caught between entreaty and horror, the big man crashed to the ground like a felled tree.

Nikolas darted back to snatch up the ax. But before his hand could close around it, Thera swept it out of his reach, whipping it effortlessly up through the air, then back down at him like a predatory bird diving at its prey. The labrys hit Nikolas with such force that he was thrown backward, the blade ripping through his body and striking the wall behind him.

Nicodemus fell upon Thera then and, with a courage born of desperation, grappled for her throat. Without moving, Thera flung him away. His body slammed into the altar. He made one feeble effort to raise himself up, then, clutching his chest, collapsed and was still.

Aria's relief turned to horror. She had come to save her sister, by force if necessary, but not by murder. She could feel Thera's power building faster and faster, magnifying itself by sapping her own. She tried to break the connection between them, but Thera held on.

"Michael." Aria reached for his arm. Though he couldn't help her in this struggle, he was her only link to the sane, ordinary world that was tumbling away from her.

"Michael, is it?" Thera's voice rose shrilly. "Your Michael is the one who sent them after me. The one who brought us all to this. He is the one you should run from." Her voice softened, became entreating. "Just allow yourself to be what you are. You need no man, Aria. You need only me."

Thera's pleas went unheeded; Aria was still straining to pull away. Thera turned her gaze to the spot where Nikolas had fallen and wrenched the bloodied ax from his chest. Thick red droplets splattered onto the ground and sprayed out in the air.

Aria watched as the ax flew straight at her. It wasn't possible—Thera couldn't afford to destroy her. Then she realized it wasn't aimed at her; it was meant for Michael. Summoning all her power, she envisioned a wall of energy around him and pushed. Just two feet short of its target, the ax lurched and stopped in midair, suspended precariously between the forces of the two women. Aria's head pounded with her efforts. If she faltered for even a moment, Michael would die.

"You cannot win against me," Thera called out, her tone smug with certain victory. "Very soon you will begin to weaken. This much power brings with it pain, pain I have become hardened to."

Aria said nothing. The pain Thera spoke of was devastatingly real. She wasn't sure how long she would be able to hang on to consciousness. Already the golden labrys was blurring, swimming before her eyes. There had to be another way to save him. Then with lightninglike clarity she saw it.

As her sister continued to taunt her, Aria whispered urgently to Michael. "Count to five and hit the floor."

Michael didn't question her. She was all that stood between him and death, and even if he no longer loved her, he would never sacrifice him to Thera.

Aria counted to herself. A second's miscalculation would be fatal. At four, she released her hold on the ax. She heard her sister's triumphant laugh as the weapon whistled toward its target. Beside her Michael's body slammed onto the ground. There was no time to see if he was all right. She focused on the cave roof over Thera's head and drove all of her energy into it. The ceiling exploded in a shower of flying rock and debris.

Thera was taken by surprise. Before she could shield herself, she was knocked unconscious by the falling rocks.

Aria fell to her knees, depleted. Despair and sorrow ravaged her, making her oblivious to the continuing destruction around her. She heard Michael's voice, but his words spun through her mind without meaning.

"Aria, we've got to get out of here." He pulled her up beside him and shook her. "Listen, for God's sake, don't you hear it? The whole damned mountain is coming down around us." As he dragged her toward the tunnel, she saw the others fleeing the far recesses of the cave where they had taken refuge. Their terrified screams penetrated her stupor. All at once she was aware of the ominous rumbling around them. It was as if they'd been swallowed whole by some prehistoric monster. It was her nightmare, but it was real.

Before starting through the tunnel she turned back, but a curtain of rock and detritus obscured her view of the altar.

"There's nothing you can do for them now," Michael said, answering her thoughts. He prodded her along, gripping the precious lantern as they stumbled through the rock-clogged tunnel. The ground vibrated beneath their feet, and sediment poured down on their heads, the dust filling their throats and lungs. They crept through spaces grown so narrow that the jagged rocks tore ruthlessly at their clothes and bodies. More than once the tunnel directly behind them collapsed seconds after they'd passed through.

After what seemed an endless time, they reached the mouth of the cave and crawled outside, coughing and blinking in the brilliant sunlight. The others, having found their way to safety, lay sprawled on the mountainside, unable to go farther. Aria and Michael fell among them, clinging to the trembling earth. As they watched, the cave entrance was sealed off by tons of cascading rock. Then, abruptly, the mountain quieted. In the preternatural stillness that followed, Aria sat up slowly and looked around her. Others had begun to move about cautiously, their eyes glazed with shock. She turned to Michael. He was already on his feet. Voices floated up to them from the distance as the villagers raced up the mountainside to help the survivors.

Aria held out her hand, and Michael drew her up to lean against him. They made their way slowly down the path, trying not to think about what they were leaving behind. Below them the Lassithi Plateau fanned out in dreamlike tranquillity.

34

Long Island: December 6

The brick patio was littered with the last shriveled oak leaves of autumn. They crunched underfoot as Michael and Damos carried their trays to the wrought-iron table. The large fringed umbrella had been stored at the end of summer, but the table was decked with an orange cloth that added to the springtime warmth of the day. The temperature was in the sixties, the sky a cloudless blue that had tempted them outside for one more meal before winter took hold again.

The two men unloaded the plates, utensils, and mugs, and after setting the table in a haphazard fashion, drew up chairs to wait for Helena and Aria. Michael was no longer uncomfortable around Damos. In a strange old-fashioned way he felt he had proven his worth and his love. He wished his relationship with Aria were as promising. Although she had accepted him back into her life, she seemed remote and uninvolved. Understanding that she had a lot of confusion and pain to work through, he hadn't pressed her for more than she could give. But there were moments when he wondered if he hadn't lost her after all. He had voiced this concern to Damos, and the older man had nodded and remarked that he had noticed the same distance in his own relationship with her since her return from Crete. He thought she simply needed time; too much had happened too fast. Michael had said all those things to himself, but there was a certain comfort in hearing them from someone else.

The glass doors slid open, and Helena and Aria appeared

with plates of cold cuts, a basket of crusty Italian bread, and a pitcher of hot apple cider fragrant with cinnamon.

Damos filled the mugs, and they all busied themselves fixing sandwiches. Aria watched her mother make one, then put it down untouched. Helena had always been slender, but over the past few weeks she seemed to have grown too thin and frail, her skin almost translucent, her eyes protruding above sharpened cheekbones, as if the grief of twice having lost a daughter was sucking her into herself.

Aria felt a twinge of envy. If only she could grieve for her sister, perhaps the ache would dull and dissolve. But she couldn't. She lay awake night after night, eyes wide and tearless. She knew Michael suffered from her inattention, but although she no longer blamed him for the tragedy, she didn't seem able to pick up all the pieces and get on with her life. She felt somehow suspended, as if she had heard one shoe drop and was waiting for the other to follow.

"Is the hunger strike for a good cause at least?" Michael joked, indicating Helena's and Aria's untouched plates.

Aria smiled wanly and started nibbling at her sandwich. Helena pushed hers aside.

"I'm not hungry," she said, rising from her chair. "Please enjoy yourselves. Excuse me." She walked quickly into the house.

"I'm sorry," Michael murmured. "I didn't mean to upset her. I was just trying to make conversation."

Damos shook his head. "Do not trouble yourself, Michael. It was nothing you said. Some days I only have to glance at her or say good morning to produce the same effect. But it gets better. At night now she sleeps more than she cries. We all deal with sorrow in our own way." He looked across at Aria. It was she who worried him, not Helena. She'd been too stoic, too unemotional since her return. He was not as certain of her well-being as he had led Michael to believe. While it was true that people dealt with grief in different ways, they did have to deal with it. He was concerned that Aria had barricaded herself against it. Maybe he would try to talk with her before the weekend was over.

He refilled the mugs and made an attempt at conversation. Michael did his best to keep it going, but the mood of the day had gone as dry and lifeless as the curled brown leaves that rustled around them.

Aria was stacking the dirty plates on a tray when the first hailstone hit the table. It bounced once and ricocheted onto the patio. Thinking it was an acorn or a small stone, they all looked up, expecting to see the bird that dropped it. Within seconds the balls of ice were falling everywhere, growing in size as they watched. Instead of running for cover, they stared incredulously at the placid blue sky, unmarred by even the faintest wisp of a cloud.

"Tell me I'm not seeing what I think I'm seeing," Michael said finally.

"Let's get inside and then discuss it," Damos replied, helping Aria clear away the remains of their lunch. "If this is an illusion it certainly hurts like the real thing."

Carrying the overloaded trays they ran into the kitchen. Michael shook melting hailstones from his hair, and a grin spread across his face.

"Did I miss something?" Damos inquired.

"Don't you realize what this means?"

"Yet another freakish weather system?"

"Exactly. Those ancient gods of yours have been appeased, but the weather is still as weird as ever. So the storms never did have anything to do with angry gods."

Damos thought for a moment. "It would seem you are right." He shrugged and smiled. "It will be a welcome relief to go back to believing in science and art and nothing more."

Aria was loading the dishwasher. She glanced over her shoulder at Michael. There was no relief or joy in her face. And although she was staring at him, her eyes seemed to be focused not on him but on some inner conflict. His own smile evaporated. "Aria, what is it?"

"For a scientist you're too easily convinced," she said, turning back to the dishwasher.

Damos was frowning now, too. "What is that supposed to mean?"

Aria immediately regretted her comment. There was no point in worrying her father. She had no substantial proof one way or the other. But Michael's complacency had rattled her.

She forced a smile for Damos. "Just teasing a little." Damos nodded, though he wasn't convinced. And Michael noticed that the corners of her mouth quivered as if she were about to cry.

They were given the same rooms they'd stayed in on the night of the hurricane. Out of deference to Damos and Helena they didn't argue. Once the house was quiet, Michael told Aria he would come to her room and stay with her until dawn.

While she waited in her bed, she tried to remember how she'd felt the night Thera shared this room with her. But she couldn't seem to recapture the undiluted joy of it. The memory had been mutilated, destroyed by what had followed. She loved Thera and hated her. Missed her and blamed her. And Aria finally understood why she couldn't grieve for her sister.

Michael appeared in the doorway, framed by the hallway light. Aria was glad he was there. She didn't want to be alone tonight. He closed the door behind him, throwing the room into total darkness. There was a dull thud, and she heard him curse softly. Then he was sliding under the covers, his body pressed against hers in the narrow twin bed. He kissed her.

"Are you all right?" he whispered, propping himself up on one elbow.

"Um-hum."

"But you weren't teasing this afternoon. Something upset you."

Aria wanted to deny it. He'd already gone through too much because of her. But she needed to talk to someone. And maybe he would help her see things more clearly, prove that she was wrong. She wished there were a way to approach the subject gradually, but she couldn't think of one. Finally she just blurted it out.

"I'm not so sure Thera is dead."

Michael hesitated for a moment, but when he spoke his voice was calm and even. "No one could have survived that cave-in."

"No ordinary person, maybe. But Thera isn't ordinary. It would explain a lot that I can't explain any other way. I've been having extended dreams and strange sensations, the same ones I used to have when she was still in Crete and I didn't know about her. If she were dead I don't think that would be happening. I would know without question that she was gone."

Michael was troubled by the unexpected admission. She hadn't mentioned any of this before. "The dreams could be a sort of phantom pain," he said, trying to keep a rational perspective. "The way a person can still feel a limb after it's been amputated."

"I thought of that, too, and I almost had myself convinced, until that hailstorm today."

"It's just weather, Aria," he said, lying down again and drawing her into his arms. "You don't really believe in all that angry-god stuff, do you?"

"They know she's alive."

"There are logical explanations for all of it."

Aria rested her head on Michael's chest and wished she could be as sure of that as he seemed to be. But there was something she still hadn't told him, something that went beyond the realm of simple logic. Since their return home, nearly all of her dreams had been identical. She saw herself being buried alive as the cave collapsed around her. Battered and dazed, barely able to breathe, she struggled to dig her way out. Aria had tried to convince herself that her mind was only working through the trauma of what she had experienced. But what tortured her the most was not knowing if she was really seeing herself in those dreams or if she was seeing her sister. She wondered what Michael would say, given this last bit of information.

She raised her head. "Michael?" she whispered. "Michael?"

He didn't answer, and she realized by the even rhythm of his breathing that he was asleep. It was just as well. She wouldn't wake him. There would be time enough for him to worry. Time enough for him to know.